BUILT TO LAST

By the Author

Winter's Harbor

Built to Last

Visit us at www.boldstrokesbooks.com

BUILT TO LAST

by
Aurora Rey

2016

BUILT TO LAST

ISBN 13: 978-1-62639-552-7

THIS TRADE PAPERBACK ORIGINAL IS PUBLISHED BY
BOLD STROKES BOOKS, INC.
P.O. BOX 249
VALLEY FALLS, NY 12185

FIRST EDITION: APRIL 2016

CREDITS
EDITOR: ASHLEY TILLMAN
PRODUCTION DESIGN: STACIA SEAMAN
COVER DESIGN BY MELODY POND

Acknowledgments

I remain so grateful to everyone at Bold Strokes Books. It's a remarkable community of smart and talented people who have made me a better writer and a better person. Special thanks to my editor, Ashley Bartlett, who has taught me more than I'd like to admit.

When I started this book, it grew from a fantasy of having an old farmhouse in the country. By the time the first draft was complete, the farmhouse had become a reality. While the house didn't need a complete overhaul, it's proven to be plenty adventurous. I'm so grateful for my partner, Andie. I can't imagine playing gentlewoman farmer with anyone else, even though we've yet to get those goats.

For AMH. Home is wherever you are.

CHAPTER ONE

The house was too big, older, and farther out of town than Olivia wanted. The photos in the listing were terrible. There were only a couple of them to begin with and they didn't do much to show the character of the house, or its condition. But still. Something about it spoke to her. It had a porch and a fireplace; it had promise. Olivia asked her Realtor to schedule a showing.

The whole house hunting process had proven beyond frustrating. Everyone had warned her about the Ithaca market and, unfortunately, everyone was right. She'd been at it for four months and every house she'd seen was either completely generic or full of once-trendy add-ons—no personality or the kind of personality you'd try to avoid at parties. The rest were either dilapidated college student rental properties or completely out of her price range.

Except for this one. Definitely worn, but it seemed sturdy, reliable. It reminded her of a favorite sweater, frayed but comfortable, or the copy of *The Optimist's Daughter* that she'd toted around since high school. When they pulled into the driveway, Olivia felt a flutter in her chest.

Set back from the road, it was a farmhouse that didn't have any farm left to it. It had what appeared to be an overgrown vegetable garden and a small barn that had been halfheartedly converted into a garage. The white paint was peeling and one of the dark green shutters hung at a precarious angle. A wide porch spanned the front and wrapped all the way around the side of the house. Sure it was roped off with yellow caution tape, but that didn't stop her from imagining a big swing and a pair of rocking chairs, or what it would be like to sip a glass of wine and watch the sun set into the rolling hills.

It was the kind of house she'd dreamed about as a little girl.

Scott, her Realtor, led her around to the back door because, according to the note in the listing, the porch was in danger of collapsing. He retrieved the key from the lockbox and unlocked the deadbolt. Olivia couldn't tell if he needed to lean his full weight against the door to get it to open or if he was being dramatic. She didn't ask. They stepped into the kitchen. While Scott made a show of pushing the door closed behind them, Olivia took in wide-plank wood floors that were original but badly scarred, an old farmhouse sink, peeling wallpaper. She looked past the dated appliances and dingy cabinets and envisioned a wrought iron pot rack hanging over a huge island and toile curtains on the windows. She loved it.

"This," he made a circle with his finger to indicate their surroundings, "is not what we discussed."

Had it been anyone but Scott, with his hipster glasses and silver hair, she might have taken offense. Because it was Scott, Olivia hung her head and sighed. "I know."

Scott dug around in his messenger bag and pulled out a spiral notepad. "Let's see. I have my notes right here: not too big, low maintenance, twenty minutes or less to campus. Honey, you're not even one for three."

"But the others are all so boring." Olivia drew out the last word to a solid four syllables, allowing herself to sound extra whiny.

Scott tsked. "When it comes to houses, boring is shorthand for reliable, undemanding, and easy. But, yes, I agree. Clearly, you've seen my house."

Olivia smiled. In the two years she'd lived in Ithaca, she'd spent quite a lot of time at the house Scott shared with his partner Dan, a linguistics professor whose office was down the hall from hers. The gorgeous old Craftsman sat on the prettiest street in the Fall Creek neighborhood. The couple had spent six years on the renovations and joked that they still weren't done.

"I want you to be happy." Scott put his hands on his hips. "But with great character comes great responsibility."

Olivia rolled her eyes. "I've always been the practical one, but maybe I want original woodwork more than I want a new, high-efficiency water heater."

"Mmm-hmm. You tell yourself that when you're taking an ice-cold shower in February."

Olivia tried to hide the shiver that rippled through her at the thought. "Come on, voice of reason, let's see the rest of it."

As they walked through the downstairs, she fell more in love. Each room offered more of the same—charming details and craftsmanship showing signs of wear and very bad decor. The living room boasted a large brick fireplace and garishly mauve walls, while the powder room felt like a bad beach vacation. Upstairs, the only full bathroom was home to an antique claw-foot tub and sea-foam green tile. With four bedrooms, Olivia wondered how expensive it would be to take out a wall to make it feel more like a master bath, maybe build a walk-in closet. She didn't mention her idea to Scott.

"I want it."

Scott shook his head. "I knew you were going to say that. Since it's been on the market nearly three months already, I think we can go in below asking price and, you know, bold, italicize, and underline the home inspection clause."

Although his tone remained stern, Olivia could see the playfulness in his eyes. She felt like she'd won over a skeptical parent. "Thank you, Scott!"

"Don't thank me yet, honey. Save it for when we verify she isn't going to collapse on closing day."

While Scott locked up, Olivia stood in the driveway and tried to figure out how far back the property line was. She was going to have a lot to mow. She imagined toodling around on a lawn tractor in a floppy straw hat. There were always goats. Maybe she'd look into goats.

She didn't mention goats as they got into Scott's car and drove to Gimme! Coffee to fill out the paperwork. She went to the counter to order lattes while Scott claimed a table. By the time she joined him, an oversize mug in each hand, he had the offer of sale form filled out and ready to go.

"I'm going to be up half the night," he said after taking a long sip. "It's so worth it, though."

Olivia sipped her own coffee and sighed. "So worth it."

"So, I may have already pulled some comps."

Olivia was pretty sure that part of the process came after she'd found a house she wanted. "What do you mean?"

"I had a gut feeling about this place, so I went ahead and pulled comps in case you decided to put in an offer."

Olivia narrowed her eyes. "But you gave me such a hard time about it."

Scott shrugged. "I had to tease you a little. Besides, I couldn't risk influencing you."

She loved having a real estate agent who was also a friend. "Well played."

"Thank you. I've been doing this a while."

They spent half an hour poring over homes that were at least somewhat similar in square footage and state of disrepair. After settling on an offer price fifteen percent below asking, Scott walked her through the various clauses and contingencies, including the ever-important home inspection.

"Are you sure it isn't too low?" She was afraid of offending the sellers and ending negotiations even before they started. She knew she wasn't supposed to get too attached at this point in the process, but that didn't seem to stop her.

"Given how long it's been on the market and the fact that it's empty, I'm confident this is a good starting point."

Olivia took a deep breath, suddenly aware of what a big deal this was. "Okay."

"Okay."

"Now what?"

"Now I submit it to the seller. Then we wait. They can accept, reject, or counter. The latter is the most likely and then, hopefully, we meet somewhere in the middle."

"Right. Okay. Good."

"I've already got you on speed dial." He offered a reassuring smile. "I will call you the second I hear something."

It turned out that the sellers, siblings who'd inherited the house from an aunt, were keen on getting rid of it. With no other offers on the table, they halfheartedly counteroffered two thousand above Olivia's initial offer. When she got the news from Scott, she indulged in a brief happy dance and didn't bother continuing negotiations.

The minute she stopped dancing, she started the process of fretting about the inspection.

There was so much that could go wrong. The house could have termites. Or a crumbling foundation. Or asbestos. It could need all new plumbing. It could have all of that. As willing as she was to take on projects, there were things that were—that had to be—deal breakers. If that happened, and she had to walk away, she would be heartbroken.

The whole thing felt like a high-stakes version of the old game show, *Press Your Luck*. As Olivia dialed the number Scott gave her for the home inspector, she repeated the phrase "no whammy, no whammy" to herself over and over. When a cheerful voice answered the phone, Olivia's heart jumped in her chest. She'd worked herself into quite a trance.

"Good morning. Bauer and Sons Construction, this is Daphne. How may I help you?"

"Good morning." Olivia took a deep breath. "I would like to schedule an inspection."

Olivia offered a description of the house, including the fact that it hadn't been lived in for almost two years. She held her breath, afraid the woman might turn her down on the spot.

"That sounds great. I'm going to schedule you with Ben. He's a big fan of old houses."

Of course they wouldn't turn her down. It was what they did for a living. "Wonderful."

"You don't need to be there, but some people prefer to. The report will be thorough, but seeing things on the walk-through can make the report easier to digest, especially if you're a visual person."

"I'll be there," Olivia said without hesitation. She gave the address and set a time for the following Wednesday morning.

"Sounds good. You're all set, then."

"Thank you so much."

"You're welcome. Thank you for choosing Bauer and Sons. Have a great day."

"You, too."

Olivia hung up the phone and looked around her office. Now all she had to do was spend the next five days not obsessing about everything that could go wrong.

CHAPTER TWO

Joss stood at the kitchen sink, looking out the window at her backyard. She'd built the deck the previous summer, along with the wooden fence that was more about having a place for the dog to run than privacy. It had been the final project on the little Craftsman she'd bought to renovate in her downtime. The view never failed to make her smile.

She noticed that a couple of the plants she had in large pots along the rail were sporting perfectly ripe tomatoes. She'd need to pick those when she got home from work that afternoon. She imagined thick slices of red and yellow tomato with fresh mozzarella and basil, a little balsamic vinegar, and decided that was what she'd be having for dinner.

She was just finishing her second cup of coffee when the phone rang. The theme song from *The Golden Girls* began to play and Ben's face appeared on the screen. He'd downloaded and programmed it when she wasn't looking, then cranked the volume and called while they were picking up supplies for a project. Joss was in the middle of the lumber aisle when "Thank You for Being a Friend" began blaring out of her pocket. Ben was so amused by his prank that Joss had kept the song as his personal ring tone.

Joss swiped a finger across the screen. "It's never good when I hear from you at this hour."

"Good morning to you, too, sunshine." The voice on the other end sounded more like a two-pack-a-day smoker than her brother.

"Oh, man, you sound terrible. Are you okay?"

"Just a cold, I think, but I can't seem to take a deep breath without coughing. What do you have going on this morning?"

Joss conjured the image of her desk calendar. "Nothing scheduled. I was about to head to the office to work on the plans for the Sanderson kitchen reno. I can cover whatever you need."

"You're the best. It's an inspection, old house out on Davis Road."

"Not a problem. I want to tell you that you owe me one, but I don't even have the heart." There was also the fact that she really liked doing inspections. She got to poke around and play detective while helping people make informed decisions.

"One of the many reasons I love you. It's at nine. The address is fourteen-forty."

"I'm on it. Get some rest."

"Thanks, homes. Smell you later."

Joss rolled her eyes. "One, don't say that. It's not 1994 and you are not the Fresh Prince of Bel-Air. Two, I don't think you're going to be smelling anything for a while."

Ben started to laugh, but it quickly morphed into a fit of coughing. It took him a full thirty seconds to stop. When he finally did, he said, "You're horrible. You did that on purpose."

"Nope. You already said I'm the best. Now, go back to bed and I'll text you this afternoon."

After hanging up the phone, Joss put her mug into the dishwasher and headed upstairs. Not that she was happy to see her brother under the weather, but the prospect of exploring an old house instead of sitting at her desk put a spring in her step. In the shower, she whistled *The Golden Girls* song.

After getting dressed, she headed out to her truck, checking to make sure she had all the tools she needed for an inspection. Happy she wouldn't have to stop by the office, she double-checked the address and headed out.

Half an hour later, Joss pulled up to the house and smiled. She loved old houses. In part, she simply preferred the look and feel of them. Really, though, she appreciated the craftsmanship. More often than not, old houses were well-built. Even ones that appeared to be crumbling usually boasted more structural integrity and attention to detail than those built in the last thirty years.

This one was no different. If she had to guess, Joss would peg it as having been built between 1890 and 1910. The porch appeared to be falling off, a fact she would have spotted even without the yellow caution tape. The roof looked old, but the parts she could see didn't seem to have any holes—a good sign, since water damage was the single biggest enemy of old houses.

She pulled her truck into the gravel driveway and parked behind a red hybrid hatchback. She shook her head and chuckled. Only in Ithaca did people simultaneously buy hybrid cars and drafty old houses. That wasn't fair; they probably did that in Portland, too.

Joss climbed out and studied the exterior of the house. The windows looked original, which wasn't necessarily a bad thing. The yard was unkempt, but it had a good slope. Hopefully, that meant the basement was dry.

She made her way to the back door and peered in. The kitchen was just as she'd expected—a bit of a mess, but not a lost cause. The floors and trim looked original and, thankfully, hadn't been painted. It was just the sort of house she'd love to get her hands on. If she played her cards right, maybe she'd get the chance.

Joss turned her attention to the woman who was standing in the middle of the room with her back turned. She was wearing a navy blue sundress and matching shoes, the kind with ribbons that went around her ankles and tied in neat little bows. Her hair was a fiery red, pulled up into some sort of twist that exposed her neck.

Joss wasn't a monk by any means, but the intensity of her reaction took her by surprise. Maybe it was the contrast of the tired space that made the woman seem so striking. That had to be it. Of course, it didn't help that she was dancing. It was subtle, for sure, but there was definitely a sway in her hips. Joss's fingers itched to feel the movement. *Get a hold of yourself. She's a client, and likely married.* Deciding she needed to get out more, Joss shook off the strange surge of desire and knocked firmly on the door.

Olivia had arranged to have Scott let her into the house half an hour before the scheduled time for the inspection. It guaranteed she would be early—she had strong feelings about being early—and gave her the chance to poke around and daydream. If the sale went through, she'd have enough in her budget for a fair amount of renovation. If the house wasn't in need of major structural work, she had plenty of ideas on how she'd like to spend the money.

She was fantasizing about a six-burner stove when the knock on the door scared the living daylights out of her. The fact that she was expecting someone hadn't seemed to make a lick of difference. She wrenched open the back door, hoping the person on the other side hadn't heard her yelp.

"I'm sorry. I didn't mean to startle you."

Olivia winced. "Was I that obvious?"

"Well, you probably don't have a good seal on this door, but still. I could hear your scream out here."

She looked at the person standing in the doorway. No, that wasn't accurate. Olivia looked at the incredibly gorgeous woman standing in the doorway. She was wearing khaki pants and a navy and white gingham shirt, scuffed work boots. Her light brown hair was cut short, not quite military close, but just as neat. Really, though, it was all about the eyes. She had the most beautiful hazel eyes Olivia had ever seen. And Olivia was already acting like an idiot.

"Right. Well, then."

"I'm Joss Bauer and I'm here to do your structural inspection."

That didn't sound right, but she accepted the offered hand anyway. "I'm Olivia Bennett. It's nice to meet you."

As though sensing her confusion, Joss offered a smile. "You were scheduled to meet with my brother, Ben, but he's a bit under the weather."

"Ah, okay. Thank you for coming out." Olivia took a deep breath, willing her heart rate to slow. She hadn't felt that instantly attracted to someone in a long time, but it didn't mean she needed to act like a silly teenager.

"My pleasure. So, are you the buyer?"

She shifted her nervousness back to the house. "I'm hoping to be. It will depend on what you find."

"Fair enough. Are we expecting anyone else?"

Olivia shook her head. "Nope. It's just me."

Joss nodded. "Okay, then, let's get started. We'll start with the interior and work our way out. You don't have to join me, but if you do, I'll explain things as I go. Everything will be in the report, but sometimes it's easier to understand things if you have the visual to go with it."

Olivia smiled. "I agree. I'll follow you and try not to ask too many questions."

"No such thing, I promise. Since we're in the kitchen, let's start here."

Joss set down her toolbox and clipboard. Olivia tried not to drool. She took out a small instrument and started poking the outlets scattered around the room. "It looks like everything, in here at least, has been updated to three-prong. We'll see if they upgraded the circuit breaker as well."

Olivia nodded, doing her best to pay attention to Joss's words instead of the way her hands handled the tools or the way her khakis hung on her hips. "My Kitchen Aid mixer will be grateful."

They moved to the living room next. There, only a couple of the outlets had been converted from the old two-prong. Joss walked around, seeming to check the stability of the floor. She pulled a marble from her pocket and set it down, repeating the process in different spots. "The floors are pretty level. That bodes well for the state of the foundation."

"That's the best news I've heard all day."

Joss got on her hands and knees and stuck her head into the fireplace. "It needs a good cleaning, but it looks okay. I'll check the chimney when I'm on the roof."

They went through the half-bath and first-floor sitting room before heading upstairs. Again, the worst of it seemed to be bad taste. Olivia tried not to get too excited. "I'm hoping there is hardwood under this atrocious carpet. Do you think that's likely?"

Joss smiled at her. "You mean you don't like the blue shag? I think it's swingin'."

Olivia let out a snort, then coughed to try to cover up the sound. "I think the swing has swung on this one. Really, though, what do you think?"

"Why don't we take a peek?"

"You can do that?"

Joss was already in a closet, on her knees. "I'll pull up a little corner in here. I can tuck it back in and it won't even show. This won't tell you what shape they're in, but you'll be able to see if it's hardwood or just subflooring."

Olivia stood behind Joss and got a faint whiff of sandalwood. Seriously, this woman was going to push her to distraction. "What is it? What do you see?"

"I see something that is going to make you very happy."

Is it you without a shirt on? "Yeah?"

"More wide-plank pine. You're welcome."

"I really want to hug you right now." She meant it, for more reasons than the floor.

"You should save it until I've checked out the basement and the roof."

Olivia couldn't tell if there was a hint of flirtation in Joss's voice. She was afraid it might be wishful thinking on her part. Other than the one fix-up Scott and Dan had orchestrated—that hadn't ended well— she'd not dated at all since moving to Ithaca. She decided to go out on a limb. "I don't know. I'm feeling kind of lucky."

The look Joss shot her made her insides go hot. This was shaping up to be a banner day.

The basement, while damp and likely prone to flooding in the spring, wasn't in terrible shape and boasted a functional sump pump. The electrical box had been redone within the last twenty years, so that was good. The furnace was a different matter. After poking around it for a minute, Joss said, "It still works, but it's far from efficient. You should consider replacing it, especially since you're on propane out here. A newer model will pay for itself in a few years."

They climbed the stairs and went out the side door. "Sounds like a good investment to me."

"I'm going to grab a ladder from my truck."

"Okay. Do you need a hand?"

"I've got it, but thanks."

Olivia couldn't decide if Joss's smirk was at the offer of help, or who was doing the offering. She watched Joss saunter down to her truck and adeptly unhook and lift the extension ladder to the ground. If Olivia had been the swooning type, that would have done it. Joss carried the ladder back to the house and positioned it against the lowest part of the roof.

"I don't want to tell you not to come up on the roof with me, but—"

"No need. I trust your judgment and I'm clearly not dressed for it." Olivia figured it was better to decline than be told she shouldn't. In truth, she had no desire to be on the roof anyway.

Joss climbed up the ladder and disappeared. Olivia decided the view of Joss's rear end was another good reason to stay on the ground. She heard some scraping and a bit of banging and then Joss was on her way back down.

"The porch roof is a mess. The pitch is bad and water's just been sitting on it, which is probably why the porch itself is in such bad shape. Otherwise, I'd estimate you're about fifteen years into a thirty-year shingle. It's not as good as having the original slate, but it's not bad."

As far as Olivia could tell, they'd looked over everything and there were no major disasters. She allowed herself to be optimistic. "Thank you. So, in your professional opinion, is it a reasonable thing to take on?"

Joss seemed to consider for a moment. "Well, it's in good shape considering its age. None of the work is major, but it does need work. If you understand that and you're willing to put that work in, it should stand for another hundred years."

Music to Olivia's ears. "I can't tell you how happy I am to hear that."

Joss offered a smile that made Olivia go weak in the knees. "I love being the bearer of good news. For the record, Bauer and Sons is primarily a residential construction company. This is exactly the kind of project we love to take on."

"Is that so?" Olivia had a flash of Joss at her house, day in and day out, building stuff.

"It is. I hope you'll consider requesting a bid from us if you do end up with the house."

It was Olivia's turn to flash a smile. "I most definitely will."

"Great. So, I'll email you the full inspection report later today. It will have photos and notations about the areas that require immediate attention."

"That sounds good. My purse is in the kitchen. Let me go grab it so I can write you a check."

"I'll follow you. Some of my things are still inside."

"Oh, right."

They went back to the side door and into the kitchen. Joss scribbled a few more notes, then handed her an invoice from the clipboard. "So are you new to Ithaca?"

Olivia looked up from her checkbook. "Sort of. I've been here for just about two years, renting while I settled into the area."

"Ah. So what do you do?"

"I teach at Cornell. English department."

"Oh." Joss visibly tensed. Olivia wondered if there was an actual drop in temperature or if it merely felt like it.

"I just survived my two-year review. In academia, that's code for 'it's no longer taboo to buy a house.'" Joss either didn't get the joke or didn't find it funny. Olivia didn't know what to make of it. She handed Joss the check. "Thank you again for coming out. I learned a lot, about this house and about houses in general."

"You're welcome. I'm glad you found it useful." Joss's voice was flat and detached.

"Absolutely. Knock on wood." Olivia rapped her knuckles against one of the cabinets. "I'll be calling you again soon about a renovation project."

Joss nodded. "The company would welcome your business."

Olivia tried not to scowl about the awkward formality in Joss's tone. "I'll be in touch."

"Good luck, and thanks for choosing us for your inspection." Joss extended a hand.

Olivia shook it. Although the gesture felt stiff, she couldn't help but respond to the sexy roughness of Joss's skin. "Thanks. I've got a good feeling."

Joss gathered her things. Olivia opened the side door for her. Joss nodded curtly. "Thanks. Have a good day."

"You, too."

Olivia watched Joss pull away. That was weird. Instead of stewing about it, however, she turned her attention back to the house. The inspection had gone even better than she'd hoped. The house was going to be hers.

CHAPTER THREE

Joss drove back to the shop, her jaw clenching involuntarily. She should have figured this woman was faculty. Who else came to town and bought a big old house by herself? People with more money than brains, or, at least, not the kind of brains she considered useful. And she was Southern. Despite the alluring drawl, she was probably conservative, too.

Joss made a mental note to make Ben repay this favor when he was feeling better.

As she pulled into the parking lot, Ben was coming out of the main office. Joss was preparing to give him a piece of her mind when she saw his whole body jerk. Although she couldn't hear him, it was obvious that Ben was sneezing and her annoyance was replaced by sympathy. She climbed out of her truck and he offered her a wave.

"You should be home and in bed, my man," Joss said to him.

"Bah. I was just getting some files." He punctuated the sentence with a sneeze.

"You sound horrible. Stay away from me." Joss made an "X" with her fingers and aimed it in his direction.

"I'm fine."

"Mmm-hmm. When 'fine' sounds like 'find,' you are not fine."

Ben scowled. "I'm going home."

"Homb?"

"You're a jerk."

"Sorry, sorry. I'm just cranky."

"Did a pretty girl neglect to call you back?" Ben started to chuckle, but it quickly turned into a cough.

"No, just another college professor who thinks it would be charming to buy a farmhouse. English professor, of all things. And she's Southern." Joss didn't mention the fact that Olivia was sexy as hell. Or that her drawl made Joss all hot and bothered.

"You do understand that more than half of our client base comes from people who work at one of the colleges. And farmhouses are charming. I think that's your official motto."

Joss rolled her eyes. She knew it, but she didn't have to like it. "She got all awkward when I wasn't the 'Ben' she was expecting, like she didn't know what to do with a woman in a tool belt."

"Aren't we quick to judge, today? Let me guess, she was really hot, too."

"I hardly noticed." Joss certainly had noticed. She'd noticed how flirtatious Olivia had been, too, but it felt cheap and kind of fake now.

Ben raised an eyebrow. "I'm pretty sure you're incapable of not noticing."

Joss huffed. He was right. When the two of them went out together, she was more inclined to notice women. In a completely appreciative and respectful way, of course. "Fine. She was gorgeous, but that's beside the point."

Ben laughed again, and again it triggered a coughing fit.

"Go home, man. Get some rest and try not to show your face until you're no longer contagious."

Ben tipped the worn Phillies cap he was wearing. "Yes, ma'am."

Joss elbowed him as they crossed paths. "Don't call me ma'am."

"Yes, ma'am." He started to walk away, then turned back. "Hey, Joss."

"Yeah?"

"Would I like her?"

Joss rolled her eyes. "Well, she's definitely more your type than mine."

Ben headed to his truck and Joss walked into the office. Daphne, their sister, was on the phone. From the tone of her voice, she was talking with one of the suppliers. Daphne had a way of charming her way into better-than-average terms and conditions with most of the supply companies they contracted with. On the other side of the office, her mother, Sandra, sat at a computer with headphones on. A wizard with the books, she considered any day she didn't have to speak to anyone on the phone a good day.

Joss offered each of them a wave before flopping down at her desk. She sat for a moment, turning Ben's words over in her mind. She wasn't judgmental. She could read people, and she knew a type when she saw it. It didn't interfere with her professionalism, or her ability to get the job done.

She flipped on her computer, then walked over to the coffeepot while it booted. She poured herself a cup and turned to Daphne, who'd finished her phone call. "Good morning, Daph."

Daphne stopped entering things into the computer. "Same to you, although I think it's officially afternoon now."

Joss glanced at the clock. It was a little after noon. "So it is. How are you? No cold for you?"

Daphne raised her hand, showing crossed fingers. "Here's hoping. I'm one with echinacea, with some vitamin C and zinc thrown in for good measure."

"I hope it does the trick. Lord knows you don't want to be sick at the same time as Ben."

Daphne smiled. "He means well."

"Indeed he does. Did I miss anything this morning?"

"Nothing important. How was the inspection?"

Joss rolled her eyes.

"That bad?"

Even more annoying than Olivia was the fact that she was allowing Olivia to get under her skin. "No, it was fine. The house needs work, but it's in surprisingly good shape. We might get the renovation job if the buyer makes it to closing."

"So why are you irritated?"

"I'm not."

Daphne continued to look at her, but didn't say anything.

"Okay, I'm irritated, but only a little. Clueless professor type. I'm fine now." Joss realized she was scowling. She forced herself to smile and walked back to her desk.

Joss's mother looked up from her computer screen, seeming to realize just then that Joss was there. She took off her headphones and gave Joss a questioning look. "What happened? Why are you scowling?"

She flopped in her chair again. "I'm not scowling."

"Yes, she is. Her inspection this morning was with a college professor." Daphne's phone pinged and she looked down at the screen. She lifted her phone and pointed at it. "And according to Ben, it was a pretty lady professor."

Sandra gave Joss an exasperated look. "Joss."

"Mom, I'm fine. It was fine. We might get a pretty big project if she buys the house."

The look of exasperation softened. "I know you're fine. I just wish you wouldn't let them get to you."

Joss shook her head. She'd had the bad fortune of falling for an environmental engineering grad student when she was in her early twenties. Her name was Cora and, eight months into their relationship, she got a fellowship working on a conservation project in Belize. She left town without looking back and Joss never heard from her again. It certainly wasn't the only reason she didn't care for the academic types, but it hadn't helped matters. "Mom, really. It's all good. She rubbed me the wrong way a little, but it's not a big deal."

"Okay, honey. We'll let it go." Sandra glanced at Daphne.

"Right. I've already forgotten what we were talking about." Daphne turned back to her computer and started typing away.

Joss looked back at her mother, who'd already put her headphones back on. That, apparently, was that. Joss set down her coffee and logged into her computer. Although she always got inspection reports out within twenty-four hours, she wanted to get this one done immediately. She was a professional, after all. She also wanted to put the very beautiful and very irritating Olivia Bennett out of her mind.

It took her about an hour to type everything up, complete with photos and coding for the seriousness of the various issues and concerns. She attached the nineteen-page document to an email and then spent another twenty minutes constructing the perfect four-sentence message. In the end, she thought the result was professional, friendly enough to ensure Olivia considered Bauer and Sons for the renovation job if she bought the house, but devoid of any of the flirtation she may have otherwise been tempted to throw in.

She might not like the woman, but she'd be damned if she'd lose a job because of it. She hit the send button, then kicked back in her chair and crossed her feet on the desk. It was, she decided, a very productive morning.

❖

Although tempted to linger at the house, revel in it, Olivia dutifully locked the door and returned the key to the lockbox hanging from the doorknob. Hanging around wouldn't make it hers any quicker. She drove to campus, noting with pleasure that it only took about twenty-five minutes to get to her usual parking lot. Even with morning traffic, she should be able to do it in a little over half an hour.

Olivia didn't feel the need to wait for the inspection report to call Scott. She dialed his number as she started the walk to her office. When he answered the phone, she barely waited for him to say hello before launching in.

"No major surprises or problems at the inspection. What do we do next?"

"Slow down, honey. Back up a minute and tell me how it went."

Olivia ran through the highlights of what she'd learned. Scott listened, throwing in an "okay" and "mmm-hmm" here and there. She concluded by adding, "And the company does remodeling, too. I might be able to hire them to do the work."

Scott chuckled. "You don't waste any time. Before you start ripping out kitchen cabinets, let's go over your options."

Olivia rolled her eyes, but smiled. "Yes, sir."

"Technically, you can ask the sellers to do some of the repairs, or to credit you back some of the purchase price to cover them. Given that there wasn't anything unexpected, I wouldn't necessarily recommend it, but it's my job to make sure you're informed."

"I appreciate that, Scott. I think I'm good. The price is reasonable and most of the work is getting folded into the renovations I want anyway, so it seems wrong to split hairs."

"I couldn't agree more."

"So how quickly can we close?"

"I get the sense that the sellers are ready when you are. Call your mortgage agent and your attorney and they'll get the ball rolling."

"I'll do it right away. I'd hoped to be moved into a new place by now."

"I know. You'll get there. Keep me posted and I'll have champagne chilling."

"Thanks, Scott. You're the best."

"I know."

Olivia laughed and ended the call. She paused outside her building to send a text to her friend Gina.

Inspection great. Inspector seriously hot. Fingers crossed I'll be out of your guest room soon. See you this evening.

During the summer, G.S. Hall was a bit of a ghost town. Even the tables near the entrance—bustling during the week with students and faculty meeting, working, having lunch—were empty. Olivia walked up the staircase to the second floor and down the hall to her office. When she opened the door, the smell of old books mingled with the almond oil diffuser she kept on the windowsill. Books, old and new and everything in between, filled the four bookcases she'd managed to cram into the space. It was the epitome of a crusty old literature professor's office and she loved it.

She sat down at the chunky wooden desk and booted up her anything-but-crusty laptop. She drafted an email to her mortgage adviser at the credit union and the real estate attorney she'd hired to handle the legal aspects of the closing.

Once they were sent, she looked at her phone and sighed. She'd put off calling her parents for more than a week. At least now she had good news. She initiated the call, then closed her eyes and took a deep, calming breath. "Hi, Mama."

"Hello, darling. How are you?"

"I'm doing well. And you?"

"Oh, I'm just fine. Your father's playing an early round of golf with Beau. Tara and I are going to meet them at the club for brunch. What about you? What are you up to?"

Of course her perfect sister and her husband would be joining her parents at the club. If she felt a hint of jealousy that she was never included in such things, it was overshadowed by relief. "I'm at the office, doing a little work."

"The office? I thought one of the points of becoming a professor was that you wouldn't have to work in the summer."

"I'm trying to finish revising an article so I can submit it to the *Journal of Southern Literature* before the semester starts."

"Oh, honey, I'm just teasing. I know you're like a little mouse in a wheel until you get tenure."

Even though Olivia knew her mother was trying to be playful, it was hard not to bristle, at least a bit. "It's really not so bad. I'm on track according to the two-year review I had in the spring. I just want to have this article accepted by the end of the year."

"And you will. You accomplish everything you put your mind to."

Although her mother didn't necessarily mean it as a compliment, Olivia took it as such. She decided to change the subject while she was ahead. "So, I finally found a house. The closing should be in a couple of weeks."

"Oh, darling, that's wonderful. Did you find something in that cute little neighborhood you were talking about? Small Creek?"

Olivia smiled. "Fall Creek. Not exactly. This one's a little ways out in the country, but still less than a half hour from campus."

"The country? Are you sure that's such a good idea? A young woman, living on her own."

Olivia rolled her eyes. "It's fine, Mama. Perfectly safe."

"If you say so. I still don't really like the thought of you—"

"It needs a bit of work, so I'm going to get to design it exactly the way I want." Olivia hoped shifting the conversation to decor would distract her mother.

"A bit of work? How much work?"

"It's an old farmhouse, so it's very solid. Mostly freshening up, but I'm going to put in a new kitchen, update the baths." She opted not to mention the collapsed front porch.

"Olivia, that sounds like an awfully big project."

"I'm going to hire professionals to do most of it." She had a flash of Joss standing in her kitchen, wearing a tool belt and cutting wood.

"Still, an old, run-down house in the middle of nowhere. I just don't know what on earth you're thinking."

The scolding tone pulled Olivia back to reality. Even though her mother couldn't see her, Olivia straightened her posture and squared her shoulders. "It's a great house and a good investment. It's going to be beautiful when it's done."

"Okay, darling. I'm sure you're right. I need to get ready to go meet your father."

"Okay, Mama. Give him my love. Tara and Beau, too."

"Of course. Don't you work too hard. Bye."

"Bye."

Olivia ended the call and drummed her fingers on her desk. Despite the fact that she was thirty-two, her mother had such a way of getting to her. It wasn't like she needed her parents' approval. But still. She didn't like having her choices, her judgment, questioned.

She turned to her computer and tried to focus. Her mother's words continued to echo in her mind. Olivia was just going to have to prove that she'd made a good decision, even if it was different from what her parents would have chosen. She'd always been the one to go against their wishes anyway. It made being right—being successful—all the more satisfying.

CHAPTER FOUR

Olivia sat on a stool at the kitchen island while Gina and Kel bustled around. She wanted to help, but would probably just be in the way. Kel, already dressed for work in gray pants and a slate blue button-down, pulled mugs from one of the cabinets and poured three matching cups of coffee.

Without a word, Gina, who'd been rifling in the fridge, stuck out an arm holding the carton of half-and-half. Kel took it, added some to each mug, and returned it to Gina's outstretched hand. Olivia smiled. The way they shared the space was seamless and completely adorable. After another moment, Gina emerged with an armful of bags and containers. She dumped everything on the counter and went back for more.

"What are you doing?" Olivia asked.

"I'm making Kel's lunch." Her perky tone made Olivia smile.

Gina added another armful of stuff to the pile. Olivia raised her eyebrow. That was some lunch.

Kel leaned against the sink and sipped her coffee. "I keep telling her it isn't necessary."

Gina blew an errant curl from in front of her eye. "You say that, but I know you skip lunch more days than not and that isn't okay anymore. I figure if I slave over it, you'll eat it to avoid hurting my feelings."

"You do need to eat, you know," Olivia said. Kel was four months pregnant and just starting to show, but her ebony skin had that glow. Between that and her expertly tailored, perfectly butch outfit, it was hard not to stare at just how gorgeous she looked.

Kel rolled her eyes. "I know. I've been told as much by Gina, the nurse at the clinic, my O.B., the doula, and Gina again. I'll add your name to the list."

Gina walked over to where Kel stood and kissed her firmly on the mouth. "So many women doting on you, it must be rough."

Kel quickly turned, pinning Gina against the counter. She kissed her long and slow. "You are an amazing wife, and I love you."

Gina's eyes fluttered open. "You're pretty amazing yourself, and I love you, too."

Olivia sighed. She'd never seen a couple with so much mutual love and respect who still had such passion for one another. Her sister didn't. Her parents certainly didn't. As much as it pained her not to have it, she liked knowing that kind of relationship was possible.

"So, what time is the closing again?" Gina asked.

"Three. Scott said it shouldn't take more than two hours."

"You're okay going by yourself?"

"I won't be by myself. Both Scott and my attorney will be there. There's nothing left to sort out. It's just me signing my name a billion times."

Kel nodded. "Good practice for when you break onto the *New York Times* Best Seller list for the first time."

"You understand I've not actually written a novel, right?"

"A technicality. I still consider you the most likely candidate of everyone I know."

"That's sweet, I think."

"In the meantime, we'll have to celebrate something else. Gina and I want to take you out tonight after the closing."

Olivia found herself oddly emotional. When she left everyone she knew and moved nearly a thousand miles away, she couldn't have imagined making a better pair of friends than Gina and Kel had turned out to be. "I would love that."

"Just a Taste? We can meet right when they open at 5:30, have tapas, a little wine, then decide if we want dinner, too."

The restaurant was Olivia's favorite. "I'll be there."

❖

Scott hadn't exaggerated. By the time Olivia left the closing, it was a little after five, and she estimated that she'd signed or initialed at least two hundred pieces of paper. The keys were in her purse, though, and the house was hers. She was equal parts giddy and shell-shocked.

She drove back downtown, parked on Aurora Street, and walked the few blocks to Just a Taste. It was 5:20 and there were a couple of people already waiting at the door. Gina and Kel appeared a moment later. She gave them the highlights of the two hours she spent signing her name and handing over a large chunk of her savings. When the restaurant door opened, Olivia's attention shifted.

M.J., one of the students from her American Lit survey course, was the hostess. After taking the first group to a table near the bar, she returned. When Olivia caught her eye, M.J. broke into a big smile.

"Dr. B! It's so good to see you. How's your summer been?"

"Really good, M.J. How about you?"

"Awesome. I've been interning at the State Theater and working. I'm so glad I decided not to go home for the summer."

Olivia thought back to her summers in college. After her freshman year, she took a job as a summer R.A., in part to be able to take a summer class, but mostly to avoid three months with her parents. "I know what you mean."

"Table inside or out?"

"We'll take the patio, please. There are three of us."

M.J. took menus from the podium and led them through the restaurant to the outdoor seating area in the back. "I signed up for your Southern writers course for the fall. I'm really looking forward to it."

Olivia smiled. "I'm looking forward to having you. I know you're busy now, but let's catch up. I'll be in my office most of the week before classes start. Stop in anytime."

"I will, thanks. Enjoy your dinner."

They ordered a smattering of small plates from the huge selection of seasonal tapas. Kel stuck to water, but both Olivia and Gina ordered from the selection of wine flights. "I'm going for the one with a couple of sparkling whites. It seems the most celebratory."

After toasting the house closing, they started sampling their food selections. There was a beet salad, a cheese plate, garlicky focaccia, lamb meatballs. "I always think the portions are going to be small and we should order more," Gina said, "but I'm stuffed."

"Same here," Olivia said.

Kel shrugged. "I was kind of hoping for dessert."

Gina reached over and patted her belly. "I love that being pregnant has given you a sweet tooth."

"Order whatever you want and we'll have a bite." Olivia always had room for a bite of dessert. Always.

Once the order for blackberry gelato was in, Gina turned to Olivia. "Are you sure you won't stay with us a bit longer, just until most of the work is done? You can't really want to live in a construction zone."

"I really don't want to think about moving once the semester starts. Besides, it'll be an adventure. I want to be there, in the thick of it, you know?"

Gina laughed. "No, I don't know. I think your house will be lovely when it's done, but I can't fathom wanting to sleep and shower there in the meantime."

Olivia shook her head. "You're such a princess."

"You bet I am."

"I've got movers scheduled for the end of the week to get the essentials in—nothing that can't be worked around. I'll set up a makeshift bedroom downstairs. I'm excited to get started on the work."

"Speaking of work, are you going to hire that sexy contractor who did your inspection? You know, if she's working for you, you probably shouldn't sleep with her."

Kel lifted a hand. "Wait, wait, wait. No one told me about a sexy contractor."

Gina cocked her head. "Well, I haven't seen her, so I'm only going on what Olivia told me."

All eyes turned to Olivia. "She's very nice to look at. I'll be the first to admit it. But it seems like her family's company does a lot of residential renovations in the area. Great reviews everywhere I look."

"Wait a minute." Gina's eyes narrowed. "Is that why you're so keen on staying there? You want to hang around so you can watch her work. I should have known you had an ulterior motive."

Olivia sighed. "That's not why I'm staying there. It's my home. I want to get a feel for it before I make some of the design decisions. I can't do that if I'm only stopping by for half an hour at a time."

"Mmm-hmm. Likely story."

"So you aren't going to sleep with her?" Kel asked.

"Well, I never said that." Olivia winked at her.

"But you are going to hire her," Gina said.

Olivia shrugged. "Probably. I did some research and the company has an impeccable reputation. I sent her my general ideas and scheduled a walk-through for tomorrow. If I like what she has to say, and the price, I don't see why I wouldn't."

Kel laughed and Gina shook her head. "Hard to argue with that logic."

Gina and Kel insisted on paying the bill, despite Olivia's protests that she wanted to thank them for putting her up for the last month and a half. Had it not been for their hospitality, she would have had to move into a hotel, or worse, sublet some student apartment, when her lease expired. She'd been beyond nervous to encroach on their space for such a long period of time, but it had been surprisingly easy, fun even, to stay with them.

That night, in the room that would soon become a nursery for Gina and Kel's twin boys, Olivia lay awake. She'd bought a house. In the country. That needed work. And had four acres of land. For the first time since she'd laid eyes on it over a month ago, Olivia found herself wondering if she'd gotten in over her head. When she finally fell asleep, she dreamed of blown fuses and leaking pipes.

CHAPTER FIVE

When Olivia emailed about getting an estimate for the work on her soon-to-be home, Joss was surprised. Based on how their first interaction had gone, Joss figured she was the last person Olivia would want to hire. But the email was friendly, flirtatious almost, and indicated a hope that they would work together. Joss decided to channel her annoyance into focus, spending extra time sketching out Olivia's ideas and working up a competitive bid for the project. At this point, getting the project was a matter of principle.

She showed up at the house twenty minutes before they were scheduled to meet, in part to look at the exterior with a designer's eye rather than an inspector's. She also wanted to be waiting when Olivia arrived. Again, it was a matter of principle.

Joss parked out front and took in the view. The house really was a charmer. With the front porch repaired, a coat of paint, and new shutters, it would look fresh and inviting while maintaining its historical character. Joss could see herself taking in the view of the yard from a nice old rocking chair. The image was strangely vivid and Joss had to shake her head to clear it from her mind. Olivia would probably hire a service to tend the yard and never bother to enjoy it.

Just as she was starting to feel annoyed again, Olivia pulled into the driveway. Joss got out of her truck and grabbed her sketches, reminding herself that she wanted this job.

"I'm so sorry if I kept you waiting," Olivia said as she walked toward the front of the house.

"Not at all. I was early." Joss observed that, once again, Olivia was wearing a dress. This one had a vintage feel to it, black with white polka dots. It was flouncy and hugged Olivia's curves in all the right spots. She liked the style—feminine in a way that made her think of old-school pinup girls instead of supermodels. She tried to focus on the fact that it was inappropriate attire for their walk-through, as well as the fact that she didn't use the word "flouncy."

Olivia shook her hand and smiled. "Well, I signed away my savings, and perhaps my firstborn. There were a lot of forms, I can't be sure. Either way, she's all mine."

"Congratulations." Joss was amused by the comment, even if she didn't want to be. "And don't worry. I've been to a couple of closings and I don't think the signing away of offspring is one of the standard documents."

Olivia laughed; it was a rich and easy sound that went straight to Joss's gut. "Oh, good. Since I don't have any offspring, that might have proved problematic. Shall we?"

Joss nodded. Why was Olivia being playful? That was not part of the equation. Joss balled her fists, resolving not to flirt with the woman she'd decided not to like. She followed Olivia around to the side door, the one not attached to the crumbling porch. Olivia pulled the key out of her purse and slipped it into the lock. She turned the knob, but just stood there.

"Is it stuck?" Joss asked.

"No. I mean, yes, but it's not…I just…"

Joss realized Olivia's hands were shaking. Well, hell. It was impossible not to go soft on a woman who was trembling, especially about buying a house. She placed her hand lightly on Olivia's arm and said, "It's okay. This is a really big deal."

"Was I that obvious?" Olivia shook her head, but smiled. "We're good. I'm good."

"Good." Joss stepped back and tried not to think about the way Olivia's hair smelled like almonds and cherries or the light dusting of freckles on her cheeks that she hadn't noticed before.

Olivia gave the door a good shove with her hip and stepped inside. It looked exactly as it did the day she'd been there for the inspection. Sunlight streamed in through the windows over the sink and in the small breakfast nook. Dust motes danced around in the beams of light. A mouse, clearly not expecting the intrusion, scurried under the door to the basement.

Joss, with a voice that sounded more gentle than professional, said, "It's a great house."

Olivia relaxed, reassured by Joss's words. "Thanks. I think you're right. Good bones."

"Good bones." Joss nodded her agreement. "Let me show you what I think we can do with these bones."

Joss led the way to the counter nearest the windows and unrolled a set of drawings. The first one was the floor plan for upstairs. The only change they'd discussed was knocking out a wall to combine the tiny fourth bedroom and bath into a larger bathroom and walk-in closet.

"The cost for this isn't huge," she said, "because we aren't going to move any of the plumbing. The tub will stay exactly where it is and we'll tie into the existing lines for the shower enclosure."

Although the blueprint only had circles and squares and lines to represent fixtures and walls and doors, Olivia could envision it perfectly. "Yes, it's exactly what I want."

"Technically, you could be hurting your resale value by taking it from four bedrooms to three, but I think it's worth it."

"I agree, and I certainly don't need four bedrooms."

"Right. Now, for the main attraction."

Joss shuffled the papers to reveal a blueprint for the main level of the house. Olivia took in the images, overwhelmed by how perfect they were. Joss had taken everything she said in her email and created a plan that opened up the space while maintaining the integrity of the original design. Half of the wall between the kitchen and living room was gone. In its place was a massive island that literally doubled the work surfaces in the kitchen.

"Doing it this way means you shouldn't have to compensate for any load-bearing walls. Although I wouldn't necessarily lay out the appliances this way, it's functional, and not moving anything is going to save you on plumbing and electric."

Olivia could see it, and she loved it. "It's absolutely perfect."

Joss couldn't help but smile, at least a little. The house was going to be amazing, there was no doubt about it. Olivia's face glowed with excitement; the sincerity of it proved irresistible. Joss pulled herself back to reality so that they could talk materials. This would be telling.

"You don't have to decide everything now, but knowing your general thoughts will allow me to give you a more precise estimate."

She expected Olivia to want granite counters and all the other must-have upgrades that seemed to be featured on every episode of every show on the HGTV channel.

"My big indulgence is going to be high-end appliances. I want the six-burner gas stove, the refrigerator with French doors, the whole thing."

"Okay."

"Everything else is about balance. I want it to look nice and be durable, especially when it comes to things like counters and bathroom fixtures, but I don't have my heart set on anything. I'd rather keep with the traditional farmhouse aesthetic than do anything really modern or trendy. Does that make sense?"

Joss nodded. Damn it all if it wasn't exactly what she would do. She scribbled some notes, punched numbers into her calculator, made more notes. When she looked up, Olivia was staring at her with what appeared to be a mixture of anticipation and dread. She handed her the paper with her estimate for the entire project. Olivia looked at it, looked at her, looked at it again.

"This is for materials and labor?"

It was a very competitive estimate. If Olivia balked, Joss was prepared to walk away and wash her hands of the whole thing. Knowing that most of the other companies in town wouldn't come close, or would do subpar work, would be her consolation.

After what seemed like a long time, Olivia tapped her fingers together. "Let's say, then, that I wanted to do the upstairs floors as well. If I rip out the carpet myself, how much to sand and refinish them?"

Joss studied Olivia for a moment. It was hard to imagine this pretty woman, with her pretty dresses and pretty drawl, on her hands and knees with a crowbar. "Rip up the carpet, including the padding, pull out all the staples, and fill all the holes?"

Joss enjoyed a small satisfaction in seeing Olivia's eyes get big. To her credit, she regained her composure quickly. Whether it was pride or naiveté, Joss couldn't be sure.

"Yes."

"Full second floor minus the bathroom, including new thresholds and quarter-round where needed, stain of your choice, two coats of polyurethane, and you sign with me to do the rest of the work. Eighteen hundred more."

Olivia stuck out her hand. "Deal."

Once they'd shaken hands, Olivia cracked a grin. Joss got the distinct impression that she was on the verge of a happy dance. They'd see how happy she was after her fiftieth splinter.

"We're just finishing up a project. We should be able to start by the middle of next week. Will that work for you?"

"The sooner the better."

The smile Olivia flashed was enough to send a jolt of heat right to Joss's core. It was okay. She'd probably hardly have to see her. She'd do amazing work on this beautiful house that deserved to be restored, then she'd be on her way and that would be the end of it. "We do our best to stay on schedule."

"I'm sure you do. Oh, I should probably mention that I'll be living here during the reno."

"What?" It wasn't unheard of by any means, but given the extent of the work, it didn't seem like the best idea. Plus, Olivia was so girly. In Joss's mind, girly meant high maintenance.

"I know it sounds crazy, but my lease was up a few weeks ago and I've been staying with friends. I really don't want to impose on their hospitality any longer than I have to. Plus, I'd rather not move in the middle of the semester if I don't have to."

"You realize there will be days where you have no running water, no electricity?"

Olivia's smile didn't falter. "If there are a couple of days I need to stay with them again, I certainly can. And I'll be leaving most of my furniture in storage so it won't be in your way. Don't worry about me. I like to be in the thick of things."

"If you say so." Joss told herself not to worry about it. After two days of sawdust and hammering, Olivia would be running for the hills.

"I'm tougher than I look." Olivia winked at her.

"Okay, then. Let's tentatively set next Wednesday as our start day. We'll take measurements and poke around, then demo will start on Thursday."

That was still two weeks before the semester started. "Sounds perfect."

"Great. I'll plan to see you at eight. You can also decide whether you want to be here to let us in and out or give me a key for the duration of the work."

"I start teaching again in a couple of weeks, so I'll give you a copy. Thank you."

"And thank you for choosing Bauer and Sons. We appreciate your business."

Whatever casual rapport they had while chatting about the house was gone and Joss was, once again, all business. Olivia sighed. It was okay. Joss would do good work and she'd still be nice to look at.

They shook hands and Olivia watched Joss leave. She then broke into the happy dance she'd been holding in since she saw Joss's plan for the house, and the estimated cost. Between the money her grandparents had left her and her own savings, she wouldn't have to finance any of the work. And since she was going to pick out all the details herself, it was much more exciting than buying a more expensive house in the first place.

She took a few minutes to walk around, soaking in the fact that the house was now hers. She decided the small sitting room downstairs, the one she was planning to use as an office, would be a perfect makeshift bedroom. Since it only needed a fresh coat of paint and to have the floors refinished, it would be one of the last rooms done. By that time, hopefully the upstairs would be finished and she could move into her actual bedroom.

Olivia returned to the kitchen. Since she didn't plan on keeping it, she realized she hadn't even bothered to check and see if the refrigerator worked. She plugged it in, fiddled with the thermostat knob, and heard the compressor rumble to life. Fortunately, someone had thought to clean it and leave the door open, so it didn't even smell bad.

Olivia closed the door and put her hands on her hips. She looked around the room again and nodded. This was going to be so much fun.

❖

Moving in was almost anticlimactic. When the movers showed up at the storage facility, Olivia was ruthless. She had them load her smaller guest bed, one chest of drawers, a futon for the living room, and a small rolling cart and folding table for the kitchen. The truck seemed oddly empty and she was pretty sure the movers thought she was crazy. She had them throw in a couple boxes of books and some basic kitchenware.

Gina, who'd come to help, raised a brow. "That's it?"

Olivia shrugged. "I'm being practical. The less I bring now, the less I have to move around for Joss's crew to work."

"I get it. I mean, I don't know how you're going to do it, but I get it."

Olivia smiled. "Do you still want to come and see the house even though there's nothing for you to do?"

Gina slung an arm over her shoulder. "Woman, that's why I offered in the first place."

It took longer to drive back to her house than it did for them to unload everything. Since the movers seemed almost bothered by having so little to do, Olivia had them carry in the suitcases of clothes from her car that she'd had at Gina and Kel's. That took them all of six minutes. Olivia smiled and shrugged, promising to call them again when she moved in earnest. She tipped them generously and sent them on their way.

She spent half an hour showing Gina around, pointing out the wall that would be coming out and where the new kitchen island would be. Gina was enthusiastic, if a bit skeptical.

"It's not that I don't believe it will be fabulous."

"But?" Olivia worried that Gina had picked up on something she'd missed in her giddiness and her vision of what it could be.

"No but. I just can't imagine starting with this. I don't have a DIY bone in my body."

Olivia laughed. "You have so many other talents."

"Thanks. Really, though, do you know how to do any of this stuff?"

"I'm leaving all the serious work to the professionals. Painting is easy and I like it. Wallpaper and carpet removal probably won't be fun, but I want to get my hands in it, get dirty. You know?"

Gina shook her head. "If you say so."

"And let's not forget the sexy contractor."

"Right. You're looking for some opportunities to brush up against her. Literally."

"If that happens to be a side effect of things, I certainly wouldn't complain."

"I look forward to the tales of your exploits."

"And I look forward to having exploits worthy of tales."

After Gina left, Olivia stood in the kitchen. It felt nearly as empty as it did before. Olivia had a moment of alarm that this was how she was going to live for the next couple of months, but she brushed it off. It was all good. She was excited for her minimalist adventure.

She thought Joss would be happy that she hadn't clogged up the rooms with unnecessary stuff. Happy and impressed. She wanted Joss to be impressed. And to like her. And Olivia had a sneaking suspicion it was going to take a lot more than her usual tactics to get there.

She took a little while to put away her clothes in the dresser and downstairs closet, then realized there really wasn't anything else to unpack. Kitchen stuff would need to stay in boxes since the cabinets would be gone sooner rather than later. Since she hadn't yet bought any supplies, there weren't any projects she could start, either. As far as she was concerned, that could only mean one thing: shopping.

Olivia drove into town thinking about what she'd need to start some of her projects. She took the winding road that skirted the lake, enjoying the glimpses of water through the trees. Halfway there, she remembered she'd neglected to locate the boxes containing towels and other bathroom items. It was the perfect excuse to indulge in a few new ones, along with a shower curtain and mat to tide her over until the renovations were done.

She started at Bed Bath & Beyond, picking out a shower curtain covered in little gray whales and a matching bath mat. There were some bright pink towels on clearance and she figured why the hell not. That got her thinking about the fact that she needed a washer and dryer. Really, the sooner she bought those, the sooner she could stop dumping time and quarters into the Laundromat. It was the practical thing to do.

She stopped by one of the big box stores, found a nice high efficiency set on sale, and arranged delivery for later in the week. Then she roamed the aisles, looking at paint colors and floor samples and everything in between. Although part of her wanted to buy one of everything, she decided to start with the supplies she'd need to take down the hideous wallpaper that seemed to be covering every flat surface in the house.

After getting some advice and buying everything she thought she'd need, Olivia headed to Wegmans. While it was difficult, she managed to restrain herself from filling her cart with every spice and pantry staple she could think of. Since everything she put in her pantry would only have to come out again when the work started, she kept it to produce, things she could eat within the week, and coffee. Even with her restraint, she managed to fill five large canvas grocery bags. A lot of it was cleaning supplies, though, which made it seem better.

By the time she was home and everything was unpacked, she was exhausted. It was the good kind of exhaustion, though. She made a salad and took it outside. She'd have to get some outdoor furniture so she could enjoy the rest of the summer. In the meantime, she found a patch of grass in the shade and sat cross-legged on the ground. She ate her dinner, trying to decide if she should try to put in a vegetable garden first, or a berry patch. She'd probably need a rototiller, along with someone to teach her how to use it.

One thing at a time. Olivia chuckled, certain she'd be telling herself that a lot in the upcoming weeks.

Chapter Six

Olivia woke up in a good mood. Today Joss was coming to start pre-project exploration. Olivia didn't know what that meant, but she didn't really care. Her renovation was getting started. She was also going to see Joss, who she'd been thinking about probably more than was healthy.

She put on a casual dress and resisted the urge to fuss with her hair. In the kitchen, she put on a full pot of coffee instead of the half pot she typically made for herself. She indulged in a bit of daydreaming about how the space would look when it was all done. She wondered if it was too soon to go shopping for appliances. The sound of a car in the driveway pulled her back to the present.

Olivia approached the back door, then realized it wasn't Joss standing on the other side. It was a tall, lanky guy carrying a toolbox. That was strange. She opened the door and offered a smile. "Good morning."

"Good morning. I'm Ben Bauer, with Bauer and Sons Construction. Are you Olivia?"

"I am. Come in, please."

Ben stepped inside. "Thanks."

Olivia closed the door behind him and extended her hand. While he shook it, she studied him, trying to figure out why he looked familiar. "Have we met before?"

"No, but we were supposed to. I was scheduled to do your inspection, but I was sick that morning, so my sister, Joss, did it instead."

"Right. Ben. I remember now." Well, that explained why he looked familiar. Although Olivia couldn't put her finger on it at first, there was definitely a family resemblance. "I'm glad you're feeling better."

"Thanks. I hope you don't feel like we keep doing a bait and switch on you. Joss needed to help wrap up a project today, but we didn't want to make you wait."

It did feel like a bait and switch, but only because she'd been so looking forward to seeing Joss again, even if her manner was a little aloof. "It's fine. I really appreciate you coming."

"Of course. We really are a family operation, so you'll likely see both of us quite a bit before it's all said and done."

Olivia hoped so. Despite the odd chill that permeated her last meeting with Joss, she wanted to see more of her. As for Ben, he seemed nice enough, and really did look like the taller and skinnier male version of Joss. "That's good to know. So are you the Bauer, or the and sons?"

Ben laughed. "Technically, Joss and I are the grandchildren. Despite his sincerest wishes, my grandfather only had one child, my dad. He, in turn, had me and two girls. We all work at the company."

Olivia thought about her family business. Nothing would have thrilled her parents more than if she'd gone to law school and joined the ranks of Bennett and Associates. She shuddered at the thought. "That's quite a legacy."

"It's nice we all ended up deciding that's what we wanted to do. Anyway, I didn't come here to give you the family tree of the company."

Olivia smiled. "It's fine. I asked and it's a good story."

"Thanks." Ben seemed to get almost shy at the compliment. Olivia found it quite adorable.

"So you're here to take measurements?"

Ben quickly regained his composure. "Sort of. I'm mostly playing detective. Since your plan involves taking out a couple of walls, I'm here to figure out what's load bearing and make sure there aren't any surprises."

"You can do that?"

"Absolutely. After working on enough houses, you get a feel for what's where, but you never really know. I drill a few holes, put in my little camera, and poof—no guesswork."

"That's really cool." Olivia thought of all the home improvement shows she watched. People always seemed to go tearing into walls first, then freak out when they discovered the main sewer line in the way.

"Well, it gives you a lot more control. If we find something we weren't expecting, we can estimate the cost so you can decide if you want to absorb it or change the plans. It's less dramatic than what you see on TV, but generally better for the home owner."

The fact that he seemed to be reading her thoughts made Olivia laugh. "I appreciate that."

Ben flashed a winning smile. "We do want our clients to be happy. You're welcome to watch, but I'm fine if there is something else you'd like to do. I also have the key you gave Joss. If you need to leave, I'm happy to lock up when I'm done."

Olivia thought for a moment. She'd considered going to her office for a few hours, but there wasn't anything that was immediately pressing. If she stayed, she could tackle the wallpaper on the walls that weren't going anywhere. She'd also know the results of Ben's poking around. "I don't want to be in your way. I'll work on a couple of projects and you can let me know if you find anything of note."

"Sounds like a plan. I'll holler if there's something you should see."

"Perfect." Olivia went to her makeshift bedroom to put on appropriate work clothes. When she arrived back in the kitchen, Ben was scribbling something on a notepad.

"So far so good," he said.

"Music to my ears. Would you like a cup of coffee?"

His eyes lit up. "Really? That would be great."

Olivia poured two cups. "Cream and sugar?"

"Only if it's not too much trouble."

She added both and handed it to him. "No trouble at all. Even in a construction zone, coffee is a must."

Ben lifted his mug. "I'll drink to that."

"I'll be in the living room fighting with wallpaper if you need me."

"Thank you. I'll let you know what I find."

Olivia took her coffee and headed into the living room. If she had to guess, she'd have dated the decor around 1983. The wallpaper was mauve and gray, with large, faux brush strokes hinting at floral shapes. It reminded her of the very first living room of her childhood.

Her mother had redecorated often, always in whatever look was both trendy and expensive.

She took the spray bottle of adhesive remover she'd bought and gave a ten-foot section of wall the once-over. Once it was saturated, she wedged a putty knife under one of the seams. She grabbed a corner and pulled. She pulled and pulled, growing more and more excited as an entire strip came away in one large piece. Excitement quickly turned to dismay when she looked at the wall and realized only the top layer of paper had come off. The wall remained coated in a soggy, sticky mess.

"Fuck."

"Is everything okay in there?" Ben's question made Olivia realize she'd spoken out loud.

"Fine, fine." She clearly wasn't very convincing, because the next thing she knew Ben was hovering in the doorway.

"Something wrong?"

Olivia sighed. "Only that this is harder and grosser than I'd expected."

Ben laughed. "I think hard and gross is the definition of wallpaper removal."

She arched a brow. "Thanks, Mr. Merriam. Or are you Webster?"

"Can I give you a hand?"

"Do I really look that helpless?" She hated the perception that she was some hapless female who couldn't handle projects on her own.

"Not at all. You look exceedingly capable." He winked at her.

Ben's smile seemed genuine. So did the rest of him. And he was nice and chatty—so different from Joss. "Flattery will get you everywhere."

"Your technique is very good. If you wet it down just a little more, you can take your scraper and get most of the goop in one sweep. May I?"

"By all means." Olivia handed over the spray bottle and putty knife.

Ben spritzed a small area, waited for maybe a count of ten, then scraped the wall. As promised, the residue came off in a gooey blob. Hallelujah.

"Besides getting it really wet, you want to make sure you hold the blade at a forty-five-degree angle."

"That I can do."

Ben looked at her. "You'll still need to give it a good wash, but that should be it. Would you like a hand? I don't need to be anywhere for another hour or so."

Olivia thought about Joss. She'd looked so incredulous when Olivia negotiated some of her DIY projects into the contract. At the time, her push had been as much about wanting to get her hands dirty as it had been about saving money. Now, it felt like a matter of principle. "I think I can manage, but I appreciate the offer."

Ben cocked his head. "Are you sure? It could be our little secret."

It was as though he'd been reading her mind. Olivia had to laugh. "Okay, but only just a little."

They devised a system in which Olivia sprayed and Ben scraped. In less than a half hour, they'd done the better part of a wall. Olivia stepped back to admire the progress.

"Not bad, right?" Ben said.

"Not bad at all. Thank you so much for the advice and the help. I really don't want to keep you."

"My pleasure, really. I'm sorry now that I have to leave."

Olivia gave him a sideways look. "Okay, now you're just being silly."

"I mean it. Of course, I might be talking about the company more than the work."

"Well, that seems far more plausible." Olivia enjoyed the banter. It was exactly the kind of easy, almost flirtatious back-and-forth she wanted with Joss. Why did Joss have to make it so difficult?

"Would you like to have dinner, or maybe drinks, sometime?"

Olivia was so caught up in thinking about Joss that she barely caught the question. It sounded like Ben was asking her on a date, and that couldn't be right. "Excuse me?"

"I asked if you might join me for dinner or a drink sometime. I don't normally mix business with pleasure, but since this is really Joss's project, I don't think it counts."

She hadn't misheard. Well, hell. She could barely get Joss to give her the time of day and here was her brother asking her out on a date. Not that he wasn't good-looking, and far more charming than his sister had turned out to be, but really. The universe was playing a little joke on her.

"I, uh, I'm flattered, really." She had a fair amount of practice in deflecting male interest, but Ben had caught her by surprise and she struggled to find the right words.

"Hey, no worries. I just couldn't resist asking."

For some reason, she felt the need to explain. She liked Ben and didn't want there to be any awkwardness between them. She had enough of that with Joss. "It's just that I..." Why was it hard to spit out the words suddenly? "I'm a lesbian."

Ben let out a sound that was something between a laugh and a guffaw. Olivia narrowed her eyes at him.

"Sorry, sorry," he said quickly. "Well, that's ironic."

Olivia was used to being read as straight. It irritated her, but if people weren't asses about it, she took it with a grain of salt. She wasn't sure why Ben was laughing, or why he found it ironic, for that matter. "I'm sorry?"

Ben scratched his temple. "No, it's me who should be sorry. It's just...my sister made some comment about you being more my type than hers. I figured she had something concrete to base it on."

Realizing her hands were fisted on her hips, Olivia made a point of dropping them to her sides and unclenching. She probably shouldn't respond, but she couldn't contain herself. "I can assure you I gave her no such thing."

Olivia started putting the pieces together. If Joss assumed she was straight, that might explain why she was so standoffish. On one hand, it was a relief. On the other, it was infuriating. It was one thing to be invisible. It was another to be presumed straight and essentially judged for it. By another lesbian.

Olivia liked to think she possessed some fundamental essence of gayness. That, combined with a certain look—or smile—should be enough to create a blip on the gaydar. And she'd given Joss plenty of looks, and smiles.

"Look, I'm sure there was some misunderstanding. I meant no harm, and I can assure you my sister didn't either."

Olivia tried to regain her composure. It wasn't his fault that his sister played into such ridiculous and annoying stereotypes. "It's fine, really. Clearly, some signals got crossed somewhere along the way."

"Are you sure? I feel really bad now." Ben looked so sheepish,

Olivia couldn't hold it against him. Especially since it wasn't his fault in the first place.

"I'm sure. I'm not bothered that you asked me out, I promise." He didn't look relieved. Olivia shook her head. "It's that Joss assumed I was straight."

"Oh. I see."

Olivia wasn't sure he did, but she didn't want to belabor the point. Nor did she want to make him any more uncomfortable than he already was. "It's all good. Don't you have somewhere to be?"

The look on his face made Olivia think he'd completely forgotten. "Right. I do. I should go. Joss will be here in the morning to do all the prep work for demo."

Great. "That sounds good. I'll be here, at least in the morning for a bit."

"Okay. I'll see you later in the week, likely. I really am sorry."

"No need. It's water under the bridge."

Whether it was her assurance or the fact that he was leaving, Ben finally looked relieved. "Thanks. Good luck with the rest of your wallpaper."

"Thanks. I'm going to need it."

Olivia closed the door behind him as he left. She stood at the window and watched as he pulled out of the driveway and down the street. She shook her head again, then went back to work.

Three hours later, Olivia's arms ached and she was covered in a combination of sweat and wallpaper residue. The living room was done, however, except for the wall that was coming out. The walls were discolored and a little sad, but they weren't in terrible shape. She was pleased with the results and quite satisfied with herself, even if she'd had a little help.

After taking a shower, she made herself a late lunch and took it outside. Since the porch was off-limits, she'd set up a plastic patio set in the backyard. It would tide her over until she could put a pair of big, old rocking chairs out front. There was a light breeze and it was, by all accounts, a gorgeous late summer afternoon.

Still, Olivia couldn't quite seem to relax. Something about the whole interaction with Ben continued to nag at her. It was Joss—her quick assessment and ready dismissal. In principle, it infuriated her. In reality, it felt hugely disappointing. She'd been attracted to Joss, more so than she'd been to anyone since moving to New York. Clearly, the feeling was not mutual.

❖

Joss pulled into the parking lot of Bauer and Sons. The sun was shining, John Cougar was pumping from the speakers, and the Sharpstein project was finished a day ahead of schedule. Seeing Ben's truck in its usual spot was icing on the cake. It meant he'd survived the discovery work and measurements at Olivia's house. She pulled in next to him and climbed out of her truck. On her way into the office, she mentally corrected herself. It was the Bennett house, no different than any other project.

She walked into the office and found Daphne laughing and Ben shaking his head. She'd either missed a good joke or Ben making an ass of himself. Either way, she wanted to know what it was.

"Dude, you were so wrong." Ben continued shaking his head while Daphne tried, unsuccessfully, to stop laughing.

"What? What was I wrong about?" Joss wondered if maybe she'd estimated the supplies for a project wrong, but it seemed unlikely that would cause such a stir.

"Your little professor, the Southern one you seem to dislike so much."

Joss felt the muscles in her jaw twitch. "I don't dislike her. She's a paying client, which means I like her just fine."

"She's also a lesbian."

"What? What are you talking about?"

Daphne jumped in. "Casanova here decided to put the moves on her and she shut him down."

Joss felt an involuntary tightening in her chest. "What?"

Ben huffed. "I didn't put the moves on her. I asked her, very casually, if she might like to have a drink sometime."

"I thought we agreed not to date clients." The mental image of Ben getting cozy with Olivia made her queasy.

"You agreed. I only acknowledged it was probably a good idea. Besides, this is primarily your project."

"But you're missing the best part," Daphne said. "She turned him down because she's a lesbian."

Joss tried to process everything that was happening. Olivia wasn't straight. That, in itself, was...something. Joss thought back to the first time she'd seen Olivia, swaying in her kitchen to imaginary music. Joss had been attracted to her—instantly and intensely—but those feelings were quashed when she learned what Olivia did for a living, where she was from. It had never occurred to her that, in spite of those things, or maybe in addition to them, Olivia might be gay.

"And she was pretty annoyed that I'd assumed she was straight because of you."

Joss pinched the bridge of her nose. "Hold up. Start over, from the beginning, and tell me everything."

Ben shrugged. "There isn't that much to tell. I showed up and she was there, wearing this dress that made her look like a fifties housewife, only sexy."

Joss interrupted him; these were mental pictures she did not need. "Okay, maybe not everything."

Ben rolled his eyes. "We chatted. She followed me around, asking questions. She was warm and funny and I decided to ask her out. I didn't really think it through."

Of course he didn't think it through. Ben asked women out at the drop of a hat. Even when he got rejected, he seemed to enjoy the asking. "Then what?"

"She politely deflected, which was cool, but then she told me she was a lesbian. I think she was trying to make me not feel bad, which was sweet. I apologized and told her I'd gotten the wrong impression from you. That part really seemed to irritate her."

This was the last thing she needed. "Shit. What exactly did you say I told you?"

"Only that you thought she was more my type than yours, which were your exact words, I'm pretty sure."

Joss shook her head. This was not good. What had been a mildly uncomfortable situation was now going to be painfully awkward. Olivia knew that Joss thought she was straight, and not in some passing, didn't even think about it way. She knew that, at least a little, there'd been conversation about whose type she was. And Joss was going to have to show up at her house the next morning and face her.

"I don't understand what the problem is," Daphne said. "Shouldn't being lesbians give you something in common? Make it easier to work together?"

Joss glared at her sister. "It doesn't work like that."

"Really? Why not?"

Ben laughed. "Because Joss is bound and determined not to like this woman. It was one thing when Joss thought she was attractive, which she is, by the way. The fact that she's both attractive and gay makes things more complicated."

"Thank you for that in-depth analysis." Joss's voice dripped sarcasm.

"So what are you going to do?" Daphne asked.

Joss squared her shoulders, more than ready for this conversation to be over. "I'm going to do the job." When her brother and sister both raised a brow, she added, "And do my best not to put my foot in my mouth. Again."

CHAPTER SEVEN

Olivia paced back and forth in her kitchen. Joss was due to arrive any minute. Her conversation with Ben from the day before played through her mind. To her way of thinking, she had two options. The first option was to ignore the situation entirely, pretend it never happened and keep all of her interactions with Joss to a bare minimum. That wasn't her style. The other option was to confront it head-on, force Joss to admit she was wrong. It didn't need to be an argument, but she did need Joss to acknowledge that she'd jumped to conclusions and that those conclusions had been completely wrong.

Then the whole mess would be behind them. With the air cleared, maybe the awkward tension between them would go away. Maybe they could be friends or, even better, enjoy a little casual flirtation. Meeting Joss had reminded Olivia just how much she missed that.

As if on cue, Joss pulled into the driveway. She waited until Joss was about ten feet from the back door before opening it. She offered her most welcoming smile.

"Joss, it's so nice to see you again."

Joss returned the smile, but there were nerves behind it. "Good morning, Olivia. It's nice to see you, too."

Olivia stepped aside so Joss could enter the kitchen. "It was such a pleasure meeting your brother yesterday."

Joss looked exceedingly ill at ease. "Yeah, about that. I'm sorry he asked you out. Hitting on clients is not what Bauer and Sons is about."

Olivia waved her hand. "Oh, that's no big deal. Ben and I sorted it out and we're good."

"Okay, good. I didn't want you to have the wrong idea."

Olivia looked Joss in the eyes. "Just like I don't want you to have the wrong idea."

Joss winced slightly and looked down. "Yeah. I'm sorry about that, too."

It wasn't enough of an answer to satisfy her. "I don't understand why you would tell your brother I was straight. What made you so sure?"

Joss shrugged, but refused to make eye contact with her. "It wasn't like that. We didn't sit around discussing it. I wasn't sure, but I didn't get gay vibes from you, and my gaydar is pretty reliable. Combined with the fact that you're so girly. And Southern."

Olivia huffed. "There are just as many lesbians down there as there are up here."

"Of course there are." The way she said it made Olivia think the idea had never occurred to her.

Olivia sighed. It was one thing to get that kind of reaction from crusty old administrators and straight guys. It was another, and entirely obnoxious, thing to get it from a fellow lesbian. To get it from a hot lesbian she was attracted to, well, that was simply demoralizing. Which was why she was having such a hard time letting it go.

She narrowed her eyes at Joss. "Is that why you don't like me? You assumed I was straight?"

"No."

"So there's a different reason that you don't like me."

"Yes. I mean, no."

Joss looked beyond uncomfortable at this point. As much as she wanted to enjoy watching Joss squirm, her upbringing compelled her to smooth feathers whenever they were ruffled. And she needed to make nice if she wanted the chance to get flirty—or more. She clasped her hands together and offered a smile. "It's not a test, and I'm not trying to make you feel bad."

Joss looked far from convinced.

"Really. I get annoyed when I'm read as straight because of how I choose to look or dress. I also get annoyed when people hear my accent and figure I'm some airhead debutante."

"So you weren't a debutante?"

It was Olivia's turn to look away. "I wasn't an airhead."

"Shit, I was kidding. You seriously were a debutante? Big dress and a ball just for you?"

Well, hell. This was not how she wanted this conversation to go. "It wasn't like *Gone with the Wind*, if that's what you're thinking. And don't change the subject. We're talking about why you don't like me."

"I think those things are one and the same, darling." The second the words were out of her mouth, Joss looked horrified, as though she couldn't believe she'd just said that.

Olivia narrowed her eyes. "What is that supposed to mean?"

Joss seemed to regain her composure. "Nothing. I only meant that we don't have anything in common."

Olivia felt her pulse start to thud in her head and heat rise to make her entire face flush. "You don't know anything about me."

It looked like Joss was going to hurl another insult, but she didn't. Olivia saw her take a deep breath and clench her jaw. "Look, forget I said anything. We're going to be working together for at least the next few weeks. Let's try to keep it professional and things will go a lot more smoothly."

Olivia looked at the woman about whom she'd already had more than one erotic dream. She was drawn to her awake and in sleep, and couldn't seem to shake it. She'd meant her question about Joss not liking her as a gentle tease, a way to get Joss to open up. Normally, Olivia was good—really good—at that sort of thing. Instead, she'd opened up a can of worms and started an argument. Or got sucked into an argument. She still wasn't sure which.

As much as it stung, if that was what Joss really thought of her, it was probably for the best that she know it now. She had no use for women who were judgmental and rude. "That sounds like an excellent idea. I'll let you get to work."

Olivia grabbed her purse and left the same way Joss had come in. She got in her car and pulled out of the driveway, refusing to look back. She headed toward town without a concrete destination in mind.

That was not how she'd intended things to go. Why did Joss have to be so contrary about everything? Olivia chided herself for getting pulled into a bickering match. It was the opposite of what she'd been going for. A little part of her brain told Olivia to let it go. But just like ignoring a problem, letting it go wasn't in her nature either. And there was something about Joss. She was attractive, sure, but it was something more compelling than that. Olivia couldn't put her finger on it, but it was something she couldn't—didn't want to—ignore. By the time she got into town, she'd come full circle. She was going to have to apologize. Well, she didn't have to, but if she wanted to figure out this thing with Joss, trying to make up would help. She squared her shoulders. She didn't hate apologizing, but she certainly didn't enjoy it, especially when she wasn't in the wrong.

She stopped at the grocery store. She didn't need anything, but she wasn't going to go back empty-handed and make it obvious she'd stomped out in a huff just to do it. Olivia wandered the produce department, letting the colors and smells distract her. It wouldn't be too long before she'd have a kitchen where she could cook to her heart's content.

Since that wasn't the case yet, Olivia picked up fresh salad ingredients and local blueberries. Feeling self-indulgent, she passed by the cheese counter and picked up a wedge of brie. An older man in the bakery department was putting out fresh baguettes, so she grabbed one of those as well. Feeling calmer, she paid for her things and headed home.

Olivia walked back into the house and found Joss removing trim from the doorway that separated the kitchen and dining room. She watched as Joss pried each piece off individually then added them to a neat pile in the corner. Watching her work was hot, more so than she'd imagined.

Joss must have sensed that she was being watched, because she turned. "I know it looks tedious, but the wood is original. Even if we don't need it elsewhere in the house, it has value."

Olivia picked up on a defensive edge in Joss's voice. She decided to use it as an opportunity to be conciliatory. "I completely agree. I appreciate that you're taking so much care. If you don't use it, I'll invent a project to give it a purpose."

"It would be perfect if you ever wanted to turn some bookshelves into built-ins."

Olivia couldn't tell if Joss was throwing her a bone or if she simply couldn't resist imagining a project. In either case, it was the right thing to say. "Oh, my God. Yes. That would be amazing."

"I'd be happy to add it to the project if you'd like." Could that be Joss attempting to make nice, too?

Olivia offered her a smile. "Seriously? I've got so many books that have been languishing in boxes. I can't squeeze any more into my office."

"I'll sketch out a couple of options and bring them to you later this week."

"Thank you."

"No problem."

Joss started to turn away. Olivia took a deep breath. "Joss, I'm sorry I got testy with you earlier."

Joss looked down, as though her hammer was the most fascinating thing she'd ever seen. "You don't need to apologize."

Olivia realized she'd fisted her hands on her hips and forced herself to drop them to her sides. "I do. I get irritated when I'm read as straight, especially by..." She glanced away, then back and Joss. "Well, you know."

Joss merely raised an eyebrow.

Olivia plowed on. "I'm just saying that was one thing. And then the whole debutante thing on top, it really set me off."

Joss went from looking dubious to downright uncomfortable. "Okay, well, I'm sorry I pushed your buttons."

"Thank you. I have a lot of ambivalence about certain parts of my upbringing. I became a professor, moved here, to escape a lot of that. I guess I'm still sensitive about it." She hadn't planned on baring her soul, but it sort of came out.

"Okay." Joss nodded, but still seemed uneasy.

"I just really don't want there to be any tension between us. We're going to be crossing paths a lot over the next few weeks."

"I agree."

"Truce?"

"Truce."

Olivia stuck out her hand and Joss shook it. Olivia smiled again. It was a step in the right direction. "I'm so glad. I'll let you get back to work. I'm going to go change and get back to the never-ending wallpaper."

Joss watched Olivia disappear into the sitting room she'd claimed as her bedroom. She shook her head, not entirely sure what had just happened. Whatever it was, she hoped it would help the project go more smoothly. She put in her ear buds, cranked some classic rock, and got back to work.

An hour later, Joss had finished removing the trim and baseboards. She'd also removed outlets and capped the wiring in the walls slated to come down. She contemplated leaving without saying anything, but doing so after Olivia's overture seemed rude. She put her tools away and went in search.

"Olivia?"

"In here." The sound came from the small half-bath off the formal sitting room.

Joss followed it and found Olivia ankle-deep in torn-up wallpaper. She'd changed from the skirt she'd been wearing and was in an Emory T-shirt and a pair of athletic shorts. Her hair was pulled into a messy bun and there were bits of wallpaper stuck in it. For some inexplicable reason, Joss found that look even sexier than when Olivia was all dressed up. Joss shook her head at the absurdity of it. "I just wanted to let you know that I was leaving."

"Thanks, and thank you for all your hard work today."

Joss shrugged. "That's what you're paying me for."

"I know, but I'm still thankful for the work—both the quality and the quantity."

The compliment caught her off guard. "Okay. You're welcome then. Ben and I will both be here tomorrow to start demo. I'll warn you now that it's going to be loud and dusty."

"Thanks for that, but I'll be here. I'll stay out of your way, though. My goal is to get all the upstairs carpet done before the semester starts."

Joss couldn't tell if she was relieved or perturbed that Olivia would be around. "We'll be here around eight."

Olivia flashed a smile. "I'll have plenty of coffee."

"Great. Good luck in here." Joss gestured to the small space.

"Thanks, I think I'm going to need it."

Joss backed out of the room and headed to the kitchen. She made sure all her things were neatly tucked away, then let herself out. The afternoon was gorgeous, so she rolled down the windows of her truck and turned on the radio.

As she drove, Joss replayed the conversation with Olivia in her mind. It certainly wasn't what she'd expected after their tense interaction that morning. Still, the idea of letting her guard down made Joss uneasy. The fact that Olivia was a lesbian only added to that feeling. It created a mix of things that didn't go together in Joss's mind. It made things complicated, and Joss was the kind of woman who preferred things simple and straightforward.

CHAPTER EIGHT

Ripping up carpet couldn't be that difficult. Olivia had watched several YouTube videos in preparation. She'd spent a solid twenty minutes with a very nice man at Home Depot discussing strategies and tools. She'd bought a brand-new crowbar, along with pliers, a utility knife, and some construction-grade garbage bags.

She decided to start early in the morning, when neither Joss nor her crew would be around. That way, she could take her time and not worry about a running commentary or, worse, behind-her-back snickers. She put on shorts and a tank top, gathered her new tools, and headed to what would become her master bedroom.

As promised in the videos, the carpet came up easily. After prying a corner from under the baseboard, it was easy to pull back nearly half of what covered the room. Cutting it into manageable pieces proved to be another matter entirely. It was heavy and stiff and the crumbling backing made her sneeze and itch.

Half an hour later, she sat in the middle of the room, sweating and swearing. She'd cut off two pieces and crammed them into one of the bags. The bag was full and the room was less than a quarter done. This was not going to cut it.

Olivia stood and looked around. There had to be an easier way. A glance out the window gave her a glimpse of the Dumpster Joss's company had delivered to haul away the materials pulled out during the project. She'd planned to throw her bags of carpet into it. Of course, that involved stuffing it into bags in the first place and dragging those bags down the stairs.

She walked over to the window and, after some jimmying and a little more swearing, got it open. She cut a single line down the middle of the room and rolled one of the halves. She couldn't quite lift it, so she pulled it over to the window. After propping one end on the sill, she hefted the other end and started shoving. It only took a few pushes to send the roll flying.

It landed with a satisfying thwack. The thwack was followed by the sound of car doors and some cheers and clapping. Olivia peered out the window and found Joss, Ben, and a guy she assumed was on their crew staring up at her.

Ben nodded up at her. "You show that carpet who's boss!"

She figured she had two choices. She could be embarrassed, act stern, and try to pretend that nothing happened. Or she could work it. She grabbed the smaller pieces she'd cut and sent them out the same way. After, she stuck her arm out and shook her fist. When there were more whoops, she felt satisfied she'd made the right decision.

She left her work in progress and headed downstairs to greet the crew. "Morning, guys."

Ben grinned at her. "Good morning to you, handywoman. You're up and at 'em early today."

Olivia looked over at Joss, who was specifically not looking at her. "I'm just trying to hold up my end of the bargain."

Ben looked confused, so Olivia was about to offer an explanation when Joss decided to join the conversation. "When Olivia requested a quote to refinish the floors upstairs, she did so with the condition that she remove the carpet herself."

"I see," Ben said. "And did you explain to her what the process entailed?"

Joss shrugged. "She seemed to understand."

Olivia flashed back to their conversation about the overall budget for the project. It had taken place during the walk-through, when Joss assumed she was some straight little priss. Joss had probably been amused by the whole thing. She likely figured that, after a halfhearted attempt, Olivia would throw her hands up and beg the professionals to take over. The thought of it made her lift her chin. There was no way she was going to be the butt of some joke about how clueless and incapable she was.

Olivia offered her most confident smile and prepared to blatantly lie. "Oh, I knew what I was signing up for."

Ben nodded, as though weighing whether or not he wanted to get more involved than he already was. "Well, I approve of your methods. We'll be sure to steer clear of your windows. I'll even have Jack toss what you throw into the Dumpster."

Olivia thought she detected a hint of an eye roll from Joss. It was beyond irritating. She put her hands on her hips. "Thanks, Ben, but I can do it. A deal is a deal, after all."

Ben and Joss exchanged silent glances, after which Joss said, "It's no big deal. We'll be hauling stuff out from the first floor and loading up the Dumpster anyway."

She tried to decide whether continuing to refuse would make her look petulant instead of independent. "Okay, thank you. If y'all don't get to it, I'll take care of it later. I know there's a lot of demo to do today."

"There sure is. We'll get started and let you get back to work." Ben offered her a playful salute while Joss went back to ignoring her.

"Okay. Coffee and cups are on the counter. Help yourself and holler if you need me for anything." She took a deep breath and headed back upstairs.

With her new system of shoving large pieces out the easiest window, she made pretty quick progress. By around eleven, she was pulling up the carpet in the final small bedroom, the one that was going to become a walk-in closet and the rest of her master bathroom. She pried open the window and sent it sailing. The sound it made as it landed was noticeably different from the rest. She leaned out the window and peered down. There was a large rectangle of blue shag covering part of the roof of her dilapidated front porch.

"Shit." It didn't really matter, given that both the porch and its roof were being torn down within the week. Mostly, it was a matter of principle. The last thing she wanted was to give Joss the satisfaction of knowing she'd been lazy or sloppy in her work. She'd deal with it later, she decided, and went to work on the padding.

While just as disgusting as the carpet in terms of dust and itchiness, the padding came up much more quickly. It was light and squishy and she was easily able to fold it up and chuck it outside. She allowed herself to feel smug for a moment, until her eye caught six rows of tiny tufts of foam still attached to the floor with staples. There had to be over a hundred in this room alone.

Olivia picked up her crowbar and wedged it under one of the staples. She pushed down to lever it out. It loosened somewhat, then gave way, causing her to fall back on her ass. She looked down and found, not a nice neat hole where the staple had been, but two uneven bits of metal sticking up from the floor. The staple had broken in half.

"Son of a..." She grabbed the pliers. After a minute of twisting and yanking, she'd managed to pull the two pieces free. She sat back on the floor and surveyed what would likely be hours of tedious and uncomfortable work. Perhaps Joss would get the last laugh after all.

Joss stood in the doorway. She'd come up to give Olivia an update, but had stopped short when she heard her swear. As loath as she'd be to admit it, she couldn't resist watching Olivia wrestle with the crowbar. When she fell back, Joss had to bite her cheek to keep from laughing out loud. Perhaps this little Southern Miss had more spunk than she'd given her credit for. Knowing she'd get caught if she just kept staring, Joss cleared her throat.

Olivia jumped, then whipped her head around. Seeing Joss, she narrowed her eyes. "How long have you been standing there?"

Embarrassed that she'd been watching, she looked away. "Not long at all. I just came up to tell you we're about to take out the kitchen wall and to see if you wanted to take a swing or two with the sledgehammer."

Olivia continued to look at her. Joss didn't know whether or not Olivia believed her, but it seemed as though she wasn't going to press it. "You mean like they do on television?"

Joss rolled her eyes. The rise of home improvement shows was both a blessing and a curse to her profession. While it got people interested in the ways old houses could have new life, it also gave a ridiculously false sense of the work involved. "Yes, just like they do on TV."

Olivia stood up and Joss tried not to notice the way she brushed the dust from her rear end. "Well, I wouldn't want to miss that."

Olivia brushed past her and led the way downstairs. When she did so, her breasts just barely touched Joss's arm. The touch, which couldn't have lasted more than a second, sent a jolt right to Joss's gut. She tried to shake it off as she followed. This was going to be a long eight weeks.

Downstairs, Jack carried the last of the kitchen cabinets out to the Dumpster, along with the stove that no longer worked. Most of the counters were gone and the refrigerator had been relocated to the dining area. Ben stood in the middle of the room holding a sledgehammer. He smiled at Olivia. "So, do you want to watch, or do you want to swing?"

"Oh, I definitely want to swing."

There was a gleam in Olivia's eyes that made Joss's stomach twist uncomfortably. No, that wasn't accurate. It wasn't discomfort Joss was feeling; it was desire. What the hell had gotten into her?

"I was really hoping you'd say that." Ben handed Olivia the sledgehammer.

Joss snagged a pair of safety glasses from her toolbox and thrust them at Olivia. "You should wear these."

"Thanks," Olivia said, then winked at her. "Safety first."

It didn't seem like Ben was going to offer any guidance, so Joss figured she should. The last thing she wanted was Olivia hurting herself. "Just take a nice swing. Try to use your legs more than your back, like if you're lifting something heavy."

Olivia nodded intently. "Okay. Should I aim for anything in particular?"

"Nope. Anywhere on the wall is fine. If you hit a stud, not much will happen, but when you get straight drywall, it should go right through."

"Got it." Olivia adjusted the glasses and took the sledgehammer in both hands. She swung it over her right shoulder, then thrust it into the wall.

As much as Joss might not want to admit it, it wasn't a bad swing. She watched as Olivia freed the head from the hole she'd created and took another swing. She did it twice more before looking to Joss. "How's that?"

Joss's throat had gone dry. "It's, uh, it's good," she managed.

Ben jumped in. "It's really good, actually. Are you sure you haven't done this before?"

Olivia beamed. "I haven't. It's awfully satisfying, isn't it?"

Joss managed to find her voice. "Indeed it is. Just wait until you kick through the other side."

"Well, by all means, let's do that."

Joss stepped forward and pulled at the hole Olivia had created. Large chunks of drywall came away, revealing studs and the back of the opposite drywall. When she'd created a big enough space, she stepped back and gestured to Olivia. "It's all yours."

Olivia stepped forward. Without being coached, she grabbed onto two of the studs to brace herself. It took a couple of tries, but Olivia pushed her sneaker-clad foot through the other side. She stood back and rubbed her hands together. "This is officially my new favorite hobby."

When the drywall was cleared, Olivia turned again to Joss. "Now what?"

"Now we knock out these studs and frame in the new opening between your kitchen and living room."

Olivia frowned. It looked like a pout for a second, but then she squared her shoulders. "I suppose that means I should get back to the floors."

Joss sighed. She was so going to regret this. "You know, we can fold that into the project. It isn't going to affect your final cost by much at all."

Olivia planted her fists on her hips. Joss was starting to realize it was a habitual stance for her. "I appreciate that, but I said I would do it and I will. For me, it's more about having a hand in the work than it is about the money."

Joss expected her to be stubborn. Olivia's comment about the work, however, took her by surprise. Between that and her ability to swing a hammer, Joss found herself looking at Olivia differently. Of course, that, combined with Joss's physical reaction to her, could prove to be downright dangerous.

Since she hadn't said anything, Ben stepped in. "That's a commendable stance. We won't step on your toes, but we're more than happy to help. Isn't that right, Joss?"

Joss cleared her throat. "Absolutely."

"Thanks, both of y'all. I'm fine for now, but I reserve the right to change my mind after I've yanked out a thousand staples. Deal?"

"Deal." Joss and Ben spoke in unison.

"I wouldn't say no to one little favor, though."

"What's that?" Joss asked, wondering what Olivia considered a little favor.

"There's a big piece of shag carpet on the porch roof. Could you," Olivia waved her hands back and forth, "do something about that?"

Ben laughed and Joss couldn't help but crack a smile. "We'll take care of it."

"Great. I'm going to head back upstairs. I appreciate you letting me take out a wall. I'm sure it slowed you down."

"Homeowner's prerogative," Joss said.

Olivia's voice came down the stairway. "I like that."

When it was clear she was out of earshot, Ben looked at Joss. "What was that?"

"What?"

"That whole interaction. You were acting like the class nerd getting attention from the cheerleader."

Joss scowled at him. "Stop it." She hadn't been that obvious, had she?

"I'm just saying it seemed like you had a crush on her more than you couldn't stand being in the same room as her."

"You're being ridiculous. Neither one of those is true."

"If you say so."

"I do. Can we get back to work, please?"

"Whatever you say, boss."

CHAPTER NINE

Joss loved her crew, but she truly enjoyed the days she got to work solo. She liked the quiet and the ability to set her own pace. That was especially true when framing walls. Measure, mark, cut. When she had five or six pieces of wood done, she'd stop and carry them over to where they needed to go. Measure, position, install. It was methodical and precise and so easy to see progress.

The house was quiet, too. She'd seen Olivia when she arrived and they'd chatted for a bit. She'd gone upstairs to work on her floors, though, and they only crossed paths a few times, mostly when Olivia was coming and going from the kitchen.

At about four in the afternoon, something started to smell good. Given the state of the kitchen, Joss couldn't help but be curious. She wandered in the direction of the aroma, but found no sign of Olivia. She spied a slow cooker set up on a rolling kitchen cart that was standing in for counter space. Joss walked over to it and lifted the lid so she could peek inside. Chicken and vegetables—onions and sweet potatoes and some kind of greens—simmered away in a sauce that hinted at cumin and ginger and maybe cloves.

"Hungry?"

At the sound of Olivia's voice, Joss jumped and barely held on to the lid in her hand. She replaced it quickly and put her hands behind her back. "Sorry."

Olivia smiled and Joss realized she was more amused than annoyed. "No need to apologize. That won't be ready for a couple of hours, but if you're hungry, I'd be happy to make you a snack."

"No, no. I'm fine. I was just curious." After a pause, she added, "It smells really good."

Olivia laughed. "I know, right? I can't take credit, though. It came from the ready-to-cook case."

"Ah." That made a lot more sense.

Olivia put her hands on her hips. "Not that I can't cook, mind you. I'm just trying to be reasonable given the state of things around here."

Joss couldn't fault her for that. "That's why I was curious. I couldn't figure out where you were chopping vegetables or hiding all your spices."

"It's my compromise. I accept not making things from scratch so I don't have to live on takeout."

"That's really smart. I'd definitely grill, but I don't know if I'd think to use a slow cooker."

Olivia raised a brow at her. "Are you paying me a compliment?"

Joss felt a flash of discomfort before realizing that Olivia was teasing her. "I think I am."

"A banner day indeed." Her eyes danced with playfulness. "Are you sure I can't make you a snack?"

"I'm fine, really, but thanks. I was actually just finishing up for the day."

"Oh. Okay." Joss couldn't be sure, but she thought Olivia sounded disappointed.

"I'll be back first thing tomorrow. I'll finish the framing in the morning and schedule the code enforcer to come and do his inspection. Once that's done, we can start hanging drywall."

"That sounds great. Thanks."

Joss finished putting away her tools. "So I'll see you in the morning, then?"

Olivia's smile had returned. "I'll be here."

Joss offered a wave as she climbed into her truck. As she drove home, she thought about how things with Olivia had shifted. They seemed to have moved past the awkward tension. Or, at least, the initial tension. It had been replaced by something else. An entirely different kind of tension.

Joss had a vague feeling that Olivia might be flirting with her. She was usually pretty good at reading that kind of thing, but something about Olivia threw her off. Olivia smiled at her a lot. And she had a way of touching Joss's arm if Joss was close to her, pointing something out or giving an explanation of how something worked.

What Joss couldn't figure out was whether that was how Olivia was with everyone, or if it was specific to her. Not knowing irritated her. It was about as irritating as Joss's own reaction. Olivia had a way of looking at her that made her insides fluttery, and Joss didn't do fluttery. And when they did have any sort of physical contact, Joss's body responded. Not a spark so much as a flash of heat that traveled from the point of contact to her core, where it then radiated back through her entire being. It was a physical attraction for sure, but it seemed like it was something else, too. Something more.

Joss had no idea what it was and even less of an idea what to do about it. Olivia was not the sort of person she got involved with. On top of that, she was a client. Ben teased her about her code of never dating clients, but Joss stuck to it. There was way too much potential for complicating a project, not to mention the potential for complicating her life.

❖

"I can't believe you're cooking in the middle of this." Gina drank old vine zinfandel from a paper cup and wandered around the gutted kitchen.

Olivia shrugged. "Well, I'm not going to live on takeout until the renovation is done. I keep it simple. If it can go in the slow cooker or on the grill, I'm good to go."

"Well, don't tell Kel that. If you can put a meal together in these conditions, she'll never let me redo our kitchen."

Olivia laughed. "I promise. You're not planning to do your kitchen anytime soon, are you?"

Gina refilled her cup, then did the same for Olivia. "Ah, no. That project has been put on hold for the foreseeable future. Something about expecting two babies makes other large expenditures seem like not the best idea."

Olivia poked a wooden spoon at her. "You know, I thought hell was going to freeze over when Kel got pregnant, but I was wrong. It's freezing over now. The two of you are on a budget."

Gina huffed. "If you weren't right, I'd hit you. I still can't believe we're going to need two of everything."

"How is Kel holding up? I haven't seen her in weeks."

"Well, we crossed the pants line right after you moved out. That wasn't pretty."

"Pants line? You'll have to explain. I don't speak pregnant lady."

"It's the moment during pregnancy when one's pants no longer fit. Kel took it pretty hard. She knew maternity clothes were part of the arrangement, but I don't think she'd actually laid eyes on a pair of maternity pants before. So much elastic."

Olivia nodded. "Right, right. And the whole floppy sweater and leggings thing isn't really her style."

"Not even a little. Now that we've passed twenty weeks, she's really showing. It's going to be a long few months."

Olivia bit her lip, halfheartedly trying to cover a smile. "Is she moody?"

"It's better now that the morning sickness has passed. That was a nightmare. You know, I have moments of wanting to tease her, but the rest of the time, I still can't believe she's doing this." Gina leaned against one of the stools Olivia bought to go with the yet to be built kitchen island. "She's carrying our babies."

Olivia put down her spoon and walked over to where Gina was standing. "She loves you, and she wants this family as much as you do."

Gina sniffed. "I know."

"You're going to be amazing moms. And I'm going to be an amazing auntie."

"You're going to spoil them rotten."

"That's my plan."

Gina shook her head, but laughed. "So tell me about you. Clearly, the work is coming along. How's the hot contractor?"

"This needs another half hour. Let's go sit outside."

"Okay." Gina followed her out the side door to her makeshift patio area.

"The house is great. I don't even mind living in the chaos because every day I can see a change. Something goes out, something comes in. The contractor," Olivia rolled her eyes, "remains a work in progress."

"Oh, do tell."

"She's seriously hot. Not to be cliché, but when she's walking around in jeans and a tool belt, it's all I can do not to drool."

Gina's eyes lit up. "I really need to meet this woman. But it sounds like there might be a catch."

Olivia sighed. "She doesn't like me, or at least she didn't."

"Why on earth would she not like you? You're almost annoyingly likable."

Olivia had to laugh at the characterization. "I don't know if it was because I'm Southern, or maybe that I'm a professor? I think she figured I was a snob."

"That's ridiculous."

"Oh, she thought I was straight, too."

Gina made a slow, exaggerated nod. "Oh."

"Which made me mad."

"Of course."

"So we argued."

"Naturally."

"But we made up."

"Did you apologize or did she?" Gina leaned forward, as if she were an investigative reporter.

"I did first, but then she did, too."

"I see. And now?"

"That's just it. She's polite, friendly even, but formal. But then I think I catch her staring at me."

"You mean when you're not staring at her?"

Olivia smirked. "Funny. True, but still funny."

"You want to win her over, don't you?"

She really did. "Is that bad?"

"Not at all. I'm curious, though. Do you want her to like you or do you want her to sleep with you?"

Olivia shrugged and tried her best to look innocent. "Is it wrong to want both?"

Gina smiled and lifted her paper cup in a toast. "Never."

Olivia went back into the house to serve up dinner. It was a Moroccan stew that came all prepped and ready for the slow cooker. She sampled it and was pleasantly surprised. She added a bit of pepper then ladled it into bowls, tucking half a pita into each. When she turned, Gina was hovering in the doorway. "Need any help?"

"We are all set." Olivia handed her one of the bowls and grabbed spoons from the plastic bin where she was storing her utensils. They returned to the table outside. Olivia raised her wine. "Here's to our last week without students."

Gina curled her lip. "Could you not? I am not ready."

Olivia shook her head and chuckled. "I think it's a little late for that now."

"I know, but I don't have to like it." Gina took a bite of her food. "Hey, this is good."

"Right? No prep whatsoever. I was going to recommend them to you, given your thoughts on cooking."

"You know me so well." Gina seemed to think for a moment. "Maybe I can get it cooking and hide the package, convince Kel I made it from scratch."

"Your secret would be safe with me."

"So I don't think we were done talking about your contractor. What's her name?"

"Joss."

"Joss. That's a great name. I don't think we were done talking about Joss."

"We weren't?"

"No. We established that you want to sleep with her, but we didn't establish whether or not it was going to happen."

Olivia considered it. "I don't know. I don't think she's the type who's readily seduced. And I wouldn't want it to be like a conquest anyway. That feels so skeevy."

Gina took a bite and then pointed with her spoon. "You know what you need? A reverse seduction."

"Excuse me?"

"A reverse seduction. You seduce her, but make her think she's seducing you. Classic femme move."

Olivia frowned. "I don't think she's a seducer, either. She strikes me more as the old-fashioned, chivalrous type."

Gina huffed. "Well, I didn't mean seduction seduction. I meant flirt, go on a date, then maybe sleep together. I only meant that you should make her think it's her idea."

Olivia had to laugh at Gina's description. "You make it sound so reasonable."

"I am reasonable," Gina insisted.

Olivia raised a brow in response.

"I am. You haven't dated anyone since I've known you. You haven't even been interested in anyone really."

"That's not true. I went on three dates with Marissa."

It was Gina's turn to raise a brow. "You did that because Scott set you up and you didn't want him to feel bad. Didn't she lick your face?"

Olivia cringed, remembering her third—and final—date with Marissa. What had started out as a normal kiss had gotten really weird, really fast. "Yes."

"So, as I was saying, you haven't been interested in anyone since you moved to Ithaca. I think it's high time."

Gina had a point. Not only had she not dated since moving to Ithaca, she'd hardly dated since breaking up with Amanda, the cardiology resident her parents thought was the best thing since sliced bread. "You're right. I'm just not sure if setting my sights on a woman who seems bound and determined not to like me is the way to go."

Gina shrugged. "I guess you'll have to win her over."

They finished dinner and Gina headed home. Olivia contemplated working on the floors upstairs, but decided to give herself the night off. Instead, she wandered around the house with the paint chips she'd picked up. Her mother and sister leaned toward pastels. Olivia made a point of selecting bolder colors. Nothing too loud, but the last thing she wanted was for everything to blend into a boring oblivion.

Maybe she should ask Joss about colors. It would be the perfect conversation starter and a way to ask some semi-personal questions. Besides, Joss had surely seen plenty of bad choices and could steer her away from things that looked great on a small piece of cardboard, but terrible on a wall. She'd probably even know a thing or two about shades that would go with the style and era of the house. As much as she'd become enamored with her old farmhouse, she didn't know all that much about them in general.

If she could get Joss to start talking about things in her comfort zone, who knew where it might lead?

Olivia congratulated herself on her plan and looked at the choices she'd made so far. The powder room on the first floor would be a sagey green, but she couldn't decide between one that was more gray and another that was more blue. She really wanted to do the kitchen in a dark red. In her mind, it felt French country, but she was afraid it might be too intense for the space.

The room giving her the most trouble was her bedroom. She'd picked up a dozen different options, including a blue-gray, a sea green, and something called salted caramel. She'd even picked up a shade of lavender, although she couldn't imagine actually picking it. Knowing she wasn't likely to make any decisions, Olivia arranged her samples by room. She made stacks and placed them on the kitchen cart.

Since she wasn't doing any work on the house, Olivia decided she should attempt something productive before going to bed. Her syllabi and plans for the first couple weeks of classes were set, but she could always do some future planning before she had stacks of papers to grade. She picked up her work bag and took out the books she'd brought home from her office—poetry collections of Audre Lorde and Minnie Bruce Pratt. She'd been wanting to add some more modern work to her American lit survey course and was leaning toward poetry. If she could use some of her favorite works, and throw in some conversation about race, class, and gender, so much the better.

Olivia took her books and a pad of sticky notes to her makeshift bedroom. After getting undressed, she slid between the covers and smiled. Cool, clean cotton sheets on bare skin was in her top ten of favorite sensations and a luxury she never planned to take for granted. She angled the lamp that was sitting on a stack of boxes and opened the first book.

Two hours and about a dozen sticky notes later, Olivia had the beginnings of a unit, complete with a framework for class discussion on the juxtaposition of "self" and "other." Happy with her progress, she set her books aside and turned off the light.

There was a full moon and it shined through the temporary paper shades she'd stuck on the windows. As her eyes adjusted to the silvery light, Olivia found her mind wandering to Joss. It was so easy to imagine Joss there, in the room with her. Her skin would look pale in the light, but it would be warm and smooth. Olivia's fingers would trace the lines of well-defined muscles, her mouth would seek the places where Joss was soft.

It startled Olivia how easily she could picture it, how quickly she'd become aroused. She hadn't felt that flash of desire in a while. She hadn't realized how much she missed it.

CHAPTER TEN

The next morning, Joss again arrived at Olivia's by herself. The electrician showed up mid-morning to finish the upgrades to the outlets and add a couple of new breakers to the electric panel, but otherwise, it was just the two of them. Olivia enjoyed the relative quiet of only Joss working. It felt homey, intimate.

Olivia plowed ahead with project carpet removal, making slow but steady progress. She'd finally devised a pry and wiggle method that helped her get most of the staples out in one piece. She could only do it for a couple of hours at a time, though. In addition to testing the muscles in her arms, it was killing her knees. Since painting was another of her big projects, she decided it was a perfect time to seek Joss's expert opinion.

She went downstairs and found Joss scoring drywall. Not wanting to break her concentration, Olivia waited until she put the blade down. "Hi."

Something flashed in Joss's eyes when she looked up. Olivia thought for a second it might be desire, but it might have been wishful thinking on her part. "Hi."

"I don't want to interrupt your work, but I'd love to get your opinion on something when you have a moment."

"Now is as good a time as any. What's up?"

Suddenly, Olivia felt silly. Too late to back out now. "I wanted to start painting in the rooms that weren't going to have any work done but the floors."

Joss nodded. "That's smart. Since we'll be sanding, it won't matter if you get any drips."

Since Joss seemed to think it was a good idea, Olivia decided not to tell her it was because she needed a break from the staples. "Oh, good. I…Actually, I was hoping you might be willing to look at some of the paint colors I was considering, give me your opinion."

Joss looked surprised, but not turned off by the request. "Sure."

"I picked out some I like, but I'm not sure how they'll translate to walls. I'm sure you have a lot of experience with that."

"I most certainly do."

"I also would like to pick things that aren't too far off the mark for the age and style of the house."

"I definitely have a feel for that sort of thing, but if you want real authenticity, you should consider talking to an expert."

Olivia smiled. "You're enough of an expert for me."

Joss looked at her like she was trying to decipher a double meaning. Perfect. "Okay, then. Show me what you have."

Olivia spread out her paint chips on the makeshift table created by Joss's sawhorses and the drywall. Joss went with the more gray of the greens for the downstairs bathroom and a honey tone for the one upstairs. "I like the gray, but it feels rather modern."

Olivia nodded in agreement. "What about the kitchen? Is this red too dark?"

Joss studied it for a moment. "You know, I don't think so. Between the cabinets and the windows, there isn't so much wall space that it would be overwhelming."

Olivia put her hand on Joss's arm. "I am so happy to hear you say that."

Joss looked at her arm and then cleared her throat. "You'll, uh, want to make sure you go with something lighter, but complementary for the living and dining rooms, since they'll all be visible at the same time."

"Like maybe something mushroomy?" Was "mushroomy" a word?

"Absolutely. Just make sure it's got warm undertones instead of cool."

"Right." Olivia took her hand away and looked right into Joss's eyes. "My real dilemma is the bedroom."

"Oh? Why is that?"

"I can't seem to settle on anything."

"All right. What kind of feel are you going for?"

"I definitely want it to be a relaxing space. Sensual, but not in an obvious sort of way." Olivia looked away, then back at Joss. "Does that make sense?"

"It does."

Olivia wasn't sure about Joss, but it felt like they were talking about a lot more than paint. "So do you have any wisdom to impart?"

"It's all about the bed."

Olivia had no idea if Joss was speaking literally or figuratively, but either way, her heart rate jumped considerably. "How so?"

It was Joss's turn to offer a smile. It seemed playful almost, and full of promise. "Pick out your bedding first. I learned the hard way that it's a lot harder to find a quilt or duvet cover you like. Once you have that, you can find a paint color that works with it."

"Oh." Okay, so not entirely full of promise, but it made a lot of sense. "That's a really good idea."

Joss shrugged but didn't break eye contact. "You just need to figure out what you want your bed to say."

Olivia had intended to be only mildly flirtatious, but Joss was making that nearly impossible. "Oh, I know what I want it to say. I just have to figure out the right way to say it."

"Dare I ask?"

"I think you're going to have to wait and see. Thank you again for your advice. It's been immensely helpful."

"Happy to help."

Joss watched Olivia gather up her paint chips and disappear into the kitchen. She shook her head in an attempt to clear the fog that had settled over her brain. It did little to dispel the tingling on her arm where Olivia's hand had been or the tightness in her belly that had taken hold when Olivia held her gaze.

Joss had spent the better part of the morning convincing herself that her attraction to Olivia was a passing infatuation, fueled by the fact that Olivia was the last person on the planet she should be pursuing. She'd even congratulated herself on keeping their conversation friendly and light. How in the hell had a conversation about paint colors turned so suggestive? It wasn't at all how she wanted things with Olivia to go. But as she watched Olivia putter back and forth in the kitchen, humming a tune she couldn't quite recognize, Joss realized that she wanted more rather than less. What the hell was she supposed to do with that?

Joss forced her attention back to the work in front of her. It sort of did the trick for about an hour and a half. She resumed cutting the drywall for the wall she'd finished framing the day before. When that was done, she started securing it to the studs with long screws. She was attaching the last piece when Olivia sashayed back in.

"They're predicting rain by six, so I'm going to do my grilling now. Can I interest you in an early dinner?"

"Um..." This was a terrible idea.

"It's nothing fancy. I picked up some pre-marinated chicken and potato salad, sliced some cucumbers and tomatoes. I have far more than I can eat."

Joss nodded. "That would be great. Thank you."

"It's the least I can do after all the work you've been doing. It's also nice to have company."

"Can I give you a hand?" Sure. Because cooking with a woman wasn't intimate at all.

"No need. You finish up whatever you're doing. It'll be ready in about twenty minutes."

"That's perfect." Olivia disappeared back into the kitchen and all Joss could do was shake her head. This was probably an improvement on bickering, but it felt far more dangerous. Every time she was around Olivia, Joss seemed to have absolutely no control over what came out of her mouth.

Olivia headed out to preheat the grill, congratulating herself on getting Joss to agree to dinner. As much as she'd prefer to serve something a little nicer, Joss probably said yes in part because it seemed so casual. "Baby steps," she said to the squirrel who chattered at her from a nearby tree.

After getting the chicken on the grill, Olivia pulled out the two salads and some fresh berries. She turned to Joss. "Will you have a beer?"

"If you are, sure."

Olivia piled everything on a tray and carried it outside. She was just pulling the chicken off when Joss stepped outside, drying her hands on a paper towel. "Your timing is perfect."

"Thank you again for sharing your dinner."

"It's my pleasure. With classes starting next week, it's nice to be able to enjoy the last little bits of down time."

They sat at the plastic patio table, filling their plates from the plastic bowls and containers Olivia had brought out. She lifted her bottle. "Here's to excellent progress."

"To progress."

They talked a little about the house—what the order of projects would be, when Olivia would be able to start painting which walls. She realized that it was her enthusiasm for the work, and not just the finished product, that would win Joss over. The distinction would be important to someone like Joss. Olivia would have to remember that.

Not wanting to only talk shop, Olivia asked Joss questions about her family and what it was like to work with them.

"I started hanging around the office when I was about six. My dad took me to my first job site on my tenth birthday. He gave me my first hard hat and tool belt and I cried when my mom made me take them off for bed. I never wanted to do anything else."

Olivia didn't think she'd ever heard something so adorable. "If being a lawyer had involved a hard hat and tool belt, I might have gone into the family business, too."

"Your parents are lawyers?"

"They started their own firm after they got married. Mostly wills and trusts, some divorce thrown in for good measure. When I told them I was applying to English programs instead of law school, I honestly thought they might disown me."

"But they didn't?"

"Oh, no. They save the drama for deposition meetings and trials. When they realized I wasn't going to change my mind, it became all about getting into the best program, working with high-profile scholars."

Joss shook her head. "It sounds like a lot of pressure."

Olivia shrugged. "I sort of thrived on doing things my way. It kept things interesting."

The gray clouds had been gathering, but Olivia was resolutely ignoring them. She didn't want her time with Joss to end. And while it seemed like Joss was far from making a move, it felt like things between them had definitely shifted in the right direction.

When a rumble of thunder sounded in the distance, Joss glanced at the sky. "It looks like maybe we should—"

She didn't get to finish her sentence. The sky opened up and the rain started to fall in buckets. Fat, heavy drops pelted the table, the dishes, and the top of Olivia's head. She realized that Joss was grabbing things from the table. She followed suit and they both booked it back into the house.

Although they couldn't have been in the rain for more than a couple of minutes, they were both soaked. Olivia looked Joss up and down, appreciating the way her wet shirt clung to her shoulders and breasts. It took all of Olivia's restraint not to kiss her, to peel away the fabric and taste her. She swallowed hard and then forced a casual smile. "You were saying?"

Joss laughed. "Clearly, I was about two minutes too late."

"It's my fault. I knew it was coming."

"No worries. And dinner was delicious."

"Thanks. Can I offer you a dry shirt? I'm sure the last thing you want to do is drive home all wet and clammy."

Joss looked at Olivia, whose thin T-shirt was plastered to her skin, accentuating her breasts and revealing erect nipples. At that point, the last thing she wanted to do was go home at all. She tried to rein in the lust that had quickly taken over her body. "Yeah, that would be great."

"Okay. I'll be right back."

Olivia disappeared into her bedroom. Joss swigged what was left of her beer and tried not to think about Olivia pulling off her wet clothes. She imagined Olivia's skin, damp and smelling faintly of honeysuckle, and her breasts, soft and full in her hands. When Olivia returned in a loose-fitting black tee, Joss had a moment of being genuinely surprised.

"It might be a little snug, but it's not too girly." She handed Joss a navy Atlanta Braves shirt.

"Thanks." Joss went to the guest bathroom and changed. With the mirror gone, she had no way of knowing if the shirt looked okay. It fit well enough, though, and smelled like Olivia. She emerged from the bathroom and found Olivia in the kitchen putting away the leftover food.

Olivia looked up and smiled. "I must say, that looks way cuter on you than it does on me."

"You're just saying that."

"I'm not, I swear. You should keep it."

"I couldn't."

"Of course you could. Trust me, I have no attachment—either to the shirt or the Braves."

Joss frowned. "Not into baseball?"

"Actually, I prefer the Cubs." Joss raised a brow and Olivia shrugged playfully. "I have a soft spot for underdogs."

"You're full of surprises today, you know that?"

Olivia grinned. "I'm going to take that as a compliment."

"It was meant as such."

"Well then, thank you."

The dry clothes had done little to abate the desire Joss was feeling to kiss Olivia. "I, uh, should probably go."

Olivia crossed her arms over her chest. "I'm sorry if I kept you."

Joss shook her head vigorously. "Not at all. Thank you so much for dinner."

Olivia tilted her head to one side. "Thanks for staying. It was nice to talk to you about something other than my house."

She was right. It had been nice. More than nice. "So, I'll see you in the morning."

Olivia flashed a smile. "I'll be here."

CHAPTER ELEVEN

Joss dreamed of Olivia. When she woke up at six, her sheets were tangled and she was covered in sweat. The cold shower she took cooled her skin, but did little to ease the insistent pulsing between her thighs.

On the drive to Olivia's house, she weighed her options. On one hand, she didn't date clients. She'd always thought of it as part of her professional code. Of course, she'd never been tempted before. Tempted was an insufficient word to describe what Olivia did to her. Trying to ignore whatever was between them seemed like a losing battle.

Joss wondered if she should give into it. Maybe that would help her get it out of her system. It wasn't like she'd professed to Olivia that she didn't date clients, or academics for that matter. Really, once they'd moved past the initial friction between them, things had become quite friendly. Between the flirty banter and all the arm touching, Joss was pretty sure Olivia would say yes. And just because she wasn't really into hookups, going on a date didn't mean they were going to get married.

It was settled. Joss felt relieved. She liked having a game plan. Even if Olivia turned her down, there would no longer be this big unknown hanging between them and Joss could put her attention solely onto her work. And if Olivia said yes, well, she'd figure that out, too.

Joss made a detour to stop at Gimme!, ordering two large lattes and a couple of croissants. When she turned into Olivia's driveway, she found Olivia kneeling in one of the overgrown flower beds, pulling weeds. She must have seen or heard Joss's truck because she stood up, brushing dirt from her knees.

Joss offered her a smile. "Good morning."

"Good—oh my God, is that Gimme! coffee? Is one of them for me?"

Joss congratulated herself for thinking of it. She handed Olivia one of the white paper cups. "I have pastry, too."

"I cannot tell you how happy that makes me. Wait. Are you buttering me up? Is there bad news?"

"No bad news. I promise."

Olivia narrowed her eyes. "So you're just being nice?"

"I am nice. Do you want one of these croissants now?"

"Yes, but I need to wash my hands." Olivia headed toward the side door.

Joss followed her into the house. "Chocolate or almond?"

"Ooh. Almond, as long as you don't have a preference."

Joss opened the bag and took out one of the pastries. She wrapped it in a napkin and handed it over. "It's all yours."

Olivia took a bite and let out a small moan. "You seriously just made my morning."

"Good, because I am trying to butter you up a little."

"I knew it. What is it and how much is it going to cost me?"

Joss chuckled. "It's not going to cost you anything. I was hoping maybe you'd have dinner with me tonight?"

"Dinner?"

"Yes, dinner. Like we had last night. Only at a restaurant. And dry."

"Joss Bauer, are you asking me out on a date?"

Joss looked at Olivia, thinking back to the first time she'd seen her, standing in the kitchen alone, swaying to nonexistent music. The attraction had been immediate. And although it had been tempered by their early interactions—and if she were being honest, her own prejudices—it had never gone away. Having dinner with her the night before, getting caught in the rain, had only intensified the feeling. As much as she'd wanted to, it was something Joss could no longer ignore. "Please don't make me regret this before we even go."

Olivia's eyes, which were dancing with amusement, softened. "I'm sorry. It's rude to tease you when you're being so nice."

"So is that a yes?"

"Oh, my answer is definitely yes. I was merely trying to understand your motivation and put the invitation in the right context."

It would be so easy to backpedal. She could say she was trying to be friendly, to bury the hatchet of snarkiness that had defined her approach to dealing with Olivia. It would be the cowardly thing to do, however, and dishonest. "I'm asking you to dinner because you made me dinner." After a pause, she added, "And because I would like to get to know you beyond working on the house."

If Olivia had a witty reply on the tip of her tongue, she swallowed it. "That would be lovely. Thank you."

"I should say, however, that I have a general rule against getting involved with clients."

Olivia's eyes twinkled and she laughed. "Well, it's a good thing it's just dinner, then."

❖

Although Olivia offered to meet her at the restaurant, Joss insisted on picking her up. If she was going to take Olivia on a date, she was damn well going to do it right. Even though she'd been hesitant to use that word, it was a date. And in Joss's world, dates came with rules.

She pulled into Olivia's driveway just as the sun was setting. In the two hours since she'd left, she'd gone home, showered, and changed. She'd normally have picked up flowers, but that seemed a little clichéd for a woman like Olivia. She also didn't want to send the impression that she was in full-on courting mode.

Joss grabbed the Lowe's bag and climbed out of her truck. She resisted the urge to check her hair or tug at her shirt. She walked over to the side door and saw Olivia standing in the kitchen in almost the exact spot she'd been when Joss came to the house the first time. She was looking at the spot where there'd been a wall just a few days prior.

When she knocked, Olivia turned. A slow smile spread across her face, as though she'd just solved a puzzle that had been nagging at her. She was wearing another vintage-looking dress, this time black with a band of red around the bottom, and a pair of red high heels that made Joss's mouth water.

"Long time, no see," Olivia said when she opened the door.

"You've cleaned up very nicely." Joss hoped she sounded playful and not like she was trying to offer a backhanded compliment.

"Likewise." Olivia winked, helping Joss to relax.

She held up the bag she'd brought with her. "Normally I'd bring flowers, but that seemed silly given the state of your house right now."

Olivia peeked inside, her smile becoming a look of confusion. "Thank you, but what are they?"

"They're knee pads."

Olivia pulled the pair of chunky black things from the bag. "Knee pads?"

Joss regretted the choice. She should have known that a woman like Olivia wouldn't be impressed with such a practical, and completely ugly, gift. "They're for when you're working on your hands and knees. Given how adamant you were about finishing the staple removal upstairs, I thought they might come in handy."

"Oh."

"They're random, I know. You don't have to pretend to like them." She thought it would be a whimsical gift. Clever, even. What a fool she was. This whole thing was a terrible idea. How long until Olivia saw it, too?

"They aren't random. They're super practical and kind of funny, too." Olivia put her hand on Joss's arm, forcing her to make eye contact. "I love them. Thank you."

Joss resisted the urge to look at her feet. She was pretty sure she was blushing. Everything about Olivia ripped her so far out of her comfort zone. Just being around her felt like riding a roller coaster. "You're welcome."

"I'm having a really hard time not making a joke about being on my knees."

If Joss wasn't blushing before, she definitely was now. "Uh..."

Olivia smiled at her. "Relax, I'm resisting, if only just barely."

Joss swallowed. "Okay. I hope I didn't give the impression..."

Olivia laughed now, a rich and sexy laugh that turned Joss on in spite of herself. "I'm kidding, I promise. If anything, I'm regretting that I didn't have them sooner. The floors are killing me."

Joss took a breath. "Yeah, I'm sorry I didn't think of that."

Olivia waved a hand. "They're perfect. And since I probably shouldn't put them in water, shall we go?"

Joss relaxed enough to laugh. As much as Olivia's wittiness irritated her at first, the reality was that she was funny, and had a knack for putting people at ease. That it was genuine—and not just a means of showing off—made it a far more appealing quality. "We shall."

Joss didn't know if Olivia expected to have car doors opened for her, but she did it anyway. If there was any chance of this working, she would have to be herself and let the cards fall where they may.

"So, where are you taking me?"

"I made a reservation at Coltivare."

"The new place? I'm pretty sure they don't take reservations."

"They do if you went to high school with the guy who's managing it and you helped finish the punch list so they could open on time."

Olivia laughed. "Nice. Who knew you were so well connected?"

"I don't do many commercial spaces, so don't get your hopes up."

"Given that most of my connections to local restaurants are students who I hope liked my class enough not to spit in my salad, I'll take it."

"When you put it that way."

It only took about twenty minutes to drive from her house to the heart of downtown. They found parking on the street adjacent to the restaurant. When they got inside, it wasn't packed, but there were groups waiting in the wide hallway by the hostess stand, couples standing in the bar—all clearly waiting for tables.

She watched Joss smile at the hostess, say something quietly. The hostess looked down, nodded, returned the smile. They were seated at a table near a window in under five minutes. "I'm very impressed."

Joss shrugged. "Thank you, but I somehow get the feeling you're far more accustomed to deferential treatment than you're letting on."

"What would give you that impression? You understand that college professors are a dime a dozen in this town, right?"

"I suppose you have a point."

At Joss's suggestion, they ordered a Finger Lakes Riesling with a fig and prosciutto flatbread to share. "The roast chicken is deceptively simple, but out of this world. I've also tried the pork loin."

"Did they pay you in food?"

"No, but I happened to be here on the day the waitstaff was being trained, and it included samples."

"Good timing."

Joss nodded. Although she'd only tried a bite of each dish, she was pretty sure she'd eaten the equivalent of three meals. "It was definitely a treat."

Olivia went with the pork and Joss ordered cannelloni. And while the food was outstanding, it paled in comparison to the conversation. Olivia was warm and funny. Her interests ranged from sports and old movies to farm animals and gardening. She was down-to-earth and really enthusiastic about getting her hands dirty—the opposite of what Joss assumed when they first met.

"Have you ever had a garden before?"

Olivia sighed. "I've never even had a yard before."

Joss found that hard to believe. "Seriously?"

"My parents weren't big on yard work. We always lived in town houses, where the landscaping was painstakingly perfect and always done by someone else."

Joss shook her head. "I don't think I could ever live in a city."

"Now that I've lived here for a couple of years, I can't imagine ever moving back."

"Well, I'm not an expert by any means, but my mom is an amazing gardener and she's taught me a lot. I'd be happy to lend you a hand come spring if you'd like." It was only after she said it that Joss realized she was suggesting they spend time together more than six months in the future.

Whether Olivia picked up on that or simply liked the idea, Joss didn't know. But she smiled and put her hand over Joss's. "I am definitely going to take you up on that."

By the time they ordered a crème brûlée to share, Joss couldn't remember the last time she'd enjoyed a date more. On the drive back to Olivia's house, she realized she didn't want it to end. It was a pleasant surprise, if a little unsettling.

"Would you like to come in for a drink?"

Joss hesitated for a moment, wanting to say yes, but not wanting to give the wrong impression. "Sure."

Olivia poured them each a glass of wine and they sat on the futon that was serving as her couch while the house was under construction.

They talked a little bit about gardening. Olivia, who didn't know the difference between annuals and perennials, seemed to soak up everything Joss said like a sponge. It was endearing and Joss made a mental promise to reach out to her in the spring no matter what happened between them.

When their glasses were empty, Joss took a deep breath. "I should probably go."

"Does that mean you've decided against getting involved with the likes of me?" Olivia smiled, but there was disappointment in her eyes.

"No, it means I'm...I guess I'm just a little old-fashioned sometimes."

"Oh. I see."

Joss wasn't sure she did see. "I mean, not wait until I'm married old-fashioned, just do not stay over on the first date old-fashioned."

Olivia stood. "Does that mean I should wait for you to ask me on a second date?"

Joss couldn't tell if Olivia was being serious or teasing her. "What if I said you wouldn't have to wait very long?"

"I would say I'll start looking forward to it now."

"Well, then it's settled."

They walked to the back door. "I'll see you in the morning, then."

"That you will."

"I can't wait to try my knee pads."

Joss shook her head. "You don't have to say that."

Olivia put a hand on Joss's shoulder. "I mean it. They're a sweet gift, personal. My knees are already appreciative."

Her words were sincere, but there was a gleam in Olivia's eye that made Joss's insides clench. She was intensely aware of Olivia's hand. The touch, while casual, carried a near-electric charge. She could just make out a hint of Olivia's perfume. "You're welcome."

Olivia opened the door. A breeze had picked up and the air was cool. Joss paused, feeling even more than her usual level of caution. Something told her that getting involved with Olivia would be unlike any dating experience she'd ever had. Maybe that was okay.

She took a step forward, felt Olivia shift toward her. She swallowed. Olivia's lips parted slightly. Joss leaned in and kissed her softly. She'd meant it to be brief—a taste with a promise of more. Her body, however, had other things in mind. The next thing Joss knew, her hand was cupping the back of Olivia's neck and she was pulling her in again.

The second kiss went deeper. She pulled Olivia's bottom lip into her mouth, reveling in its softness. Olivia's hand gripped her shoulder. Joss put her other hand on the small of Olivia's back. With only gentle pressure, she pulled Olivia against her. The kiss deepened even further.

The coolness of the air and the heat of their bodies sent Joss's system into overdrive. She realized, through the haze that had settled in her brain, that she was on the verge of taking things further. She sensed that Olivia wouldn't protest if she did. That feeling of power combined with her desire dangerously.

It took all of her willpower to pull back.

"Wow."

The simple and breathless statement spoke volumes. Joss was glad to know that Olivia's reaction was similar to her own. "Yeah."

"So I'll see you in the morning then." It was clear that Olivia was letting Joss remain in the driver's seat. Given how she seemed to take control of just about everything else, Joss found that especially appealing.

"You will. And maybe we could do this," Joss waved a finger to indicate the two of them, "again next week."

Olivia smiled. "I will await your invitation."

CHAPTER TWELVE

"You went on a date?" Ben's face showed disbelief. "With Olivia?" Joss had picked Ben up on the way to Olivia's. She needed to hang large sheets of drywall and wanted to start the upstairs demo; both required an extra pair of hands. Telling him about the date with Olivia was precautionary. If Olivia mentioned it and Joss had said nothing, she'd never live it down. She was now wondering if she would live to regret the decision. "Yes. I do date, you know. I'm not a nun."

"I only thought you were pretty determined not to like her. Not to mention your prohibition on dating clients."

Joss sighed. "I wasn't determined, I just…"

Ben raised a brow.

"I jumped to conclusions. She's different than I thought when I first met her."

"So you were wrong."

"You're really enjoying this, aren't you?" Joss had to laugh. She'd given Ben a hard time plenty of times, especially when it came to women. For him to harass her now only seemed fair.

"I am. You know I don't think it's a big deal to date a client now and then, especially if they're hot."

"You realize that logic makes no sense."

Ben ignored her. "I'm glad you guys hooked up. Olivia is gorgeous and she's been making eyes at you for weeks."

"We didn't hook up. We had dinner."

"No sex?" Ben seemed incredulous.

"No. Dude, it was the first date."

"But you're not ruling out sex."

"Why are we discussing this again?"

"Because I'm your brother. I also happen to be the one who discovered Olivia was a lesbian in the first place."

"And somehow I find those things reasons to discuss this even less."

Ben shrugged. "You probably have a point. But as much as I give you a hard time, I do only want what's best for you."

Joss knew that Ben was sincere. She'd looked out for him when they were little; having three years on him made her feel responsible for her baby brother. By the time they reached high school, however, the feeling was mutual. And while nothing had ever come to blows—well, except that one time with Johnny Mancuso—they'd always had each other's backs. "I know, man."

"Are you going to go out again?"

Joss thought about how her date with Olivia ended—the kiss that nearly consumed her and the promise of a second. She was already counting the days until she could kiss Olivia again, and more. "Yeah, I think we are."

"Well, I think it's a great idea. Olivia is funny and cool."

"And she's a client."

"Yeah, but if she doesn't have a problem with that, why should you?"

"Because it's never a problem until there's a problem."

Ben shook his head. "You're borrowing trouble. You should relax. Besides, it's been too long since you've dated."

"You make it sound like I'm some sort of hermit."

"Not at all. I think sometimes you're so focused on the end game, you lose sight of the play."

Joss raised a brow. "Are you using sports analogies to discuss my love life?"

"Think about it. You want the wife and kids, the white picket fence, right?"

"I'm not partial to picket fences, but yes."

"But you're squeamish when it comes to dating someone new."

Joss frowned. "Sometimes."

"You're never going to get to one if you don't start with the other."

It was so annoying when Ben was right, especially about

relationships. "I just can't...Olivia doesn't strike me as wife material, if you know what I mean."

"Because she's a professor?"

"Because she's really independent. And because she seems used to a certain lifestyle. She probably makes more money than me."

"Weren't you just saying you jumped to conclusions about her that were wrong? You're doing the exact same thing now."

Joss resisted the urge to grumble. He was right. Again.

"You should give her a chance. You never know where it might lead."

"Yeah." Could she do that? Did she want to?

"And you should definitely sleep with her."

Joss punched him in the arm. "You're so crass."

"I just call 'em as I see 'em."

They pulled into the driveway just as Olivia was coming out the side door. She was wearing a pencil skirt and a crisp white shirt; her hair was pulled into a tidy bun. It made Joss's mouth water. As she and Ben got out of her truck, Olivia waved.

"Back in professor mode," she said by way of explanation. "I'm glad you got here before I left."

Joss remembered the feel of Olivia's lips against hers, the taste of her. She had to fight the urge to kiss her, right there in front of Ben. "Is everything okay? Do you need something?"

Olivia smiled and glanced away for a second. Was she blushing? "No, I just wanted to see you before I left."

The comment made Joss blush, probably because Ben was standing right there. The whole thing made her feel like a teenager. "I'm glad we caught you, then."

Ben made a point of walking to the back of the truck and rustling around. Olivia walked closer to Joss, standing just close enough for Joss to catch a whiff of her perfume. "I only have a meeting and my morning class today, so I'll be back early afternoon. Will you still be here?"

"I will. We're going to hang drywall and start demo upstairs."

"Excellent. I'll look forward to it." Olivia leaned in, bringing her lips close to Joss's ear. "For the record, I really want to kiss you right now."

Before Joss could respond, Olivia was walking away. "Always a pleasure to see you, Ben. I hope you're here when I return."

"Likewise," Ben said. "I can't wait to see the progress you've made."

Olivia was almost to her car before Joss found her voice. "Olivia." Olivia turned. "Yes?"

"The feeling is mutual."

She flashed a satisfied smile before getting into her car and driving away.

"What feeling is mutual?" Ben had walked up behind Joss without her realizing it.

Joss turned, annoyed that she'd let him sneak up on her. If she didn't tell him, he'd likely pester her about it all morning. Too bad. "Wouldn't you like to know."

Ben nodded appreciatively. "Knowing you don't want to tell is enough for me. I know you don't want to hear this, but she might be a keeper."

"Thank you, Dr. Phil. What do you say we get to work?"

Ben held up his tools. "I'm ready, boss."

They went inside, deciding to get the demo out of the way first. Because the tub was freestanding, they'd be able to get the wall out and reframed before having to disconnect the plumbing. While they worked, Ben's comment bounced around in Joss's mind. She pushed it aside, choosing instead to think about when she'd be able to kiss Olivia next.

❖

Normally, Olivia didn't mind assessment committee meetings. She found it satisfying to quantify and measure what students learned in English courses. It provided something tangible to establish the legitimacy of the humanities in a STEM-obsessed climate. She found her mind wandering, however, and more than once had to be pulled back into the conversation.

Class was easier. Something about standing in front of twenty-five students made it impossible to be anything but on. With the first paper due in a couple of weeks, she spent most of the time going over expectations and citation requirements. Since it was a survey course, she had a mix of students, including non-majors and a few freshmen. Being really thorough would hopefully save her some really bad papers or, worse, plagiarism issues. She lingered after to answer a few questions, but decided to head right home instead of going to her office.

When she walked in the kitchen door, she could hear Joss and Ben banging around upstairs. She quickly changed her clothes and gathered up her supplies before heading up to join them. She set down her things and walked through the door of her soon-to-be closet. The far wall was completely gone, allowing her to see into the bathroom where Joss and Ben were working.

"Looks like y'all have been busy."

Joss and Ben turned in unison. It was kind of adorable. "You're back," Ben said.

"I am, and I'm impressed with your progress."

"Good. Hold on to that feeling because we have an issue." Joss looked worried.

Olivia frowned. "What kind of issue?"

"When I did the inspection and found copper pipes in the kitchen and basement, I figured the whole house had them. For some reason, however, they used galvanized steel for the upstairs."

"I take it that's bad?"

"Not bad, but not ideal."

Ben jumped in. "It can be hard to tell what shape they're in without cutting into them."

Joss continued. "Which means they could last another twenty years or they could go next week."

Olivia had seen that on a show once. It didn't seem terrible, but no one had talked about how much it cost to fix. "So you're suggesting we replace them while the walls are open."

"It would mean breaking into one wall on the first floor that we hadn't planned to, but then you really shouldn't have to worry about plumbing issues for the foreseeable future."

Olivia crossed her arms. "Makes sense. How much?"

"About two extra days and a couple thousand dollars."

Olivia felt herself relax. In the grand scheme of things, that seemed like a small price to pay for peace of mind. It was also a lot cheaper than dealing with pipes leaking in the walls. "Let's do it."

Joss looked relieved and Ben elbowed her. "See, I told you she would be reasonable."

Olivia raised a brow at Joss. "Did you think I wouldn't be?"

"No. I just hate finding things that are going to cost the homeowner more time and money."

Olivia sighed. Of course Joss would take that kind of thing to heart. It was the sort of thing that made her attraction to Joss so much more than physical. "I appreciate that you told me what you found and gave me the options. I'm sure some people would have covered it back up to avoid dealing with it or done what they wanted and handed me a bill after the fact."

"Thanks. That makes me feel better."

"Good. Knowing my pipes aren't going to burst makes me feel better, so we're even."

"What are you up to this afternoon?" Ben asked.

"Well, I'm itching to paint, but I'm going to work on the floors for an hour or two first. I feel like I'm finally in the home stretch. Besides, I want to try out my fancy new knee pads." She winked at Joss.

Ben shook his head. "I still can't believe you're doing all of that yourself."

"Oh, she has everything under control." Joss winked back.

Olivia headed to what was going to be her guest room and got to work. It only took about an hour for her to finish the staples that were still there. The knee pads were a godsend. She was going to have to think of a good way to thank Joss for thinking of them and buying them for her. A vision of herself, on her knees in front of Joss, flashed into Olivia's mind. The arousal was so quick, it left her breathless. Olivia wondered if she was ever going to get that chance. God, she hoped so.

Feeling satisfied with her progress, she decided to switch gears and do some painting. She was so looking forward to covering up the garish pink that was there. She opened up the pack of paint rollers and slid one onto the handle, unwrapped her new brush, set a liner in the paint tray. She looked up to find Joss standing in the doorway.

"You look like quite the pro there."

Olivia stood. "Unlike pulling up carpet, I actually know how to paint walls."

"You did just fine with the carpet, especially for a first timer."

"You'll have to watch it with all the compliments. They'll go right to my head."

Joss rolled her eyes. "Oh, well, then I take it back."

"Too late." Olivia popped the lid on a gallon of paint with a screwdriver. She poured some of the creamy yellow paint into the tray liner and stood up. "I now think I'm the diva of DIY."

Joss shook her head, but smiled. "You've got the diva part right. Are you sure you don't need a hand?"

Olivia picked up her edging brush. "As you so nicely said earlier, I have this completely under control."

"We'll be downstairs if you change your mind."

"Thanks."

Joss disappeared and Olivia climbed onto her new stepladder. She dipped her brush, then trailed it slowly along the edge where wall met ceiling. She did it a second time, pausing to admire the crisp line. Even with the fancy primer-paint-in-one she'd bought, it was going to take a couple of coats. But still. It looked good. And, more importantly, it was hers.

CHAPTER THIRTEEN

The next day, Joss was back to working solo, patching the seams and holes in the drywall to get it ready for painting. Between her conversation with Ben and Olivia's flirtatious comments, she'd pretty much settled on seeing where things with Olivia might lead. With that decided, her mind was free to focus on how it should go.

Maybe she'd invite Olivia to her place, cook her dinner. It was so easy to see Olivia on her sofa with a glass of wine, naked in her bed. Apparently, her mind wasted no time. As if summoned from Joss's thoughts, Olivia appeared in the doorway. Joss shook off the haze of her fantasy and smiled.

"Does it count as a second date if I invite you to stay for dinner again?"

Joss set the putty knife on the edge of the joint compound hawk. "It depends. Are you inviting me?"

"Only if it doesn't offend your old-fashioned sensibilities." Olivia smiled at her in a way that seemed both innocent and seductive. It was a unique talent she had.

"I think I could probably handle it." It was a slight shift in her plans, but there was nothing wrong with that.

"Delightful."

"But only if I get to reciprocate later this week."

"Oh, most definitely."

Joss realized just how fun this kind of banter could be, and how long it had been since she'd experienced it. "Well, then what are we having?"

"How do you feel about clams?"

"You're going to cook clams?" Joss gestured to the shells of cabinets that had been delivered but not installed, the gaping hole where the stove should be. "In this?"

"I guess you'll have to wait and see, won't you? I'll stop at the store after class. I should be back around four."

"Okay. I should be just about done with joint compound when you get back."

"More walls to paint. Oh, goody."

"I could help, you know."

Olivia walked up and kissed her on the cheek. "You're very sweet. If we get to the point where I'm holding you up, we can discuss. Deal?"

Joss took Olivia's face into her hands and kissed her in earnest. "Deal."

Olivia blinked at her a couple of times and smiled. "I'm sorry. Do you think you might be able to do that again?"

Joss loved that Olivia seemed a little off balance. Having that effect recharged Joss's confidence, reminded her what it felt like to woo a woman. She put one hand on the back of Olivia's neck, another around her waist. Instead of the vigorous kiss she imagined Olivia was expecting, Joss began gently. She traced Olivia's bottom lip with her tongue. When Olivia's lips parted, she slid inside, letting herself sink into the taste and softness of Olivia's mouth.

When Olivia moaned softly, Joss went deeper. She teased Olivia's tongue, nibbled her bottom lip with her teeth. As much as Joss wanted to focus on Olivia's reaction, it was impossible to ignore the heat that threatened to consume her. Something about Olivia tested her control, making her feel powerful and almost a little nervous. She finally pulled away and was left feeling as shaky and hungry as Olivia looked.

"So, um, I'll see you later this afternoon, then." Was that a coherent sentence? Joss hoped so.

Olivia let out a shuddery breath. "Yes, this afternoon. I'll see you then."

Joss watched Olivia leave, then got back to work. Despite the heat in their kiss, and the unspoken promise of more, there was something about the whole thing that felt oddly homey, domestic even. Joss was a little alarmed by how easy it felt. It must be the way they were sharing space. Having never dated a client before, of course she wouldn't know what that felt like.

The hours passed quickly. After finishing the first coat of joint compound, Joss took a break for lunch. By the time she was done, the area where she started was dry and she began applying the second coat. She was washing her tools when she heard Olivia's car in the driveway. Joss dried her hands just in time to open the door for Olivia, who breezed in with a couple of canvas grocery bags.

"Why, thank you."

"Of course. Is there more?"

"No, I've got it all. Thanks." Olivia set down the bags. "Can I see what you've done?"

Joss smiled and gestured to the finished wall. "It looks messy, but it's perfectly smooth and ready for paint."

"I love it and I can't wait to get color on it." After getting encouragement from Joss, she'd picked out a shade of red from the American Heritage collection. It reminded her of antique flags, and she was excited to see how it looked in the room.

"It'll be good to go tomorrow. Even though you'll have some touch-ups, I'd suggest doing it before we hang the cabinets. It will make for a lot less edging."

"Any plan that cuts down on edging is the plan for me."

"Can I give you a hand with dinner?"

"There's not much to do, but sure. Why don't you finish whatever you were doing and meet me outside?"

"You got it." Joss cleaned up and then headed to the backyard.

Olivia was standing at the grill, putting what looked to be three or four dozen littlenecks on the grates. Once they were all on, she shut the lid and looked at her watch. She looked at Joss and smiled. "Good day?"

"It was a good day. We're moving right along. You?"

"Good. I feel like I'm getting into the groove of the semester, getting to know the students."

"Is it hard, having a new batch of students every few months?"

"It takes a little while to learn their personalities, what interests them, whether or not they're motivated. Probably not unlike getting to know new clients with every project."

"That's an interesting way of thinking about it." Joss wouldn't have said her work and Olivia's had anything in common. Olivia was right, though, they were both in the business of people.

"Only I have the luxury of the customer not always being right." Olivia winked at her.

After about five minutes, Olivia opened the grill. She set the bread she'd sliced onto the upper rack and deftly started moving the clams that had opened onto a platter. She closed it again for another minute and repeated the process. Joss was surprised by how comfortable she was wielding kitchen utensils. She should probably know by now that her assumptions about Olivia were useless.

When all the clams were off, Olivia poured the contents of a small pot over the top. "These are good to go."

Joss took the platter and carried it over to the table, setting it next to the bowl of salad. Olivia followed with a plate of bread. She poured them each a glass of Sauvignon blanc and pulled out her chair. "Bon appétit."

Joss put some salad and a few clams on her plate. She freed one from its shell and sampled it. "This is really good. What is it?"

"Butter, garlic, lemon juice, white wine, and hot sauce."

Joss nodded slowly. "Hot sauce. Genius."

Olivia shrugged. "I have a few tricks up my sleeve."

Joss chuckled. That was one way of putting it. When they were done eating, Joss helped Olivia carry the dishes inside. They washed up, then put them back in the plastic bin Olivia was using in lieu of kitchen cabinets. Olivia snapped the lid on to keep dust away and draped the dish towel over the top. Joss found the tidiness of it amusing, especially given the disarray around them.

"Since it's still light out, would you come outside with me for a minute?" Joss asked.

"Sure."

They walked out the side door and around to the front of the house. The porch, along with its roof and Olivia's errant piece of shag carpet, had been pulled down the week before. A couple of Joss's crew had a few days between big jobs and Joss thought she might have them start working on the new one while they were free.

"What am I looking at?" Olivia asked.

"I wanted you out here so you could more easily visualize the options for your porch."

Olivia turned to her and smiled. "You had me at porch."

"I know it was going to be one of the last projects, but I've got some wiggle room in the schedule and I could have a couple of guys over this week to start the framing."

"Really? That would make me so happy. Does that mean I might get to enjoy it for a little while before the weather turns?"

Joss thought about her first impressions of the house, and of Olivia. Sometimes, being proven wrong was the best possible thing. "If you don't mind shuffling one or two inside projects by a day or two, definitely."

"Yes, please. Pretty please."

"So, what I need you to do is decide how you want it to look."

Olivia's eyes sparkled with excitement. "Okay. What are my options?"

"The first would be to span just the front of the house. You'd have plenty of room for a sitting area and it would cost about a third less than the other option."

Olivia scowled. "What's my other option?"

"Rebuild it exactly as it was. Span the front and wrap around the side. It'll cost more, obviously, and I'm not sure you'd really use the added space."

"But?"

Joss couldn't help but smile. How did Olivia know there was a but? "But rebuilding it fully will look amazing and maintain one of the distinctive characteristics of the house."

"Well, then I think you have your answer."

Did she? Joss hoped Olivia would go for the full rebuild, but thought she might prefer to spend the money elsewhere. "Full porch?"

"Full porch."

"Excellent. We'll make it happen."

"Excellent. While we're out here, would you mind coming around back? I have an idea for a longer-term project and I'd love to hear your thoughts."

"Happily."

Olivia took Joss's hand and led her toward the backyard. They stopped and stood in the shade of one of the huge maple trees. "You mentioned a few days ago that you know about gardening."

"My mom is the expert, but I know some. Are you thinking of putting one in?"

"I am. I feel like the summer is when I have the most free time, so it would be conducive to having a small vegetable patch."

Joss wouldn't have thought Olivia to be the type to want to grow her own food. Then again, Olivia hadn't turned out to be at all what Joss assumed when they first met. "I think it's a great idea. What's your question?"

"I'm not sure about size or the best location."

"I think your best bet is to start small. It's better to add on a little each year than get in over your head and wind up overrun with weeds and discouraged."

"And do I seem like the kind of woman who bites off more than she can chew?"

It wasn't a suggestive question, but it stirred Joss's insides nonetheless. "You seem to handle things just fine."

"That's quite a compliment from you."

Joss shrugged. Had she really come across as such a curmudgeon? "From what I've observed, it's true."

Olivia smiled. "I'll be very responsible then and start small. Does it matter where I put it?"

Joss surveyed the yard. Olivia's property abutted corn fields on two sides and woods on the other. A few trees were scattered around. "You want something that's relatively flat and will get sun most, if not all, of the day. You're going to have to put up a fence no matter what if you don't want the deer and groundhogs to raid it."

Olivia rolled her eyes. "Deer and groundhogs. Right. This city mouse still has a lot to learn."

"I'm happy to help if you want. And if you want to turn the dirt over once this season to make it easier in the spring, I'll bring over my rototiller."

"You have a rototiller?"

"I got a good deal on a used one. I'm a bit of a sucker for tools."

"I love that. And I would love to borrow it. Thank you." Olivia leaned in and gave Joss a kiss on the cheek.

The gesture was affectionate, almost platonic. Still, it made Joss realize just how badly she wanted to kiss Olivia in an entirely different way. How much thoughts of kissing Olivia in all sorts of ways had occupied her mind almost constantly. So Joss leaned forward and kissed her again. Softly at first, then she took Olivia's face in her hands and indulged the desire that had been building in her all day.

Olivia's arms wound around Joss's neck and she leaned in, pressing her body against Joss. Joss moved her hands from Olivia's face, down her arms, and then up her sides. Olivia made a purring sound, sending Joss into overdrive, then slid her hands down Joss's body and under her shirt. The feel of Olivia's cool fingers against her skin made Joss ache.

They were standing very close to the tree. Olivia angled herself so that her back pressed against it. Joss freed one hand to brace herself against the wide trunk. Olivia still wore her work clothes—an almost prim skirt and silk blouse. Joss popped open the top two buttons to reveal a pale pink bra. Olivia's chest heaved, inviting Joss's touch. Joss slid her hand inside, feeling the heat and weight of Olivia's breast in her palm.

Olivia's hands had made their way under the hem of Joss's shirt. She traced her fingernails up Joss's spine, working her T-shirt over her head in the process. Olivia discarded it, then returned to the gentle scratching that made Joss's skin tingle.

A stiff breeze on her bare skin jerked Joss back to reality. She took a step back, realizing Olivia was nearly topless and that she'd stripped down to a sports bra. And they were standing in the middle of Olivia's yard, in full view of the road. What the hell had come over her?

"You didn't have to stop." Olivia looked disheveled and shell-shocked.

Joss thought about how consumed she'd been by the moment, how close she'd come to taking Olivia against a tree. It appalled her. "We're outside, half-naked, in broad daylight. Anyone driving down the road could see us."

Olivia laughed, making her feel better, even if only a little. "It's okay. No one drives down this road."

"Still. I didn't mean for that to happen. I'm so sorry."

Olivia watched Joss yank her shirt back on and fought off a wave of disappointment. Maybe Joss had put the brakes on because they were on the verge of getting it on in the middle of the yard. Olivia wasn't opposed to that, but she could understand Joss's hesitation. But what if Joss had done it because she didn't want to get it on in the first place?

"It's really okay."

They walked back toward the side of the house. Joss wouldn't make eye contact. "I should go."

Olivia didn't put herself out there very often, but still. She was unused to the sting of rejection. And this felt a whole lot like rejection. She couldn't decide whether or not to confront Joss about it.

"Do you need anything from inside the house?" Could she say something more useless?

Joss's reply was stilted. "Just my keys. I'll grab them."

"Okay." Olivia stayed outside, feeling unsettled and still a little aroused.

Joss walked into the kitchen and emerged a few seconds later. She looked at Olivia, her eyes full of concern. "I really am sorry. Are you okay?"

Olivia straightened her shoulders, tossed her hair, and smiled. Better to make light than turn it into a scene. She refused to be caught wallowing. "Of course. I'm sorry I pounced on you like that."

Joss shook her head. "You don't need to be sorry."

"I promise I won't tear at you like a sex-crazed teenager again."

Joss came up to her and stood very close. "I kind of liked the sex-crazed part."

"You don't have to say that."

"Olivia, I didn't stop because I don't want to have sex with you. I stopped because, when I do, I want to do it right."

"Oh."

"Call me old-fashioned, but that includes privacy and a nice bed and the luxury of all the time in the world."

Olivia swallowed. So it was just about being in the yard. "I see. When you put it that way, I have to agree."

"So, I'll see you in the morning. We can take it from there?"

Joss did want her. The twinge of disappointment became a pang of desire. Desire blended with anticipation. That she could handle. "That sounds good to me."

"Thank you for dinner."

"Of course."

Joss scratched her temple. "Thanks for the other...the...you know."

Seeing Joss scramble for words made Olivia feel infinitely better. The woman really was old-fashioned. "The feeling is entirely mutual."

Joss nodded, then got into her truck without kissing Olivia again. Olivia watched her drive away and found herself wondering why they didn't just go into the house tonight. Perhaps the mood had been ruined. She told herself not to overthink it. She had other things to worry about. Like putting the finishing touches on her reverse seduction.

Chapter Fourteen

Joss's stomach was full of nerves when she arrived at Olivia's the next morning. She wasn't sure if it was the fact that they'd almost slept together or the fact that they hadn't. She'd never come so close to such reckless abandon. It had been both exhilarating and unsettling. She'd spent much of the night tossing and turning and replaying it in her mind.

Olivia was already preparing to leave for class, which proved to be both a relief and a disappointment. She greeted Joss with a kiss and smile, making it clear she wasn't going to bring up what had happened. Joss wasn't sure what to make of it, except that Olivia seemed set on leaving Joss in charge.

Olivia asked, "Will you be here when I get home?"

Relief replaced nerves. "I think that could be arranged."

"Will you let me make you dinner again?"

"How about I grab takeout?" After the mess she made of things the day before, Joss wasn't about to make Olivia cook for her a second night in a row.

Olivia smiled. "I'll get the takeout. Any requests?"

"I like pretty much everything. Pizza to subs to Thai."

"Excellent. I'll see you later then."

"I'll be here."

Olivia gathered her things and headed to campus. Joss's words played in her mind. *When I do, I want to do it right.* Would that be tonight? The anticipation of what the evening might hold made the day drag. Only a handful of students came to her office hours. She chatted them up probably more than they wanted. It was good to get to know them better, even if part of her motivation was killing time.

After her late afternoon class, she called in an order of pad Thai and panang gai, along with some spring rolls and satay. By the time she pulled into the driveway, Olivia was more aroused than hungry. She felt a little bit nervous, too, which was strange. Maybe it had something to do with all the buildup.

Joss stood in the kitchen, drying her hands. Olivia took a deep breath and swallowed, trying to calm her skittering pulse. When she opened the door, Joss turned and smiled. "Hi."

Olivia stepped into the kitchen and set down the bag of food. "Hi, yourself."

"What did you get?"

"Thai."

"Yum."

"Yeah." Seeing Joss further reduced her desire for food.

"What's wrong?"

"Nothing. I guess I'm not all that hungry now."

"No?"

"Well, not that kind of hungry."

"I see." Joss closed the distance between them. She leaned in and kissed Olivia in a way that made her knees weak.

When Joss eased away, Olivia opened her eyes and searched Joss's. "I don't want to presume anything, but I also don't want you to have any doubts as to what I want."

Joss nodded. "I appreciate that. Just so we're one hundred percent clear, what is it you want?"

"You."

Joss took Olivia's hand and pulled her slowly to the temporary bedroom.

Once there, Olivia slipped her arms around Joss's waist. "I've wanted you. I've wanted you since the day we met."

Joss smiled. "Even when I was a jerk?"

Olivia nodded. "Even then."

"I wanted you, too, the moment I laid eyes on you."

Olivia leaned in and kissed her. "I'm so glad we got that sorted out."

"Me, too." Joss trailed a line of kisses down her neck and across her collarbone.

Olivia tilted her head to one side, reveling in the softness of each touch. One of Joss's hands slid up her back to the zipper of her dress. Joss eased the zipper down, sliding a hand inside. The roughness of Joss's fingers on her skin sent shivers all the way to her toes. Olivia moaned, unable to contain herself.

Joss eased the dress from her shoulders; it fell to the floor around her feet. She pulled Olivia with her, slowly making her way toward the bed. Olivia slid her hands between them, working at the buttons of Joss's shirt.

"One second," Olivia said, easing herself away. She darted around the room to light the candles she'd bought and set out, just in case.

Joss raised an eyebrow. "I'm sorry, did you just pause me for mood lighting?"

Olivia slipped back in front of her and slid the shirt from her shoulders. "Flattering light discourages self-consciousness."

Joss laughed. "I have a hard time imagining you as self-conscious."

"Compliments, compliments. I'd think you were trying to get me into bed."

In one fluid motion, Joss had both of them on the bed. Joss, propped on her elbows, looked down at Olivia and smiled. "I'd say I already have."

The speed and the smoothness of the move took Olivia by surprise and made her pulse race. She could feel Joss's weight pressing into her. It was a delicious feeling, one she hadn't experienced in far too long. "And what are you going to do about it?"

Joss leaned in. The kiss was excruciatingly slow. For all that she'd professed to be old-fashioned, Joss could do things with her mouth that turned Olivia's insides into a puddle of pure want. When she pulled back, Olivia had to blink several times to bring her vision back into focus. "Oh, well then."

Joss smiled. "I'm just getting started."

After running a hand down Olivia's side and up again, Joss eased behind Olivia and released the clasp of her bra. She pulled it aside and spent a moment studying Olivia's newly exposed breasts. Olivia watched Joss look at her, felt her skin grow warm and flushed. Just when Olivia felt she might spontaneously combust from the heat of it, Joss bent and took one of Olivia's nipples into her mouth.

She had no idea if it was because she hadn't been with anyone in a while or if there was something about Joss, but every nerve ending in her body seemed tied to that one sensitive point. Joss switched from making slow circles with her tongue to a gentle tug with her teeth. When Olivia thought she might not be able to take it any longer, Joss shifted to her other breast, sucking and biting and driving her completely mad.

Without stopping, Joss trailed her fingers down Olivia's stomach and between her legs. Olivia, aching and wet, opened herself for Joss's touch. When Joss's fingers slid across her throbbing center, Olivia arched into Joss and moaned.

"Fuck."

Olivia barely heard Joss's whispered expletive. It was such a sexy, unguarded moment, Olivia found herself even more aroused. When Joss's hand moved lower and she eased one, then two, fingers into her, Olivia had an expletive of her own. Joss's strokes were long and slow, her callouses creating a delicious friction. Olivia clamped around her fingers, pulling them in deeper.

Joss's mouth was at her ear, her tongue playing with Olivia's earlobe. Olivia dug her fingers into Joss's shoulders, holding on, trying to get even closer to her. She could feel Joss's muscles bunch and flex in her hands.

"Yes, Joss. God, you feel so good." Olivia mumbled the words between ragged breaths.

Joss's thrusts became more forceful. Olivia could feel Joss's knuckles pressing against her. Olivia pushed back, basking in Joss's strength and stamina. When Joss's thumb swept across her clit, an upward stroke for every thrust, Olivia started to come undone. The orgasm pulsed through her, the pressure giving way to a quivering pleasure that she felt in every muscle of her body.

It took Olivia a long time to regain her senses. Even when the tremors stopped, her heart continued to thud in her chest. When she finally caught her breath enough to speak, she opened her eyes. Joss was lying on her side, propped on an elbow and looking at her intently.

"That was fucking amazing," Olivia said.

Joss's smile was slow. Olivia couldn't be sure, but she was pretty sure it was a little bit smug, too. "You're pretty amazing."

"If I'd known it was going to be that good, I would have tried to get you into bed sooner."

Joss chuckled. "Didn't anyone ever tell you good things come to those who wait?"

Olivia rolled onto her side, surprised by how weak her body felt. "Nope. No one has ever told me that."

Joss traced Olivia's collarbone with her finger. "It's true. That said, if you make me wait much longer, I'm not sure I'll live to see tomorrow."

Olivia cupped Joss's breast in her hand. It was small and firm, a hint of feminine softness on her otherwise muscular form. She brushed her thumb over the nipple, enjoying the way it became erect at her touch. She shifted her gaze, looked into Joss's eyes. "We can't have that, can we?"

When Olivia took the hard nipple into her mouth, Joss groaned. Olivia lifted her hand to the other breast, rolling the nipple between her finger and thumb. Joss's hands bunched in her hair, holding her close. Olivia relished the way Joss's body responded to her, moved against her.

As much as she would have liked to worship Joss's breasts for the rest of the night, Olivia was desperate to feel Joss in her mouth, to taste her. She made a line of kisses down Joss's torso, admiring the defined ridges of her abs. She brushed her cheek across the patch of dark curls before easing her tongue into the soft folds. Joss's hips bucked and she gasped.

"Mmm…" Olivia was intoxicated by her taste. She made slow circles with her tongue, giving Joss a chance to settle in. When Joss's hips began a steady, rhythmic thrust, Olivia shifted slightly, stroking Joss's hard center. She wrapped her lips around it, sucking gently while flicking her tongue back and forth.

Joss's hands were in her hair again, a sensation Olivia adored. Joss was saying her name over and over, interspersed with "yeses" and "ohs." Olivia quickened her pace, matching the urgency of Joss's words and the movement of her body. When Joss's whole body went rigid, Olivia stayed with her, sucking and stroking as her muscles twitched and shook. Finally, Joss's body went limp. Olivia pulled away, resting her head on Joss's thigh.

After a long minute, she pulled herself up and crawled to curl up next to Joss. "Yeah, that was definitely worth the wait."

Joss wrapped an arm around her. "I told you."

Olivia lost track of time. She couldn't remember feeling so content. She'd just started drifting off to sleep when she felt Joss shift. She lifted her head. "What? What is it?"

Joss kissed her temple. "I know this sounds terrible and I really don't want you to be upset, but I have to go."

Yanked back to reality, Olivia sat up. Disappointment gripped her. "What?"

Joss lifted a hand and cupped her cheek. "I don't want to, I promise. I meant what I said about wanting to have all the time in the world, but I can't leave Ethel by herself all night and I didn't make arrangements."

The letdown became a hard knot in Olivia's stomach. "Ethel?"

Joss must have seen the look on her face because she shook her head quickly. "My dog. My dog's name is Ethel."

Olivia felt a wave of relief. "Oh. Okay. That makes me feel better. I think."

Joss smiled. "She's really old and mostly content to sleep her days away, but I can't leave her overnight."

Olivia nodded. "Of course not."

"I should have made plans for her. I don't know why I didn't. Maybe I didn't want to presume things either. I'm really sorry."

"It's okay."

"Thank you for understanding." Joss kissed her again and climbed out of bed.

Olivia watched her pull on her clothes. Although she still felt a pretty keen disappointment, Olivia couldn't hold it against her. "What kind of dog?"

"A beagle mix. Ben and I each adopted one of a pair of siblings that had been dumped in the country, about eight years ago now."

Not that she wasn't pretty far gone over Joss already, but Olivia's heart melted just a little bit more. "And you named her Ethel?"

"And Ben has Fred. The SPCA gave them those names when they were brought in. They were starting to respond to them, so it seemed mean to change to something else."

"That might be the most adorable thing I've ever heard. I've never had a dog. My mother is allergic. I'd like one, though."

Joss, now dressed, walked over to the bed and sat next to her. "I'd probably wait until the house is done, but you've definitely got a good place. I really am sorry I have to go."

Olivia smiled. "Given who the other woman is, I think I'll be okay."

"Thank you. I'm sorry we didn't get to dinner."

"I'm not."

"Me either, except that you went to the trouble to pick it up."

"Not a big deal. You can have it for lunch tomorrow."

"Thanks. Tonight was...great. I hope we can do it again soon."

"It was, and yes, let's do it again soon."

Joss kissed her. "I'll lock up on my way out. And put the food in the fridge."

"Thanks."

After she heard the back door squeak open, then closed, Olivia got up and blew out the candles that were still burning in the room. She climbed back into bed and pulled the covers up to her chin. She'd had women leave after sex before, but never to go home to a dog. At least, never to her knowledge. One more way Joss was full of surprises. Given her track record with women, maybe that wasn't such a terrible thing.

CHAPTER FIFTEEN

The next day, Olivia was already preparing to leave when Joss arrived. Joss consciously pushed aside the worry that crept into her mind. What if Olivia really was upset about the fact that she'd left the night before? Joss attempted to reason with herself. Olivia had a job. Joss did, too, for that matter, and having Olivia around would be a distraction. A delightful distraction, but a distraction nonetheless.

"We're going to pull out the upstairs plumbing fixtures today."

Olivia's eyes lit up. "Really?"

"Yep. The bathroom tile came in. So we're going to pull everything out today and lay the tile. It needs forty-eight hours to fully cure, then we can put the new fixtures and the tub back in."

"That makes me incredibly happy."

"Don't get too happy yet. While we only need to completely shut off the water for a couple of hours, you're going to be without a shower for about four days."

Olivia put her hands on her hips. Joss had come to realize it was an unconscious gesture that could mean Olivia was thinking about something, that she was irritated, or that she was being playful. Now that she knew that, it didn't make her bristle like it did when she and Olivia first met. "That's fine. Gina and Kel have just finished converting their guest room to a nursery, so I'll get a hotel."

Joss cringed inwardly. The thought had occurred to her to invite Olivia to stay at her place, but she'd effectively talked herself out of it. It was way too soon to be playing house for the better part of a week. That argument worked fine when she thought Olivia would stay with her friends. Having her go to a hotel seemed wrong.

"You know, you could stay with me." The words were out of her mouth before she knew what she was saying.

Olivia raised a brow. "Are you sure?"

Joss wasn't at all sure, but she wasn't going to take it back. It would be fine. It was the right thing to do. It didn't have to mean anything beyond that. "I mean, you don't have to, but I have plenty of space. A hotel seems unnecessary."

Olivia's response was a slow, sultry smile. The effect on Joss was strong and immediate. "That's very chivalrous of you."

Joss cleared her throat. "It just seems logical."

"Logical?"

"Since I was going to ask you over for dinner, that is. That's what I'd planned to do for our second date."

"I see. Well, since you were going to ask me over anyway."

Joss decided keeping things light would help her not freak out. "Yeah, I figured you could use a real home-cooked meal."

"Are you making fun of my kitchen setup?" Olivia gestured to the small cart that held her coffeepot and slow cooker—the extent of her appliances now that the kitchen had been emptied and the stove she ordered would take at least three weeks to arrive.

"Yes. Yes, I am." Joss was still taken aback by how easy it was to banter with Olivia, be playful. It was nice, made things feel more familiar than they would otherwise after just a couple of dates.

"I do have the grill, you know."

Joss crossed her arms over her chest, made her face stern. "Do you want to come over or not?"

Olivia crossed the room and kissed Joss on the cheek. "I would love to. Thank you for the invitation."

"You're welcome. I'm looking forward to having you there." Olivia's brow went up and Joss realized the double entendre of her words. Before she could backpedal, Olivia smiled again.

"And I'm looking forward to you having me."

Joss swallowed the lump in her throat. "I'll, um, text you the directions. I'll leave here around five to go clean up and start dinner. You're welcome whenever."

Olivia's face softened. "That sounds great. I really appreciate you offering me a place to stay."

"For the record, I don't do this with all my clients."

Olivia grinned. "Lord, I sure hope not."

"That said, please feel free to pack a bag. It's going to be a few days."

"I think I feel a U-Haul joke coming on."

Joss decided to borrow Olivia's phrase. "Lord, I sure hope not."

❖

Joss's house was about as far out of town as Olivia's, but in the opposite direction. When she pulled into the driveway, she couldn't help but sigh at how perfect it was. The style was Craftsman, probably built in the thirties. In the glow of the porch light, she could see that it was painted a deep green with cream shutters; the porch appeared to be natural pine. The landscaping looked elegant without being fussy—exactly the type of look she was planning for her own yard.

Olivia parked and walked to the front door. What a door it was—oversize with a dark stain and three small windows just above eye level. The glass looked original, wavy with age. Beneath the windows was a massive pewter knocker. It wouldn't go with the style of her house, but she was envious of it all the same.

She'd just lifted her hand to knock when the door opened. Joss stood on the other side in jeans, a plaid shirt with the sleeves rolled up, and a pair of leather deck shoes. Had the shoes been in better shape, she would have been a perfect addition to the L.L.Bean fall catalog.

"I thought I heard a car."

"Your place is gorgeous."

"Thanks. Come on in."

Olivia stepped inside and was enveloped in the aroma of fresh bread and garlic. After eating nothing more than an apple and peanut butter between classes, it was almost too much. "Oh, my God," she said, barely stifling a groan. "Your house smells amazing. What are you cooking?"

Joss took her bag and set it at the foot of the stairs. "It's just a simple pasta sauce. Oh, and bread. Thanks to my sister's cast-off bread machine, I can whip up a crusty Italian at the push of a button."

Olivia followed her into the kitchen. "Push of a button or no, I'm impressed, and starved. Between the two, I'm likely to embarrass myself with how much I eat. Consider yourself warned."

"I'm looking forward to it. Wine?" Joss walked over to the counter where a bottle and two glasses were sitting.

"Yes, please."

While Joss poured, Olivia looked around the kitchen. The walls were a rich, buttery yellow that complemented light, honey-toned cabinets. Pots hung from the ceiling and crocks of fresh herbs lined the windowsill. On the wall was a set of four paintings of citrus fruit that looked to be done by small, creative hands. It was warm and cheerful, and looked like the space of someone who did a lot of cooking.

Joss handed her a glass of wine. "I can drop the pasta anytime. Are you ready to eat?"

As if on cue, Olivia's stomach growled, apparently loud enough for Joss to hear.

"I'll take that as a yes?"

Olivia blushed and pressed a hand against her stomach. "Yes, but only if I get the tour after."

Joss nodded. "Deal. In the meantime, go say hi to Ethel." She gestured toward the living room. "She can't hear you coming, so you have to stomp the floor a little bit to get her attention."

She headed in the direction Joss indicated. "I hope she likes me."

"Once you've gotten the sniff test, she'll likely roll over. As long as you rub her belly, she'll grant you undying love and devotion."

Olivia chuckled. "I wish my students were that easy."

"Not a mental image I need to have."

Although she hadn't meant it literally, Joss's comment gave Olivia the mental image as well. She laughed. "Fair enough."

Joss's living room was the same blend of modern and traditional. A massive navy blue couch and a leather club chair faced what appeared to be the original brick fireplace. She noted with approval the stack of wood off to the side. Above the mantel was a sleek flat-screen television, big enough to make watching the game exciting without being obnoxious. On either side, built-in shelves were crammed with books and family photos. Olivia made a mental note to study them in more detail later.

On the far side of the chair, positioned in perfect proximity to the fireplace, lay a beagle sound asleep on the biggest dog bed she'd ever seen. As she approached, Olivia stomped her heel on the floor a couple of times.

Ethel opened her eyes and lifted her head. Olivia got down on her knees and extended a hand. Ethel's tail began a lazy wag. She stood up, taking her time with a long, slow stretch, before sashaying over to where Olivia waited.

Her hand got the once-over and then, as promised, Ethel flopped onto her side. She flashed a light pink belly and pawed the air a couple of times. Olivia obliged her with long, gentle strokes. Her tail began to thump softly against the hardwood floor.

"Well, that didn't take long," Joss said from the doorway.

"We speak the same language."

"I hope I speak that language, too," Joss mused. "Right now, I speak the language of spaghetti."

"That," Olivia stood up, "is my favorite language of all."

They ate pasta off of chunky earthenware plates. Olivia tried to decipher the contents of the sauce, but Joss swore it was only tomatoes, garlic, olive oil, and fresh basil. "And salt, of course."

Olivia looked at her with the expression she usually reserved for students who were spinning a tale about why their paper was late.

"And a pinch of crushed red pepper," Joss added.

"And?"

"And a pinch of sugar and a splash of red wine vinegar."

"Vinegar! That's what it is! I can't believe you were holding out on me."

Joss scowled. "I wasn't holding out. I just don't think about it."

"Likely story," Olivia said, finishing her second piece of bread. Because she was contemplating a third, she said, "Now, please, I beg you—take this away from me."

They cleared the table and Joss insisted on loading the dishwasher. After, they decided to go for a walk with Ethel. With only the tiniest sliver of moon, the sky was a dark canvas dotted with a million stars. Olivia linked arms with Joss so she wouldn't trip while she gaped at the sky. "I still can't get over how beautiful it is."

"It's my favorite part of living out in the country."

Olivia brought her gaze down and looked at Joss. "Ditto."

They meandered down the driveway and along one of the many corn fields that came right up to the road.

Ethel, who'd been loping along quietly, was suddenly on full alert.

She whined softly and pulled at the leash, nose to the ground.

"Uh-oh," Joss said. She abruptly stopped walking.

"Uh-oh, what?"

"Only two things get Ethel really excited. The first is steak on the grill."

"And the second?"

At that moment, a bushy black-and-white ball of fur emerged from between the rows of corn. Joss yanked harder on the leash, but Ethel lunged forward. She let out a frantic bark and the skunk, terrified at having his evening stroll interrupted, crouched low.

The next thing Olivia knew, her nostrils burned with the most horribly intense skunk smell she'd ever encountered. She was vaguely aware of Joss swearing as the skunk hurried—as much as skunks can hurry—across the road and back out of sight.

Ethel, traumatized by the incident, was low to the ground and whimpering. Joss began to intersperse her swearing with semi-panicked posturing about what they should do. Olivia, unable to contain herself, began to laugh. She laughed so hard that she bent over and had to gasp for breath. When she was able to regain some of her composure, she straightened herself and wiped the tears from her eyes.

"So the second is skunks?"

Joss stopped swearing and looked at her. The question broke the tension and Joss also started to laugh. It started out as a single guffaw, then grew into a full belly laugh. Hearing it set Olivia off again, and the next thing she knew, they were both sitting on the ground on the side of the road.

Ethel, finding the humans on the ground reassuring, crept over and licked Joss's chin. Joss patted her head, then cringed when she realized she was merely spreading the stink around.

"I swear to you, in the eight years I've had Ethel, she's never been skunked. Ever. It's the smell in the air that gets her all riled up."

"Well, now I feel special."

Joss rolled her eyes. "Seriously, though. What are we going to do?"

Olivia shrugged. "Google it?"

"Thanks, professor."

They hustled back toward the house. Olivia went inside for her phone while Joss kept Ethel out. She emerged a moment later. "Do you have hydrogen peroxide and baking soda?"

"Yep."

"Okay. Since you know where everything is, I'll hold her while you go mix it up." She handed Joss her phone. "This is the recipe the Humane Society recommends."

Joss accepted the phone and looked at the screen. "Sounds far less disgusting than tomato juice."

Olivia took the leash. "Holler when you're ready and we'll come inside."

Joss looked at Olivia, a little surprised by how quick she was to jump in. "You don't have to help. I know this isn't the date night you signed up for."

"Don't be ridiculous. I'm not an expert or anything, but I'm sure four hands are better than two."

She was right. "Thanks. I'll be just a minute."

Joss went inside and grabbed baking soda and dish soap from the kitchen. She snagged a bucket from the hall closet on her way to the bathroom. She only had about half the peroxide suggested, so she mixed things up the best she could. She opened the bathroom window, both for ventilation and to let Olivia know she was ready.

Once they got Ethel in the tub, Olivia dived right in. They knelt side by side, massaging the lather in then rinsing it off. They followed with Ethel's usual dog shampoo and another rinse. Ethel only shook once, but it was enough to soak both of them pretty well. After being toweled off, Ethel happily trotted out of the bathroom.

"Do you think she's okay?" Olivia asked.

"Yes, and she'll probably be asleep in about ninety seconds."

"Oh, good. Does that mean we get to take showers now?"

"Yes, and you can go first."

"That's the nicest thing you've said all day."

"Take your time. I'll grab towels and leave them here." Joss gestured to the ledge of the sink.

Joss went to the linen closet, then waited until she heard water running before opening the door to set down towels. She went downstairs to grab Olivia's bag. After a moment of hesitation, she carried it to the guest room. She wanted Olivia to be comfortable and have her own space. She also didn't want the fact that Olivia was staying over to imply that they were going to sleep together again.

When Olivia emerged a few minutes later, wrapped in a towel and with wet hair trailing down her shoulders, Joss stopped breathing for a moment. It was part desire, but part something else. She couldn't quite name it, but it felt like a casual sort of intimacy; it made her heart swell uncomfortably in her chest.

"I put your things in the bedroom down on the left. Make yourself comfortable. I'll be just a couple of minutes."

Olivia, whose skin was flushed pink from the hot water, smiled at her. "Thanks."

Joss showered, then put on the T-shirt and boxers she'd brought into the bathroom with her. When she emerged, she found Olivia standing in the hallway looking at one of the paintings on the wall. She wore a dark purple slip, the kind of thing that hovered on the line between sleepwear and lingerie. Her feet were bare and her hair still damp. The combination was insanely sexy.

"Feel better?"

Olivia turned to her. "So much better. You?"

"Same. Thank you again for the help, and for being such a good sport. It's not exactly how I expected the evening to go."

Olivia smiled. "All part of the adventure."

"I'm glad you think so."

"I hope that doesn't mean other adventures are off the table."

Joss chuckled. "I didn't want to presume anything, especially after, you know."

Olivia slid her hands under the back of Joss's shirt and started trailing her fingers up and down Joss's back. "But it's the other adventures I'm really interested in."

"Well, I don't want to disappoint."

Olivia smiled. "I imagine you rarely do."

Olivia continued the gentle scratching. She leaned forward, pressing her breasts into Joss's chest. Through the thin fabric, Joss could feel her nipples. Joss ran her hands up Olivia's sides, then around to take Olivia's breasts into her hands. "Was there something specific you had in mind?"

There was a gleam in Olivia's eye that Joss found beyond erotic.

She leaned forward, bringing her lips so close to Joss's ear that Joss could feel the warmth of her breath. What she whispered made Joss's entire body react, turning her arousal into a visceral desire. Olivia leaned back and looked at Joss with searching eyes. Joss smiled slowly. "Come to my room in ninety seconds."

Olivia nodded, but didn't speak. Joss left her standing in the hall and went to her bedroom. When Olivia joined her, she was sitting on the bed, ready. She made to get up, but Olivia lifted her hand. "Don't move."

Joss swallowed and stayed where she was. Olivia walked toward her. She flicked her gaze down as she took the cock in her hand, then looked up and locked eyes with Joss. The gentle pressure of Olivia stroking her was already driving her crazy.

Olivia bent down and kissed her, then nudged her back onto the bed. Joss allowed herself to be guided, wanting Olivia to call the shots, at least for now. Olivia knelt beside her, kissing her chest and continuing the rhythmic stroking that was pushing Joss dangerously close to the edge. Joss closed her eyes and allowed the sensations to pulse through her.

When Olivia stopped, Joss opened her eyes, unsure of how much time had passed. Olivia was staring at her intently and smiling. "I need to have you inside me now."

"Yes. Tell me what you need, what you want."

"Like I said before, don't move." Olivia shifted so that she was straddling Joss's hips. Joss took a deep breath and tried to rein in the arousal that was threatening to strip away any semblance of control. She felt Olivia position the cock and the next thing she knew, she was completely surrounded by Olivia's heat. She groaned, realizing how long it had been since she'd been with a woman like this.

"Is this okay?" Olivia's body was still and she was, again, searching Joss's eyes.

"You feel...amazing."

"I was just thinking the same thing."

Olivia started to move, slow undulations that Joss felt from the place their bodies were joined to the tips of her fingers and toes. She placed her hands on Olivia's hips, not so much to guide them, but to feel the movement. She watched Olivia's face, her eyes closed and her hair a tumble of flame-colored curls. Joss didn't think she'd ever seen anything so beautiful.

Olivia's thrusts became more urgent and she leaned forward, placing a hand on either side of Joss's head. Joss pulled her into a kiss and began thrusting back, lifting her hips to match the press of Olivia against her. The friction of their movement combined with the slide of Olivia's damp breasts against hers. Joss felt the pressure start to build and she had to fight furiously to hold herself back.

When Olivia's body began to tremble, Joss let go. Her limbs went rigid and the orgasm felt like an explosion. The heat poured out of her and flashes of light clouded her vision. She pulled herself together, only to find Olivia still on top of her, her hair curtaining both their faces. Olivia was still, save an occasional tremor.

"You okay?"

Olivia's eyes opened and she blinked a few times, as though trying to bring Joss into focus. "I am so fucking good."

Joss laughed. It was exactly how she felt, too. She loved that she'd reduced the English professor to such an unsophisticated declaration. Olivia kissed her and rolled over, flopping onto the bed next to her. Joss rolled onto her side, admiring the lines of Olivia's body and the sheen of sweat on her skin. "You really do look like a pinup girl."

Olivia raised a brow. "A pinup girl?"

Joss hadn't meant to say so out loud. "Sorry. I meant it in a good way. I swear."

"Don't apologize. That's a lovely compliment." Olivia lifted one of her knees and made a pose. "I like it."

Joss laughed. "I thought that the first time I saw you, or maybe the second. You were wearing this vintage-looking dress and your hair was all pinned up. You made my mouth water."

Olivia smiled again, but the compliment seemed to make her shy all of a sudden. "Thanks."

Joss traced the line of Olivia's jaw with her finger. She felt something inside her shift. More than attraction, more even than how much she'd started to like Olivia, Joss felt the stirrings of something much bigger. She had no idea what she was going to do about it.

Chapter Sixteen

The next morning, Joss let Olivia shower first again. As tempted as she was to climb in next to her, Joss figured doing so would make them both late to work. Olivia got dressed in what Joss had come to think of as her professor clothes and headed off to campus. Joss put on work clothes and headed over to Olivia's to work on the bathroom.

That evening, Olivia picked up Indian and they sat at the kitchen island with a bottle of wine and a half dozen takeout containers between them. They put on a football game, but spent most of the evening on the couch talking. When it was time for bed, Olivia hovered for the briefest moment at the top of the stairs. Joss tilted her head toward her bedroom; it was all the invitation Olivia needed.

The following day, Olivia had a work thing that kept her on campus until after six. Joss waited up for her downstairs, thinking Olivia might want to make use of the guest room after such a long day, but she was quickly proven wrong. After the third night, Joss was torn. On one hand, she wasn't in any hurry for Olivia to stop spending the night. Instead of feeling like too much time together, Joss craved more. It left her a little unsettled just how easily they'd slipped into a routine. She liked having Olivia around, and not just in the bedroom. On the other hand, she didn't dally with work. She liked finishing projects ahead of schedule and she was especially anxious to see Olivia's reaction to the completed bathroom.

The latter sentiment won out. With the tile grouted and the bathroom floors set, she spent the day putting in the new bathroom fixtures and reconnecting the plumbing. She'd had to hustle to be sure she would finish before Olivia left work, but she made it. She'd been thrilled to text Olivia and tell her to go home after class. Olivia's giddy reply convinced her she'd made the right decision.

Olivia was barely in the door before Joss pulled her up the stairs. Olivia's first response was to squeal. She gave Joss a kiss, then a squeeze, then another kiss. When Olivia finally let go, she stood in the doorway, making appreciative noises and a few comments about showering together. Since it was the first part of the job completely finished, Joss felt good knowing that Olivia was happy with the work.

But when they headed downstairs, Olivia seemed fidgety.

"Is something wrong?"

"Not at all. I need to talk to you about something, though."

Joss froze. She had a moment of panic that Olivia actually hated the bathroom. And since, in her mind, it was damn near perfect, Olivia hating it would not sit well. "What is it?"

"I need your help."

Joss looked at her. "Okay. With what?"

"I adopted a goat and I need to have a place to put him and I don't think the barn is up to snuff and I need you to help me build something for him."

"Wait, wait, hold on. Back up. You bought a goat?" If Joss had made a list of a hundred things Olivia could have come up with in that moment, a goat would not have been on it.

"Adopted."

"Tomato, tom-ah-to. You're telling me you are now, or will be, in possession of a goat. Yes?" It wasn't like Joss didn't understand what she said. And, technically, Olivia's decisions about what to do at her house were none of Joss's business, but Joss couldn't not press for an explanation.

"He needed a home. He's been at a petting zoo his whole life and it went out of business."

Joss shook her head. She wasn't bothered by the decision so much as dumbfounded. "You realize you aren't set up to care for livestock."

Olivia offered a winning smile. "No, but I have space. The way I see it, I can't put in a garden until spring, and constructing a chicken coop is even more of an undertaking. This is the least farmy farm thing I could do, which makes it the perfect place to start."

Even if the argument was absurd, Olivia sold it pretty well. Joss shook her head.

"I also have the services of a very accomplished carpenter."

The compliment was a nice touch, but beside the point. "That carpenter has her hands full at the moment, if you hadn't noticed."

"I was hoping I might get you to take on a small side project, with the explicit understanding it will push back the schedule on the house."

Joss couldn't decide if the idea was endearing or utterly ridiculous. Olivia seemed to have that effect on her. It also irked her, at least a little, that she'd barely put the finishing touches on the bathroom before Olivia was jumping on to a new—and completely random—project. "So let me get this straight. You, who are living in a total construction zone, would like me to stop working on your house so that I can build a shelter, or pen, or whatever, for a goat."

"When you say it like that, it sounds unreasonable." Olivia's hands went to her hips.

"I don't think it has anything to do with my phrasing."

"Please?"

"Are you...Are you batting your eyelashes at me?"

"Am I?" Olivia seemed genuinely surprised.

"Oh, my God. You are and you don't even know it. It's like it's in your DNA or something."

"Does that mean you won't do it?"

It was hard to tell if Olivia was acting or truly crestfallen. The idea of that should bother Joss, but for some reason, it didn't. That meant that either Olivia had some kind of secret charm or Joss was more far gone than she'd realized. Maybe it meant both. Joss shook her head, but smiled. "Not at all. I do my best not to turn down projects. Let me finish cleaning these tools and I'll meet you outside."

"Thank you, thank you, thank you!" Olivia kissed her on the cheek and headed toward the back door.

Joss watched her leave, the skirt of her dress swaying slightly with each step. She was struck by the realization that she'd do just about anything to put that gleeful look in Olivia's eyes.

Outside, Olivia was standing by the barn with her head cocked to one side. As Joss approached she turned and smiled. "So, I've been thinking..."

Joss knew what that meant. It meant that Olivia had taken whatever plan she'd started with and turned it into something more complicated. In truth, the ideas usually made the final result better without derailing any work that had been done already. Joss didn't know if that was due to effort on Olivia's part or sheer luck. "Tell me what you have in mind." Olivia launched into her idea for building a fenced-in area against the side wall of the barn. Using the side door that had been boarded up, the pen would lead into an indoor area that would provide protection and warmth. "If you look in the barn, a lot of the structure is still there. Whoever did the initial garage conversion left the rest of the space untouched."

"That definitely makes sense, then. In addition to building the enclosure, you'll probably want to reinforce whatever wall is separating the area for cars."

Olivia looked at her quizzically.

"Seriously? Goats. Notorious climbers. Enjoy standing on the roofs of cars." How had she gotten herself roped into this again?

"Right." Olivia closed her eyes for a moment. "Good thinking. Does that mean you'll do it?"

Joss sighed. "It does."

The next thing she knew, Olivia's arms were flung around her and she was being fiercely squeezed. "You're the best."

Joss chuckled. "I am. Now, how long do I have to do this?"

Olivia stepped back and smiled. "I said I could take Pierre by Saturday."

"Pierre?"

Olivia shrugged. "That's his name. I didn't pick it."

With a dog named Ethel, Joss wasn't about to give her a hard time. "Aren't goats herd animals?"

"Maybe." She shuffled her feet and looked at the ground.

"Meaning?"

Olivia looked up and her eyes were full of mischief. "Meaning I may have started looking for a friend for him already."

Joss scratched her temple. "You're something, you know that?"

"Why do I get the feeling that isn't a compliment?"

"Oh, it's a compliment. Mostly. Are you going to help me measure so I can go get supplies?"

"I thought you'd never ask."

They spent the next hour arguing over how much space a pair of goats would need, taking measurements, and discussing design. Joss did a quick sketch of the idea that she had in her mind. It included a couple of platforms and ramps that the new residents would be able to climb. It was a fun project—out of her wheelhouse, but in a quirky, low-pressure way.

"I love it." Olivia studied the drawing. "Are you sure you haven't done this before?"

Joss shook her head. "This is a first."

Joss put the finishing touches on her sketch, then started drafting a list of supplies. At the rate things were going, being with Olivia was going to mean plenty of firsts.

It was a good thing she'd finished the bathroom when she did. The goat pen took nearly three days to construct. Given the time crunch, Joss had to keep a pretty intense pace to meet the Saturday deadline. But each evening, after she taught her classes, Olivia came home, changed her clothes, and hammered in her fair share of nails.

By the general standards Joss used to evaluate a project, it was quite good. The lines were clean and the structure was sound. It had a good blend of character and functionality. Most importantly, Olivia was thrilled with it, and she was the one paying the bill.

As a side project, it was a pretty substantial distraction from her real work. Any irritation that caused was mitigated by Olivia's enthusiasm. In addition to helping with the project, she gushed about the bathroom at least once every time Joss saw her. Joss wasn't overly obsessed with praise, but it was different with Olivia. She went beyond the kind of things Joss would expect a client to say. Olivia went on like a girlfriend would. It was nice.

On Friday, Olivia asked her to bring Ethel and stay over so she could be there when Pierre arrived. It was a sweet gesture that Joss appreciated. She liked that Olivia wanted to include her. On Saturday morning, they lazed in bed and drank a whole pot of coffee. While Olivia showered and dressed to be ready for the goat woman, Joss took her belt sander upstairs. Even though she wasn't officially on the clock, she wanted to strip a patch of flooring so she could test out a couple of stain choices. Once Olivia settled on the color she wanted, Joss would be able to get the final upstairs project started.

Olivia pulled on jeans and a sweater to ward off the chill that came with the arrival of fall. She stood at her kitchen window, waiting. It wasn't long after that the pickup truck pulled into the driveway with a small trailer in tow. She felt a lump form in her throat. She couldn't figure out why she should be nervous. Well, aside from the fact that she didn't really know anything about goats and was about to be solely responsible for one.

"Is he here?"

Olivia jumped, unaware that Joss had come up behind her. "I think so. Unless I bought a horse and forgot about it."

"Why do I get the feeling you're only half kidding?"

"Stop it." Olivia elbowed her in the ribs and headed outside.

"Olivia?" The woman getting out of the truck looked to be in her early sixties. Her hair was cut short and she wore a pair of faded jeans and a flannel shirt. Olivia couldn't tell if she was a lesbian or the kind of earthy straight woman that was so prevalent in Ithaca.

"I am. And I take it you're Jean?"

"Yes, indeed. And I have a special delivery for you."

"Do you need a hand?" Joss asked.

Again, Olivia was surprised to find Joss standing behind her. "It depends. Are you going to laugh at me?"

Joss scoffed. "Of course not. I want to meet the little guy. I built his house, after all."

"In that case, let's go meet Monsieur Pierre."

They followed Jean to the back of the horse trailer. She opened one of the doors and stepped inside. Olivia watched as Jean unhooked the harness and slid a slip lead over the head of the newest addition to her household. With only a gentle pull, the goat followed Jean out of the trailer. He walked right up to Olivia and let out an enthusiastic bleat.

"Well, hello to you, too."

Joss watched the goat nuzzle into Olivia's outstretched hand. He was brown and white with ears that stood straight out and striking, almost gold eyes. Although she'd teased Olivia, the goat was adorable. And he'd needed a home. Joss appreciated that Olivia found a rescue instead of buying him from who knows where.

Jean handed Olivia the leash and went back to her truck. She returned with a manila envelope. Since Olivia's hands were full, she handed it to Joss. "All of his paperwork and vet records are in there, along with some notes from the shelter about what he eats, his habits, and whatnot."

Olivia smiled at her. "Perfect."

"And they talked to you about getting him a companion? Goats really do need company."

Olivia nodded and gave Joss a quick sideways glance. "Yes, I've been talking with someone at Lollypop Farm in Rochester. They've got a little guy who seems like he'll be a perfect fit. I'm driving up to meet him next week."

"Good. Well, I've got two sheep to drop off still, so I best be going."

"Jean, it was so nice to meet you. I can't thank you enough for bringing Pierre to me."

"It was no trouble at all. I'm glad he found a good home."

Olivia threaded her arm through Joss's. "We'll take excellent care of him."

Joss felt Olivia give her arm a squeeze. Joss offered Jean a wave as she climbed back into her truck. "We sure will. Thanks again."

As Jean pulled away, Joss looked at Olivia. "What was that?"

Olivia made a face that looked to be half smile, half cringe. "Sorry. I got nervous."

Joss raised a brow. "Nervous?"

"Yeah. Like I was a single parent who might be deemed not good enough. I panicked. Thanks for playing along."

"Sure." Joss didn't know whether to laugh or, well, not laugh.

"I promise I won't hold you responsible for his upbringing."

Joss did laugh then, but she also rolled her eyes. "What am I going to do with you?"

Olivia shrugged. "Have dinner with me and my best friends?"

Joss raised a brow. "What?"

"My friends Gina and Kel invited us over for dinner. Will you come?"

"Ah. Okay. Sure."

Olivia leaned in and kissed Joss on the cheek. "Awesome. They're dying to meet you. Come on, Pierre. Let's go check out the house Auntie Joss made for you."

CHAPTER SEVENTEEN

The following Tuesday, they arrived at Gina and Kel's with a box of cupcakes from Felicia's. After brief introductions, they stood around the kitchen talking about the work on Olivia's house and the impending arrival of Gina and Kel's twins.

"When are they due?" Joss asked.

"Early November, but with twins, the doctor doesn't think I'll go past Halloween."

"Someone," Gina tipped her head toward Olivia, "bought them Halloween onesies."

Olivia shrugged. "I know it's iffy they'll get to wear them, but the cuteness outweighed the risk."

Kel shook her head, but laughed. "I'm going to go start the grill. Joss, care to join me for a beer out on the deck?"

Joss shot Olivia a wink, then turned to Kel. "I'm not going to turn that down."

"Great. In the fridge behind you. Grab me one of those non-alcoholic travesties and whatever you'd like. I've got an opener out here." Kel pulled open the sliding glass door and stepped outside.

Joss rustled in the fridge briefly then emerged with two bottles. She followed Kel out to the deck and pulled the door closed. Olivia watched Kel point to a bottle opener attached to one of the posts. Joss opened both bottles and handed one to Kel. They clinked, drank, then went about setting up the grill and lighting the charcoal.

Olivia realized that both she and Gina were staring at them. Gina seemed to realize it, too. She glanced over and laughed. "It's like they've done this a thousand times together."

Olivia shook her head. "I think there must be some sort of code."

"Yes, like the lesbian version of bros."

"I'm not sure how I feel about that." Olivia glanced back at the two of them. Kel was saying something, gesturing with her barbecue tongs. Joss was nodding. They looked like the oldest and dearest of friends instead of two people who'd met less than fifteen minutes prior—a stark contrast to her first meeting with Joss.

"I think it's great. Kel doesn't warm up to just anyone, certainly not right away. Beer?"

"Yes, please." Olivia tore her eyes away and accepted the bottle Gina handed her.

"So…how goes it?"

Olivia shrugged. "So far so good."

Gina curled her lip, indicating that her answer was completely unsatisfactory. "What does that mean?"

"It means we're having fun. She's smart and has a wicked sense of humor, she does beautiful work. And now that I've convinced her not to dislike me, the sex is amazing."

"I'm still not sure about the whole dislike thing, but you do have that well-fucked glow. It looks good on you."

"It's unlike anything I've ever experienced, with Amanda or otherwise. It's so good."

Gina raised a brow. "Like, so good?"

Olivia punched her in the arm. "It's so good, I could forget the rules of grammar."

"Well, then. That is high praise indeed. Are you guys getting serious?"

Olivia sighed. "I don't know."

Gina folded her arms and gave her a look.

"No, really. We haven't talked about it. We've definitely recovered from getting off on the wrong foot. And she invited me to stay with her while I had no shower, which she didn't have to do."

"Do you want it to get serious?"

"I'm open to it, which is saying something. My last relationship was so formulaic, I'm pretty set on going with the flow. I figure when I meet the one, it will just happen." At least, that's what she'd been telling herself.

Gina scowled. "I'm not sure it works like that, but I'm not going to press the point, at least not right now. It looks like they're ready for us." Gina handed Olivia a platter of vegetable kabobs, then picked up another that held skewers of chicken, shrimp, and beef. It was enough food for probably a dozen people. "Are you sure we have enough?" Olivia asked.

Gina rolled her eyes. "I'm running out of inspiration when it comes to Kel's lunches. Having leftovers helps."

Olivia couldn't help but giggle. "That's sweet, and downright domestic of you."

"Meh. You've rubbed off on me, if only a little."

"I'll take that as a compliment."

They headed out to the deck and handed off the platters. Joss held while Kel transferred things to the grill. It was as though they'd done so a dozen times before. They chatted about random things. After a while, Olivia realized her mind had wandered. She could imagine a hundred such evenings—casual meals with best friends. She'd been part of a couple and she'd had lots of friends, but they'd never come together in symbiotic harmony.

Olivia heard her name and realized that her mind had wandered. "I'm sorry?"

"I asked about your goat." Gina was looking at her with a mixture of amusement and curiosity.

Olivia smiled. "Pierre is great. And I'm going to get him a companion next weekend."

When Gina and Kel gave her funny looks, Joss jumped in. "Goats are herd animals. They don't do well by themselves."

"Oh." Gina and Kel spoke in unison.

"Joss did an amazing job on the pen. Y'all have to come and check it out."

Joss shook her head. "I finish her bathroom and she's more excited about the goat pen."

Gina slung an arm around Olivia. "That's Olivia. Always full of surprises."

Olivia put her hands on her hips. "I'm plenty excited about the bathroom."

"You are, but I can still tease you about the goat pen."

Kel nodded. "She has a point. They might come and revoke your femme card."

Gina interjected. "Femmes can be excited about goats and claw-foot tubs, you know."

"Thank you, Gina." Olivia made a stern face at Joss and Kel. "Seriously."

"Help me set the table?" Gina angled her head back toward the kitchen.

"I'd be happy to." Olivia offered a dramatic hair toss and followed her inside.

Gina looked at Olivia for a long minute before opening a cabinet door. She handed her plates and utensils and napkins. "I've never seen you smitten before. I like it."

Olivia sighed. "I really am smitten."

"From what I can tell, the feeling is mutual."

"Thanks. I sure hope so."

"It's a good look on—what the hell?"

"What?" Olivia turned in the direction Gina was looking and saw Joss and Kel, seemingly in the middle of a screaming match. There were hand gestures and pointing and belligerent stances on both sides.

Gina yanked open the sliding door. "What is going on?"

Both Joss and Kel were instantly quiet. Hands dropped to their sides and they looked at Olivia and Gina. If she had to define it, Olivia would say they looked sheepish. When no one said anything, she prompted them. "Well?"

Kel finally spoke, looking pointedly at Olivia. "Your girlfriend has no respect."

Olivia felt a knot form in her stomach. Whether it was from the use of the word girlfriend or the accusation, she couldn't be sure. "No respect for what?"

"The Yankees. It's one thing to like a different team. Liking any team that isn't the Yankees, that's just antagonistic and—"

Joss interrupted her. "Really? That's not how you feel about, say, the Red Sox?"

"That's different." Olivia had never seen Kel look so exasperated. She glanced over at Gina, who rolled her eyes.

Gina cut them off. "God, we thought you were having a real argument."

"This is a real argument," Joss and Kel said in unison.

"Oh, look, you agree. Let's eat."

Joss and Kel pulled the remaining food from the grill while Olivia and Gina arranged the dishes on the patio table. Gina popped back inside for a bowl of fruit salad and they all took their places at the table. There was a moment of silence as they began to pass food around. Was it awkward or simply focused? Olivia couldn't tell.

Joss passed Olivia the plate of grilled vegetables and smiled. "Did you know that Kel is helping with the legalities of the tiny house village that's going to provide residences for local homeless people?"

Olivia raised a brow. "I didn't."

"I signed up to donate some materials and labor almost a year ago. It's a great project, but securing the land and the permits has become a legal obstacle course."

"Hopefully, that won't be the case much longer," Kel said.

"I'm really glad the project has someone competent on its side," Joss said. "The community needs this sooner rather than later."

"Thanks, and likewise. I'm sure there will be plenty of volunteers once they break ground, but having some professionals who know what they're doing is important."

"So, despite the yelling, you two are not, in fact, sworn enemies?" Gina vocalized what Olivia was thinking.

Kel shrugged. "Of course not. We're sworn baseball enemies, but that's not the same thing."

"Exactly." Joss lifted her beer and Kel followed. They clinked bottles good-naturedly.

Whether it was a code or a secret language, Joss and Kel seemed to have an understanding. It reminded her of when she and Gina first met. Gina stopped by Olivia's office to welcome her to the department. After a brief greeting, Gina did a casual scan of Olivia's books. She'd commented on one of the lesbian authors, as though she was testing the waters. Even in a place where being out was an easy affair, there was something powerful in the recognition, a confirmation of something shared. She and Gina had been almost immediately at ease with one another, just as Joss and Kel were now. She wondered if that lack of recognition had something to do with why things with Joss got off on such a bad foot.

When dinner was done, they devoured the cupcakes. After

enjoying her red velvet, she let Joss talk her into sharing a chocolate with peanut butter frosting. Since Gina and Kel had indulged in seconds of their own, it didn't take much convincing. Olivia was torn between not wanting the evening to end and wanting to get Joss alone.

When they left, Olivia realized how nice it felt to know Joss was coming home with her. She could see herself getting used to it. The sound of Joss's voice pulled her out of her reverie. "I'm sorry, I missed that. What?"

"I really like your friends." Joss meant it. She'd been a little nervous about dinner with Gina and Kel, based primarily on the fact that one was a professor and the other a lawyer. But they'd both been down-to-earth and funny. Aside from the whole Yankees thing, they were great. Kel grew up in Brooklyn, though, so she almost couldn't even fault her for that. Almost.

"I'm glad. I'm pretty sure you get the thumbs-up as well."

"I thought they'd be snooty, overly intellectual." Joss realized how judgmental that sounded and cringed.

"Not all academics are stuffy, you know."

"Clearly, I'm learning." She needed to be more open-minded. It was so much better than being proved wrong.

"Remember that in a couple of weeks when I drag you to the annual English Department party." Olivia looked at her with hopeful eyes.

Joss tensed. Open mind or not, a whole party of professor types might be too much. "What party? You never mentioned a party."

Olivia smiled. "I am now."

Joss huffed.

"Pretty please?"

"Give me the details, then I'll decide." Saying no would make her seem like a jerk, but she at least wanted to know what she was signing up for.

"Every fall, someone in the department hosts a cocktail party. The food is good, the drinks are better, and the company is mixed."

"Mixed as in academic and non, or mixed as in good and not so much?"

Olivia cringed. "The latter, I'm afraid. But it's at my favorite colleague's house, after Gina. Her husband is an absolute doll."

"Will Gina and Kel be there?"

"They should be."

Knowing a couple of the people who would be there helped. "All right."

"All right, you'll go?"

"All right, I'll go."

"I'm so excited." Olivia bopped back and forth in her seat.

Given what she'd just agreed to, Joss decided it was a good time to issue an invitation of her own. "So speaking of roping one another into things…"

"Is that what we were speaking of?" Olivia placed her hand delicately on her chest and made a face that was…What was it? It was coy. Olivia was being coy. And as much as Joss didn't want it to, it got her. Every damn time.

"Why, I believe it was." Joss put on an affected Southern accent. "And since I just agreed to go to your thing, you have to go to mine."

Olivia raised a brow. "Please tell me it's a party for sexy lesbian contractors."

"Hey!" Joss was feigning outrage, but Olivia's jest created a pang of jealousy that she did not appreciate.

"Kidding, kidding. What is it?"

Joss huffed, but it was more on principle than anything else. "You've been invited to dinner at my parents' house."

"Ooh, I'd love to meet your parents."

"We do a casual family dinner every Sunday. My mom thought it would be nice if you met the rest of the family." Joss was still a little uneasy about being romantically involved with a client, but her mother had simply waved her hand and said that was nonsense. Joss decided being obstinate would draw more attention to the whole thing rather than less.

Olivia smiled. "That's really sweet. I would love to."

"Ben will be there, as well as Daphne, her husband and kids."

"Wow. Full on family dinner."

"Full on. Are you sure you're up for it?" The question was for Olivia, but Joss felt like she was asking herself as well.

"Oh, I'm up for it. Is there anything I can bring?"

"My mom always cooks enough food to feed an army, so I'm going to say no. A bottle of wine is a nice gesture, I suppose."

"Excellent. I've got it covered."

CHAPTER EIGHTEEN

Joss didn't want to admit it, but she was nervous. Since it was dinner with her parents, and she did that every week, it made no sense. It wasn't like she was hoping for her parents' approval. Or blessing. Or whatever.

She stopped pacing when Olivia emerged from the bedroom. She was wearing a dress—she almost always wore a dress—that looked nice, but not too nice, like she was trying too hard. That was good. "You look great. Are you nervous?"

Olivia smiled. "Not really. Should I be?"

"No."

"Are you?" Olivia narrowed her eyes.

"Am I what?"

"Are you nervous to have me meet your parents?"

"No." It came out like more of a question than a statement, and Joss fought the urge to cringe.

"You are. Why are you nervous? Are you afraid they won't like me?"

"It's not like that."

"Then what?" Hands on hips. Joss had come to find the gesture both cute and kind of sexy. In the moment, it was simply unnerving.

"It's just, well, I've never dated a client before, so there's that. Plus, I think they're probably different from your family." Joss started to wish she hadn't brought it up in the first place.

Olivia laughed. "God, I hope so."

"I'm serious."

"I am, too. I mean, I love my family, but there's a reason I moved a thousand miles away. We have practically nothing in common." Joss thought about the little she knew of Olivia's family. Both parents lawyers, sister married to a doctor. Joss wasn't sure what made her more uncomfortable—the number of degrees they'd earned or the amount of money they had.

It wasn't that Joss was embarrassed by her family. In fact, she felt quite the opposite. It was more a worry that they wouldn't have anything to talk about. Olivia would make some esoteric joke that no one got, then everything would be weird and uncomfortable for the rest of the day. It was a ridiculous fear. Her family didn't believe in weird and uncomfortable. And Olivia had yet to act like the snooty professor Joss thought her to be when they first met. Joss let that fact sink in. Olivia had turned out to be nothing short of charming. If anyone wound up feeling awkward in this situation, it would be Joss. "You're right. Everything is going to be fine."

Olivia looked at her skeptically. "Is it me you're trying to convince? Or yourself?"

Joss rolled her eyes. "Clearly you're fine enough to make fun of me, so I'll take that as my answer."

Olivia shook her head, but then put a hand on Joss's arm. "I'm sorry. I don't mean to make light of something that is stressing you out. What can I do?"

It was silly to be worked up in the first place, wasn't it? Just because she hadn't brought a woman home in a couple of years. Just because she hadn't dated a client ever. Just because her family, instead of being judgmental, found the whole thing…what? Amusing, maybe? She hadn't even planned on introducing Olivia to her parents. But then her mother had asked and Ben and Daphne wouldn't let it go. Joss gave in to shut them up more than anything else. Besides, it was just a casual family dinner. It didn't have to have all sorts of heavy meaning attached to it. "You don't need to do anything. I'm sorry I made it seem like such a big deal."

"Okay," Olivia said, seemingly satisfied with the answer. "I'm really looking forward to it."

"Good, because we should probably go."

"I'm ready." Olivia walked to the kitchen. She picked up her purse, a bottle of wine, and a tin of some sort.

"What is that?"

"A little hostess gift for your mom."

"Not the wine, the tin."

"The wine is just what you bring. The tin is the hostess gift, or rather, what's inside it. It's a batch of pralines."

"Pralines?"

"Yes, they're a candy made from brown sugar and pecans."

"I know what they are. What I'm curious about is where you got them."

Olivia offered her a satisfied smile. "I made them. It's my great-aunt's recipe."

"Olivia, I've seen your kitchen."

Olivia huffed. "I made them yesterday at Gina's house. Since I don't know your mom's style, I didn't want to risk buying something she might not like. These are my go-to edible gift."

Joss shook her head. Just when she thought she had Olivia figured out, she went and did something that took her completely by surprise. She'd just acknowledged how charming Olivia was; maybe she needed to adjust her expectations. "I see."

"I'm Southern, Joss. I'm not going to show up as a guest at someone's home and not bring a gift, especially if those someones are my girlfriend's parents."

Olivia made it sound so obvious. Joss would have laughed, but Olivia's use of the word "girlfriend" had put a lump in her throat. It wasn't that she hadn't thought about Olivia in those terms, but hearing Olivia say it out loud made it feel official and serious all of a sudden. She wasn't about to say that, though, so she picked up her keys. "That's incredibly thoughtful. I'm sure my folks will love them."

On the ride over, Olivia made Joss quiz her on family names and details. Joss ran through her family tree, assuring Olivia for the fifth time that there wasn't going to be a test. When they pulled into the driveway, Joss put her hand on Olivia's knee. "No pressure, but you're likely to be the center of attention, at least for a little while."

"I'm good. That debutante training comes in handy every now and then." Olivia flipped her hair then climbed out of Joss's truck.

Joss's mom opened the door when they were halfway up the sidewalk. She took one of Olivia's hands in both of her own. "Olivia. It's so lovely to finally meet you. Thank you for coming."

"Thank you so much for having me. Joss has told me so much about you, including what an amazing cook you are."

"Is that so?" She raised an eyebrow playfully at Joss before pulling her into a hug. "We'll have to see if I live up to the stories."

Joss's dad was standing in the doorway. He introduced himself to Olivia before giving Joss a kiss on the cheek. "Hi, Dad. What are you up to this weekend?"

"I was finishing up that potting shed your mother wants before the weather turns."

"Why didn't you call? You know I would have come over."

He waved his hand back and forth. "Nonsense. You work hard all week long. Fred came over from next door and gave me a hand."

"You work all week, too."

"Bah. I don't do any heavy lifting anymore, not like you and your brother. It's fine. I know I can call on you when I need it."

As they stepped into the living room, Ben emerged from the kitchen. Joss sent him a nod. "Olivia, you remember my brother, Ben."

"Indeed I do. Good to see you, Ben."

"Likewise. I hear the house is really shaping up."

Olivia smiled at him. "It is. All the plumbing is done, and my bathroom is a dream."

Joss interjected. "Kitchen cabinets have arrived. You can see the progress when you help me install them."

Ben smiled. "I do love installing cabinetry."

Olivia clasped her hands together. "And you can meet Pierre."

"Who's Pierre?"

Joss groaned inwardly. She liked Pierre just fine, but she hadn't planned to bring him up at her parents' house. While she fully supported animal rescue, there was something about a woman who knew nothing about farm animals adopting a goat when her house wasn't even livable. Sure, she'd come to think of it as kind of charming, but what would her parents think? It was the kind of thing her mom would say indicated a person had more dollars than sense.

"He's the goat I rescued. Didn't Joss tell you? She spent a couple of days last week building a pen for him."

Ben let out a small snort. "She didn't mention it."

Olivia beamed. "It's a really nice pen, much nicer than what I would have designed for him."

Joss's mom chimed in. "Joss, that sounds like fun."

"It sure does," Ben said. "Joss, I can't believe you're branching out into farm work and haven't shared the details."

Joss was trying to think of a clever response when the front door swung open. "Oma! Opa! We're here!" Joss's nieces came bounding through the door. When they caught sight of Joss, they ran right to her. "Aunt Joss!"

Olivia watched the two little girls whirl around the room, doling out hugs and kisses and enthusiastic hellos. At five and three, they both had a bit of baby fat left and both of them had a head full of light brown ringlets. The older one caught sight of Olivia. She walked over to Olivia, more slowly than she'd run around the room, but without hesitation.

She stuck out a small, chubby hand. "Hi. I'm Libby."

Olivia bent down and shook the little hand. "Hello, Libby. I'm Olivia."

Emboldened by her sister, the younger one started toward Olivia, but she stopped about halfway. Olivia smiled at her. "So you must be Anna. I'm very happy to meet you."

Anna inched closer. She smacked Olivia's palm in a way that was more like giving her five than a handshake, then ran to Daphne and stood behind her legs.

"She's still a little shy," Daphne said. "We're working on it."

Libby cut in. "She's still a baby. When she's five like me, she'll be braver."

Olivia looked down at Libby, who was decked out in a pair of denim overalls and a shirt with little strawberries all over it. "I'm sure she will, especially if her very brave older sister helps her along the way."

"Libby, take your sister to the playroom. You can each pick out one toy to play with out here while the grownups visit."

Libby stretched out her hand. Anna emerged from behind Daphne. She took her sister's hand and the two of them went scurrying down the hallway. Olivia stood up and realized that a man, who must be Daphne's husband, had joined them. She offered him a smile. "You must be Mark. I'm Olivia."

"I am and it's a pleasure to meet you. It's nice to finally put a face with the name."

Olivia wondered just how much she'd been the topic of conversation lately. She didn't have long to wonder, however, as Ben turned the conversation back to her recent goat adoption. She explained how it wasn't something she was planning, but she'd made the mistake of visiting the website of a local rescue group and she'd fallen hard for a sweet little Norwegian dwarf.

Libby, who was coloring at the coffee table and seemed not to be paying attention, perked up. "You have a goat? Can we meet him?" She turned to Daphne. "Can we, Mom?"

"Olivia's very busy," she said. "But maybe when she has time, we can go over for a visit."

"I would love that," Olivia said. "If you come after next week, he'll have a friend, too."

"A friend?" Ben asked.

"Goats are herd animals. They need companions to be happy." Joss realized she was starting to sound as goat-crazy as Olivia.

Sandy, who'd disappeared into the kitchen, emerged. "Dinner is just about ready."

"Oh, I almost forgot." Olivia walked over to where she'd set down her purse and pulled out the bottle of wine and tin of pralines.

"What's all this?" Sandy asked when Olivia handed them to her.

"Just a little thank you for your hospitality. The tin is pralines, my great-aunt's recipe."

"How lovely. You certainly didn't need to go to the trouble, but we appreciate it. Don't we, Frank?"

Frank took the tin and removed the lid. He plucked one out and took a bite. "We sure do."

"Frank, we're about to have dinner." Sandy scowled, but there wasn't much force behind it.

"I'm appreciating." He looked at Olivia with a smile and wiggled his eyebrows.

Olivia laughed, in part because she couldn't even imagine her parents bantering like that. Sandy took the tin back and put the lid on. "The rest of you will have to wait until after the meal."

They moved to the table, where Olivia was seated between Joss and Ben. There was a brief pause before eating for Frank to say grace and then the dishes were passed around family-style. There was a beautiful pork roast that looked like it had been lovingly braised for hours. Bowls overflowed with vegetables, including roasted carrots, sautéed cabbage, and green beans with bacon. But the real star, at least in Olivia's mind, were the homemade noodles; they were tender and rich, tossed in a mixture of brown butter and herbs.

Although there were only nine at the table, it felt like there were at least three conversations going on at any one time. Olivia gave up trying to follow all of them, instead allowing herself to be pulled from one to another. There was no formality, but lots of laughter. After everyone ate, Olivia wasn't allowed to help with the dishes, so she lingered with Sandy in the dining room. It was clear that Joss, Ben, and Daphne had an easy rhythm born of years of shared chores.

There was a little bit of visiting after the dinner, but Daphne and Mark decided to leave so the girls could nap in their own beds. Ben wanted to take advantage of the good weather to get his lawn mowed. Joss took the lead in excusing them as well.

"Do you teach every day?" Frank asked.

"I do this semester. It's probably a good thing, since being on campus forces me to go to my office and I get other work done. When I'm home, all I want to do is work on the house."

Joss smiled. "Or play with your goat."

Olivia shrugged and wiggled her eyebrows. "That, too."

"It was so lovely to spend the afternoon with you," Sandy said. "We hope you'll come again."

"It would be a pleasure. I'd love to have you both over as well, just as soon as I have a stove."

Both Sandy and Frank laughed. And when they hugged Joss good-bye, they hugged Olivia as well. It was a real hug, too, and it made her feel like she'd passed an unspoken test.

On the drive back to her house, Olivia realized she had a slight stomachache, although she couldn't decide if it was from eating too much or laughing too hard. She also couldn't remember the last time she'd had a family day. No, that wasn't accurate. She couldn't remember the last time she'd had a family day and it had been so much fun. Joss's parents were warm and laid back. Her siblings teased her mercilessly, but with an affection that Olivia and her sister had never shared. Then there were the kids. Daphne and Mark's daughters were boisterous and sweet; within minutes of being introduced, they asked Olivia to play and treated her like a long lost member of the family.

The whole day made her feel even more connected to Joss. It also made her feel a certain longing, not for her family so much as how she wished her family was. She'd always had a vague sense of what she was missing, but spending time with the Bauers brought it into sharp focus.

"Was it too much?"

Olivia looked over at Joss. "What?"

"The dinner, the kids, the loud siblings. Was it too much for you?" Joss knew her family could be overwhelming. She loved it, but it wasn't for everyone. She'd told herself this wasn't a test—of Olivia or their relationship—but she knew deep down it was. Family was too important for it not to be.

"Not at all. I had a great time."

"Really?" Joss wanted to believe her, but she could sense something under the surface, something Olivia wasn't saying.

"I do. What makes you think I didn't?"

"You've gotten awfully quiet. I wondered if maybe you were a little shell-shocked. They can be a handful."

Olivia smiled. "If I am, it's in a good way. I was actually thinking about how much fun I had, and how different that is from spending time with my family."

That's what Joss had been afraid of. To hear Olivia say it, however, made Joss think the opposite of what she'd feared might be true. "How so?"

Olivia seemed to choose her words carefully. "My family likes to spend time together doing things that are expensive, or in locations that are expensive. If other people can see us enjoying expensive things and places, even better."

Joss mulled over Olivia's statement. It wasn't like she didn't think about money, about places she'd like to see and experiences she'd like to have. They were often things she'd like to do with her family, too, but she got the distinct impression that wasn't what Olivia meant. Still, she didn't want to come across as judgmental. "That's not necessarily a bad thing, is it?"

Olivia sighed. "It's not. It's just...It's just the focus seems to be more on doing something or being somewhere nice than it does on spending time together. Does that make sense?"

"It does."

"When I was a teenager, I figured I'd be the black sheep of my family because I was gay."

"And?"

"And it did cause tensions at first. But when I started dating a medical student from an old-money Atlanta family while I was in grad school, things seemed to smooth over quite nicely."

Joss shook her head. She'd had her own nervousness over coming out to her parents, to her brother and sister. It turned out they'd all figured as much from the time Joss had been in middle school. It was a relief for everyone to get it out in the open and had been a non-issue ever since. "So what happened?"

"She did her residency in cardiology while I finished my dissertation. She and my mother reserved the venue for our wedding before she even proposed."

"Are you serious?"

"Sadly, yes. I was on the job market, but I think she, and my parents, figured I'd give that up once she was in practice."

It was a strange concept for Joss to wrap her head around. She found it both fascinating and sad. "And do what?"

"Maybe teach at a private school or a local college, but mostly be her wife. Being a society wife can be a full-time job, especially if you throw in a bit of charity work for good measure."

It was like the 1950s had never ended. Regardless of her first impressions of Olivia, Joss couldn't imagine her in that lifestyle. Joss didn't know too much about Olivia's work, but she knew how important it was to her. And, as she'd discovered, Olivia liked getting her hands dirty. Being someone's trophy—even if it was a successful lesbian doctor—boggled her mind. "So, how did you get from there to here?"

"I applied for about twenty positions and interviewed at six universities. Cornell was definitely the most prestigious. Most schools were hiring for American lit, but Cornell actually wanted someone who specialized in Southern writers or women writers. I do both. Plus, I think the chair of the search committee had a soft spot for Eudora Welty. I just happened to have done my dissertation on Welty's work and influence on twentieth-century Southern literature."

"Wow. So you were prepared to go anywhere that offered you a job?"

"Just about. I applied mostly to places on the East Coast, nowhere too conservative. It's kind of how academe works."

Joss thought about her ex, Cora. When she'd been offered the fellowship, it never occurred to her not to take it. At the time, Joss had called her selfish and short-sighted. Now, talking with Olivia, Joss realized that maybe she'd not given enough consideration to how the system worked. Even if she didn't like it, she could at least understand that the job options looked different than in her line of work.

Joss pulled into Olivia's driveway and shut off the engine. "Well, I'm glad that you landed here."

Olivia looked at her and smiled. "Me, too."

CHAPTER NINETEEN

After spending the day driving to Rochester and back, and introducing Pierre to his new friend Bill, the last thing Joss wanted to do was go to some stuffy professor party. She'd secretly hoped Olivia would decide to back out and they could spend the evening eating pizza and watching an old movie. No such luck.

Olivia patted her knee. "There is no reason for you to be nervous."

A week after having dinner with Joss's family, they were having the same conversation, only in reverse. Joss took a deep breath. "I'm not nervous, I'm uncomfortable. That's not the same thing."

"There is no reason for you to be uncomfortable."

Joss sat in Olivia's passenger seat as they wound their way through Cayuga Heights. She'd been there plenty of times before. In her truck, for projects. It wasn't that the neighborhood was unpleasant. The homes—Colonials and Tudors and Victorians—were beautiful and well-tended. It was that half of them cost a half a million dollars and half of them cost even more. "Am I going to be the only one there who isn't a professor?"

"Of course not. Most people in my department are married to or dating non-academics."

"Okay. And whose house are we going to again?"

"Suzanne and Bert Whittaker. Suzanne is in my department and Bert is in Physics."

"Physics?" Joss imagined someone with cotton candy hair in a white lab coat and bow tie.

"Yes. Actually, I think it's technically astrophysics. He studies black holes. But he's nice and really down-to-earth."

"No pun intended?"

"That's funny. See? You're funny. You're going to do just fine."

Joss wasn't sure how a handful of mild jokes was going to get her through the evening, but she didn't say anything. The last thing she wanted was for Olivia to think she was insecure.

They pulled up to a house and Olivia parked on the street with a couple of other cars. She turned to Joss and winked. "In case we need to make a quick escape."

"Promises, promises."

Olivia grinned at her. "You look great, by the way."

"Thanks." Joss would never admit it to Olivia, but she'd tried on four different outfits before settling on one she thought was dressy enough without making it look like she was trying too hard. In the end, she went back to her initial plan of navy pants, a navy and white checked shirt, and a dark green sweater vest. Of course, even then, she'd spent twenty minutes of angst over whether or not to wear a tie. She decided against it, wanting to draw less attention to herself rather than more, but she sort of hated herself for chickening out.

They walked up a flagstone path and Olivia knocked on the door. Within seconds, it was opened by an African American man who appeared to be in his early sixties. He had salt-and-pepper hair and wore a cardigan sweater that seemed more grandpa than college professor. His smile was warm and Joss felt instantly more at ease.

"Olivia, I'm so glad you could make it."

"Bert, it's so good to see you." Olivia offered her hand and Bert took it in both of his.

"Yes, it's been far too long."

"Joss, this is Bert. He's Suzanne's husband. Bert, this is Joss."

Bert's smile remained warm as it turned to Joss. "Pleasure to meet you, Joss. Come on in and make yourselves at home."

"You as well." Joss realized that she'd become hyperaware of her grammar. She tried to shake off the feeling as they followed him inside.

The house was beautiful, the decor eclectic and cozy. In the living room, a pair of African masks shared wall space with some framed maps and what Joss guessed were photos of grandchildren. The biggest tell she was in the home of academics was the row of bookshelves that dominated one side of the room. They were overflowing with books in every color and size.

Joss pulled her attention from the space itself and tried to focus on the people in it. There were probably a dozen or so people already there. Sitting on the sofa and standing in groups, they seemed like a far more casual group than Joss was expecting. A few of them noticed the new arrivals and offered nods and waves in greeting.

"Suzanne is in the kitchen, I think. If you want to head that way, she can get you set up with a glass of wine or whatever else you'd like to wet your whistle."

"Thanks, Bert." Olivia took Joss's hand and led the way toward the back of the house.

Much like the living room, the kitchen was cozy and inviting. It had the feel of a recent remodel, but they'd kept the style original to the house. Joss approved of the choices of color and material, deciding she might be able to like Olivia's colleague and her husband just fine.

"Olivia." The woman, who Joss figured must be Suzanne, was putting crackers on a board that held a wedge of cheese and a pile of dried apricots. She stopped what she was doing and came over to where they were standing. She pulled Olivia into a hug and then turned to Joss. She extended her hand. "You must be Joss. I've heard so much about you. I'm Suzanne."

"Hi, Suzanne. It's a pleasure to meet you."

"I'm so glad you could join us. I've been hearing all about the work you're doing on Olivia's house. It's nice to be able to put a face with the name."

Joss smiled. She wondered if Suzanne was being polite or if Olivia had talked about her only in the context of the renovation. She told herself it didn't matter. "It's quite a project she's taken on, but it will be amazing when it's done."

"I have no doubt. What can I get you to drink? There's wine, some beer and soda in the fridge, stuff for mixed drinks over there." She gestured to the far counter, where there was a variety of bottles and pitchers of juice.

Olivia looked to her. Joss thought less about what she might want to drink and more about what would look the most innocuous. "Wine would be great, thanks."

Olivia considered for a moment. "Me, too."

"Red or white?" Suzanne looked at Joss first.

"Either is fine. I'll have whatever Olivia is having."

Olivia raised a brow at her, but didn't say anything. "Red, then. I can get it, Suzanne. You finish what you were doing."

"Thanks. It's right over there." Suzanne tipped her head in the direction of the counter next to the fridge.

Olivia walked over and filled two glasses from an open bottle. "Is there anything I can do to help?"

"Not at all. I was just finishing the snacks." She picked up the cheese board. "After you."

Olivia handed Joss a glass and led the way back to the living room. Joss followed. This was going to be fine. They were just people. She could make casual conversation for an hour or two and then it would be over.

Olivia made her way over to a small group standing near the bookshelves. Gina was one of them, a fact that helped Joss to relax. Everyone smiled and moved so that the circle would include them. She met Tim, Olivia's department chair. Then she was introduced to Jae, a young Asian guy who studied pop culture, and Marcella, a Medievalist who reminded Joss of the typical Ithaca hippie.

"It's good to see you," Gina said.

"Thanks. No Kel tonight?"

Gina shook her head. "She's working on a big case, so it's an excused absence."

That earned a chuckle from the group. No one seemed stodgy or conservative. In fact, conversation was about the latest political drama on Netflix, not some obscure piece of literature she'd never heard of. This really wasn't so bad.

"How far along is she?" Marcella asked.

"Thirty weeks," Gina replied. "We're hoping she gets to at least thirty-seven."

Joss had a flash of Kel tending the grill on her deck, already looking plenty pregnant. She wondered what it would be like to carry a baby—or two. Surprised by just how vivid the scenario was, she worked to shake it off and focus on the conversation at hand.

"Olivia says the work you're doing at her house is phenomenal," Tim said.

Joss smiled, pleased that Olivia thought highly enough of it to tell her colleagues. "It's a great house. I really enjoy breathing new life into places other people have written off."

"I saw what you did to the master bathroom," Gina said. "I'd say you've done a hell of a lot more than breathe new life into it."

Marcella chimed in. "I stopped by last week and saw it, too. I've already started putting together pictures of what I want you to do at my house."

"You wait your turn." Olivia's tone was stern and she pointed a finger at Marcella, earning laughs from the group.

After about half an hour, Joss offered to refresh drinks. She took Olivia's glass, as well as Marcella's, and headed to the kitchen. She poured wine for Olivia and herself, then went over to the bar to mix a gin and tonic for Marcella. A middle-aged man she hadn't been introduced to stood at the counter making what appeared to be an old fashioned. She pretended to study a work of crayon and glitter on the fridge to avoid elbowing in beside him.

"You came with Dr. Bennett, right?"

Joss realized that the man must be talking to her. She turned and saw him facing her, highball glass in hand. He wore a turtleneck and a tweed blazer with elbow patches, little wire-rimmed glasses. He looked to Joss like he'd stepped out of an Ivy League admissions brochure.

"Yes, I'm here with Olivia."

"Gerald Stevens, American literature." He offered his hand.

Gerald scrutinized her in a way that made the hairs on the back of her neck stand up. She shook his hand and tried to ignore the feeling. "Joss Bauer."

"You're the contractor, right? Bauer and Sons?"

Joss wasn't sure what he meant by "the" contractor, but she nodded. "I am a contractor, mostly residential and commercial renovations, the occasional addition. My family's company is doing the work on Olivia's new house."

Gerald nodded as though he already knew that. "So, you and Olivia are..."

He trailed off, presumably waiting for Joss to finish the sentence. Joss swallowed. Olivia wouldn't have invited her here if she was trying to keep their relationship a secret. Not answering would probably be weirder than acknowledging it. "We're dating."

"And she dragged you to some stuffy English department party."

Joss shrugged. "I'm happy to come with her."

"That's nice of you. I'm sure it's dreadfully dull, being surrounded by us academics and all of our erudite talk."

Joss got the distinct feeling that the comment was meant as an insult, not good-natured self-deprecation. "The conversation has been really interesting, actually."

"Oh, good. There's nothing worse than being stuck in a conversation where everything is over your head. Aside from that, it must be great for you."

What the hell did that mean? "Olivia is amazing. I certainly enjoy spending time with her."

"Indeed she is. Quite the rising star in the department. I was thinking more along the lines of being great for business, though. Olivia's friends, colleagues. I'm sure there are all sorts of jobs and projects she can nudge your way."

Joss narrowed her eyes. Was he trying to imply that she was using Olivia? Or the other way around? "We've never talked about it. I don't really need to drum up business, if that's what you mean."

"Well, I guess I only meant that you're so different."

Joss resisted the urge to roll her eyes. Was this guy for real? "I'd actually say we're quite complementary."

"Of course. I'm sure you've worked out an arrangement that's…" Gerald looked her up and down slowly. "Mutually beneficial."

A lengthy silence followed, mostly because Joss didn't know what to say. She knew she was insulted, but beyond that, it was hard to put a finger on what about the conversation angered her the most. Before she could sort out a response that she wouldn't regret the second it came out of her mouth, Gerald lifted his glass.

"Cheers," he said, and walked away.

Joss stood where she was for a long moment, then remembered why she'd come into the kitchen in the first place. She sloshed some gin into a glass, added ice cubes and tonic water, topped it with lime. It took effort to keep her hands from shaking as she carried the glasses back to the living room.

The conversation she'd left had broken up. Gina was nowhere to be seen and Olivia, Marcella, and Jae were now talking with Gerald and a man she hadn't met. Despite a strong desire to turn around and go back to the kitchen, or to put the drinks down and leave altogether, she walked toward them. She handed Olivia and Marcella their drinks and contemplated ways she might escape. Olivia introduced Phillip, who'd started teaching the same semester as Olivia.

When Olivia turned to Gerald, he interrupted her. "I've already met your friend, Dr. Bennett. Ms. Bauer and I were mixing drinks together, isn't that right?"

"We were." Joss opted not to elaborate.

"Ms. Bauer, we were just discussing Hemingway. Have you read any of his work?"

Joss had a vague recollection of reading *The Old Man and the Sea* in high school, but not much else. "Only a long time ago, I'm afraid."

"Well, I'm trying to get a sense of how people interpret Hemingway's personification of masculinity in relation to Foucault's assertion of exteriority. Would you care to weigh in?"

Joss knew the question was absurd for anyone not enmeshed in the study of literature. But still. That knowledge didn't stop the rise of color in her cheeks, the feeling that everyone's eyes were on her.

"You're being ridiculous, Gerald. Go harass someone else." Olivia rolled her eyes, but there was humor in her tone.

Gerald raised his hands, as if admitting defeat, and turned to join another conversation. Phillip followed, looking a bit like an eager puppy.

Marcella put a hand on Joss's arm. "We weren't actually talking about that, at least most of us weren't. Gerald's an ass."

"And pompous," Jae added.

Joss nodded. She didn't doubt their sincerity, but the idea that she needed the reassurance bristled. She looked over at Olivia, who seemed unfazed by the exchange. That fact shouldn't bother her, but it did.

Marcella rolled her eyes. "So pompous. What we were actually discussing were ridiculous student stories. I had a kid email me today asking to rewrite his first paper."

Joss didn't know how to respond. The request seemed maybe a little pushy, but not ridiculous. Maybe there was some kind of inside professor joke that she didn't get. "Really?"

"Yeah. It wasn't the asking so much as the fact that he felt the need to add how irrelevant British literature was in his life, but that getting any grade below a B would ruin his chances of getting into medical school."

"Oh." The explanation made Joss feel significantly better.

Marcella shook her head. "I'm not an idiot. I know there are students who feel that way. You'd think, though, they'd have the sense not to say as much when they're asking you for something."

Joss could relate to that. Although most of her clients were great, there were always a few pills. They had a way of being insulting and demanding at the same time—it was as baffling as it was annoying.

Jae launched into a story of a student who'd copied his entire paper from an online database, yet adamantly refused to accept plagiarism charges. Olivia had two students ask for extensions on papers because the fraternities they were pledging had required events that would take up their entire weekends. Joss relaxed enough to talk about Janice Schafer, a woman who waited until her entire kitchen back splash was put up and grouted to decide she didn't like the tile she'd picked. "When I told her she could no longer return the original materials for a refund, she yelled at me for at least twenty minutes."

Everyone laughed. Jae cocked his head to one side like he was deep in thought. "I wonder if her son goes to Cornell? She sounds a lot like a mother who yelled at me last semester for daring to make her son uncomfortable in my Race and Gender in Film course."

"How dare you." Olivia's dramatic inflection got another laugh from the group.

The rest of the party passed smoothly. Everyone else Joss encountered was friendly and seemed genuinely interested in her and what she did. Still, the nagging voice in the back of her mind remained, replaying her conversation with Gerald. Based on the artful way Olivia deflected him, Joss was pretty sure he always behaved that way. It would have been nice if Olivia had given her a little warning. Then she could have been more adept in her handling of him as well. Joss tried to shove her irritation aside, but the uneasy feeling kept coming back. Part of it was irritation. The other part was harder to put her finger on, but it felt an awful lot like doubt.

By the time they left, Joss had worked herself into a state. She plastered a fake smile on her face and thanked Bert and Suzanne for their hospitality. She climbed into Olivia's car, trying to focus on being relieved the whole thing was over.

CHAPTER TWENTY

Olivia drove, bopping along to the 80s music on the radio. Joss clenched and unclenched her jaw, weighing whether or not to say anything. Olivia looked over at her and smiled.

"I really appreciate you coming with me. I know those folks aren't your speed."

Not her speed? The choice of words made Joss flinch. "What's that supposed to mean?"

"Academics. I know you don't really feel like you can relate to them. It was nice of you to try."

"Are you saying I can't keep up with them?"

Olivia made a face. "That's not what I'm saying at all. What's gotten into you?"

Joss had been stewing for the better part of the last hour. She'd never let Olivia be blindsided like that. It was the fact that Olivia seemed so oblivious to the whole thing that made it worse, made it impossible for her to let it go. It also made Joss feel justified in venting her frustration. "Why did you even invite me? Was I a curiosity? Comic relief?"

"What are you talking about?"

"That whole Hemingway thing? You'd honestly tell me your friend Gerald wasn't trying to make me the butt of his joke?"

Olivia squared her shoulders defensively. "First of all, Gerald is not my friend. He's a self-involved prick. Second of all, it was one stupid comment. He was showing off."

"Which he seems to do all the time." Joss flashed back to her conversation in the kitchen, the innuendo that her relationship with Olivia couldn't possibly exist outside of some sort of quid pro quo. "You didn't seem too bothered by it in the moment."

"That's not fair."

"Isn't it? You practically giggled at him." It was a low blow, and Joss regretted sinking to that level.

"That is both untrue and unfair. I don't know what's put you in such a foul mood, but I refuse to accept responsibility for some asinine comment by some guy I can't even stand."

"That's not what I said."

"Really? That's how it sounded. I knew you weren't crazy about academic types, but I had no idea you'd be so derailed by them. I'm sorry I didn't swoop in and defend you against the department bully."

Olivia clearly didn't get it, or didn't want to. Joss regretted saying anything. "I don't need you to defend me."

"Well, then what do you need? Because right now, I'll be damned if I know."

There was an angry reply on the tip of Joss's tongue, but she swallowed it. What did she need? What did she want? For so long, she thought she'd known. Knowing, and the confidence of knowing, had been such a divining rod in her life. Since she'd opened herself to Olivia, all of that had changed. Maybe that was the real problem. "I needed a heads-up about what I was walking into, but it's too late for that now."

That seemed to stop Olivia in her tracks. "Oh."

"I can hold my own, but it would have been nice to feel like we're on the same team."

"Joss." Olivia's tone softened. "I'm sorry."

"Thanks, but it's not just tonight. It's everything. It's us." Joss's irritation had morphed into something bigger, even more unsettling.

"Joss, come on. What happened tonight? It was something, and you're not telling me."

"Nothing happened. The last couple of weeks have been really intense."

"Intense bad? I thought things were going well."

"Not intense bad, just intense. I'm realizing exactly how involved we've become without ever actually deciding what that should look like." Really, that was freaking her out more than anything Gerald had said. They were hurtling down a path and she'd been so busy enjoying the ride, she hadn't realized how far they'd gone.

Olivia looked at Joss. She realized with a jolt how strong her feelings had become. For all intents and purposes, Olivia was in love with her. The idea that Joss was trying to withdraw—both literally and emotionally—made her a little panicky. Freaking out would only make matters worse. She needed to get Joss to talk, not run. Olivia took a deep breath and tried to calm down. "You're right."

"I am?" Joss seemed surprised by her quick admission.

"The last couple of weeks have been a little nutty. Lots of worlds colliding."

Joss let out a half chuckle. "Colliding. That sure is what it feels like."

Olivia's irritation morphed into guilt. "And the people in my department can be overwhelming. Most of them mean well, but a couple are real assholes. Gerald especially. I should have warned you."

Joss didn't look comforted by that. "I can handle myself."

"Of course you can. It still doesn't mean you should have to. It was a party, for Pete's sake." A party that had been a mistake. She should have known better than to throw Joss into that. Olivia had been so caught up in how much she wanted Joss with her, she hadn't stopped to think about the consequences of it not going well. "It's a lot to navigate when we're still trying to get to know each other."

Joss tilted her head, as if in agreement, but didn't say anything.

"I can't tell you how much it means that you came with me." Olivia pulled into her driveway and cut the engine. Joss didn't move to get out, so she didn't either.

"Do you think I'm using you?"

Olivia searched Joss's face for meaning. Nothing in Gerald's little dig should have led to that. "What? Where did that come from?"

"I clearly don't move in the same circles that you do. Do you think I came with you tonight so I could get access to potential customers?"

At first, Olivia thought she must be joking. Then she was annoyed, since the question held in it the implication that she either wouldn't know the difference or didn't care. She glanced over, though, and saw the pained look in Joss's eyes. Olivia turned in the seat so she was facing Joss, took one of Joss's hands in her own. "Of course I don't think that. First, you seem to have more business than you know what to do with."

Joss shrugged.

"Second, and more importantly, you've given me absolutely no reason to doubt your sincerity, or your integrity."

"Thanks."

"Third, I'm not an idiot. And my bullshit detector is pretty good. If you think otherwise, then you're not giving me enough credit and we need to talk about that."

Joss sighed. "You're right."

"Fourth, if you were angling to use me for my connections, you would have been nicer to me when you found out where I worked, not meaner. And you would have jumped at the chance to go tonight instead of dragging your feet like a seven-year-old at bedtime."

Joss shook her head and smiled. "Okay, I think you've made your point."

"Where did that come from?" She needed to know. Almost more than making Joss feel better, Olivia needed to understand what started it in the first place.

"Nowhere. Forget I said anything."

"Joss, please. Don't shut me out."

Joss sighed. "I ran into Gerald in the kitchen. He insinuated that the only reason I was dating you was to get access to potential clients."

"Fucking Gerald." Olivia ground her teeth together. It wasn't the first time he'd entertained himself at her expense. It was a wonder Joss hadn't walked out of the party altogether.

"Yeah. I'm sorry I let him get to me."

Olivia fought the urge to rail against him. It would be satisfying, but it probably wasn't what Joss needed. In that moment, what Joss needed was far more important. "It's okay. He's got a rare talent for it. Are we okay?"

"We're okay."

Joss seemed to mean it. Olivia was relieved, if not entirely assured. "Good. Does that mean you're staying over?"

Joss sighed again and shrugged. "If you'll have me."

"Oh, I'll have you all right. Come on." Olivia climbed out of her car, glad that Joss immediately followed. As they walked to the side door, Olivia took Joss's hand.

Joss gave her hand a squeeze. "I'm sorry I asked you that."

Olivia unlocked the door and pulled Joss inside with her. "I'm sorry you felt compelled to ask."

"Yeah."

Joss looked miserable again, so Olivia decided to lighten the mood. "Besides, if anyone was using anyone, it would be me using you."

"You using me? What for? You're paying for the work, unless I missed the memo."

Olivia grabbed the front of Joss's shirt and pulled her close. "No, silly. I'd be using you for your body. You're seriously hot."

Joss raised a brow and smirked. "Cute. You're cute."

"I am, but I'm serious, too. I wanted to get my hands on you the moment we first met."

Joss's face softened and she smiled. "The feeling was mutual."

"Stop it. You didn't even like me when we first met. And you thought I was straight."

There was a playful gleam in Joss's eye. "It doesn't mean I didn't still want to get my hands on you."

"Touché. Take me to bed, please, and put your hands all over me."

"I thought you'd never ask." Joss grabbed her hand and pulled her down the hallway.

The second they were in the bedroom, Olivia started pulling at Joss's clothes. Suddenly, she was desperate to touch, to have her hands on Joss's skin. It was as though the physical contact would chase away the panic that had risen when Joss tried to pull away.

Joss's mouth was warm, firm, insistent. She teased Olivia's tongue with hers, coaxing her to be assertive and insistent in return. Joss's grip on her tightened. She pressed her body—her lean, hard, amazing body—into Olivia. The heat, the demand, of it made Olivia feel as though she were being swallowed whole.

They tumbled to the bed, mostly naked. Olivia gripped the tight muscles of Joss's rear end, pulling their bodies together. Joss ground her pelvis into Olivia, creating a friction that made Olivia long to be filled. She tugged at Joss's boxers. "You have to get these off. I have to feel you."

Joss pulled away long enough to comply. As Joss crawled back up the bed, Olivia scooted herself down, positioning herself beneath the apex of Joss's thighs.

"Olivia." Joss's voice was rough and unsteady.

"Please. Let me."

Already feeling intoxicated by the urgency that had taken over them, Olivia drank in Joss's scent and felt herself grow even more aroused. She plunged her tongue into Joss's heat, heard her groan. Olivia wrapped her arms around Joss's thighs, keeping Joss close. When she slid her tongue higher, she found Joss hard and swollen. Olivia took her with long, firm strokes. She let Joss control the pace, matching her movements to the slow thrusts of Joss's hips.

She could tell that Joss was close. Olivia longed for the release as though it was her own. When she felt Joss's legs begin to quiver, Olivia quickened her mouth, willing Joss to tumble over the edge. When Joss screamed her name, Olivia held her tight, riding the wave of pleasure with her and nearly having an orgasm of her own.

Joss collapsed onto the bed next to her. Olivia caressed her side, enjoying the way Joss's skin was damp from exertion. "I don't think I will ever get enough of you."

Joss moved with surprising speed, rolling on top of her. "You know, I was just thinking the same thing."

Before Olivia could respond, Joss was between her legs. She traced her thumb over Olivia's swollen labia, making Olivia realize just how wet she was. Joss slid two fingers into her and Olivia clamped down, feeling her body tense and her mind relax. "You feel amazing."

Olivia opened her eyes and found Joss smiling at her. "You know, I was just thinking the same thing."

Joss bent her head and Olivia felt her mouth slide over her. Each thrust was matched with a press of tongue. Olivia rose to meet her, aching for more. When Joss added a third finger, filling her completely, Olivia fisted her hands in the sheets, trying to hold back the orgasm that was building low in her belly. When Joss's last finger started to circle her tight opening, she nearly arched off the bed. Olivia came with a violent intensity; it left her entire body weak and trembling.

The next thing she knew, Joss's arms were around her, holding her tight. They lay like that a long time. Olivia slowly regained her breath, though her limbs still felt like jelly.

"Was that okay?" Joss's voice was soft, but still a little husky.
Olivia lifted her head and looked at her. "If by okay, you mean
mind-shatteringly good, then yes. Yes, it was okay."

Joss smiled. "I just wanted to make sure. It felt a little...primal."

Olivia chuckled. "That's a good word for it. It was amazing. I
loved everything about it."

Joss brushed a curl from Olivia's forehead. "Okay. Good."

They cuddled a while longer. Olivia felt surprisingly awake, wired
almost. She could tell from Joss's breathing that she was still awake,
too. Olivia propped herself on her elbow and rested her chin in her
hand. "Can I tell you something?"

"Of course."

"In my very first faculty meeting, Gerald baited me into an
argument. I fell for it and I ended up looking like a complete fool."

"Are you telling me this to make me feel better?"

Olivia laughed. "Maybe a little. He's condescending to just about
everyone, but especially women. Even more so when he knows the
women wouldn't be interested in him."

"That's gross."

"I know. I just wanted you to know that's how he is. It has
nothing, or at least hardly anything, to do with the fact that you're not
an academic. He's a button pusher of the lowest order and doesn't even
bother with being subtle."

Joss seemed to mull over what Olivia said. "Thanks, I appreciate
that."

Olivia sighed. There was more, and Joss deserved to hear it. "It's
also why I don't engage him. Calling him out only makes him more
difficult, both in the moment and at some point in the future when you
least expect it."

"That makes sense. I'm all for picking one's battles."

"Well, I don't like being a placater. I should have stood up for
you."

Joss reached out and stroked her hair. "I meant what I said about
not needing you to defend me. I've handled guys like him and worse. It
was how it made me feel about us that got under my skin."

Olivia wasn't sure she wanted the answer to that question, but she
knew she needed to ask. "And how are you feeling about us?"

"To be honest, I'm not entirely sure."

Olivia tried to ignore the knot that had formed in her stomach. "Do you want to talk about it?"

Joss rolled onto her back. "Don't take this the wrong way, but no." Olivia felt the disappointment wash over her. "Okay."

Joss rolled over again and looked her in the eye. "Can I convince you that's not a bad thing?"

Olivia didn't think so, but didn't say as much.

Joss continued. "When we started dating, I felt like it wasn't going to go anywhere. I figured we'd ride out the physical chemistry and then go our separate ways."

Olivia nodded. It shouldn't surprise her to hear that, considering how their first interactions had gone.

"It feels like maybe more than that now, but I'm not sure what that means, or what it should mean. I'm not one of those women who sorts out her feelings by talking about them. I need to think it through first. Does that make sense?"

It did. Although not knowing made her almost as uncomfortable as being let down, Olivia understood. "Yes, it does."

"I promise I'm not trying to avoid having a conversation altogether."

Olivia wasn't convinced, but she desperately wanted to give Joss the benefit of the doubt. "Okay."

Joss leaned over and kissed her. Olivia couldn't tell if it was meant to be reassuring or was Joss's way of ending the conversation. Either way, Olivia allowed herself to sink into it. When Joss's arm slipped around her waist, she let herself be pulled close. And when Joss's hands began to roam, Olivia gave herself over to the part of their relationship she knew worked just fine.

CHAPTER TWENTY-ONE

The knock at the door ripped Olivia from the erotic daydream she'd been indulging in. It wasn't the first time that had happened in the last few days. Although she and Joss were specifically not talking about feelings, there was nothing amiss in their physical connection. Olivia wouldn't have thought it possible, but the sex was even better than when they'd gotten together in the first place. She shook off the reverie and turned her attention back to her office and whoever had done the knocking.

She looked to the doorway and found M.J. hovering, waiting to be asked in. M.J.'s hair, purple this week, stood up in jaunty spikes. It was a stark contrast to the dejected look on her face.

"Hi M.J. What's up?"

M.J. looked as though she might burst into tears. "Do you have a minute, Dr. B?"

"Of course. Come in." Olivia knew it couldn't be M.J.'s performance in class that was upsetting her. She'd aced the first paper and was one of the most reliable participants in class discussion.

M.J. stepped the rest of the way into the office, closed the door behind her, and flopped in the chair across from the desk. Olivia waited a long moment, but M.J. didn't speak.

"Is something…"

"My parents are going to disown me."

Olivia's heart sank. M.J. had come out to her the previous spring and, as far as Olivia knew, had yet to come out to her family. "Tell me what happened."

"I went home for my brother's birthday and my mom wouldn't

stop pestering me about my hair and my clothes. She said I wasn't ever going to get a boyfriend if I didn't start acting like a girl."

Olivia winced. It wasn't unlike conversations she'd had with her own mother. Although Olivia had always gravitated toward feminine clothes, she refused to show any interest in boys. Her mother was relentless, threatening a long life as a proud but lonely old maid. "I can imagine that was very hard."

"I kept my mouth shut for two days. I finally couldn't take it anymore. I told her I didn't want a boyfriend and that my girlfriend was perfectly happy with how I looked."

It was hard not to smile at her verve. "Probably not the ideal way to come out to one's parents."

"Understatement of the century. My mother started crying and my father started yelling about how I was breaking her heart."

"And then what?"

"Then I started crying and I locked myself in my room. I couldn't stand sticking around, so I took the bus back by myself."

Olivia breathed an internal sigh of relief. As traumatic as it probably felt, it didn't sound like M.J.'s parents were on the cusp of shunning their only daughter. She needed to convince M.J. of that without being dismissive. "So, have you not spoken to them since?"

M.J. shrugged. "My dad texted to make sure I got back okay, but I haven't called them. I don't know what I'd even say."

Olivia remembered coming out to her parents. At first, they'd hardly said anything. Then they'd had a very civilized conversation about the kind of gay person she could be that wouldn't be too embarrassing for everyone. In retrospect, she probably would have preferred it if there'd been some crying. Or feeling, at least, of some sort or other. "Well, it sounds like they were caught off guard."

M.J. threw her hands up in the air. "I don't even get how that's possible. I mean, seriously, look at me."

Olivia couldn't stifle a smile this time. "I'm sure they see their little girl, the one they've known and loved and, unfortunately, had assumptions about her whole life."

"You're not kidding."

"I'm sure it must have been very hard to have them react that way." More than anything, she needed to provide empathy. If needed, they could deal with finding solutions later.

"I thought it would be satisfying, to finally turn all of their nosy, know-it-all lectures back on them."

"But it wasn't."

"I wanted to crawl in a hole and die. If they'd just been mad, it would be different. They seemed so...hurt." Olivia passed over the box of tissues from her desk. M.J. yanked out a few and swiped at her eyes. "It's a disaster."

This was the moment to step in. "It might not be a complete disaster."

M.J. looked completely unconvinced. "You didn't see their faces."

"True. They didn't say you had to leave, though, did they?"

She sighed. "No."

"And they didn't say you weren't their daughter anymore."

"They didn't."

"So, they're upset. That sucks, but it's not the end of the world."

M.J. looked the tiniest bit hopeful. "You think?"

"I think. Parents are funny. Even if you feel like you've been obviously gay your whole life, it doesn't mean they saw it."

M.J. shook her head. "You're going to tell me I should call them, aren't you?"

It was Olivia's turn to shrug. "I'm saying that there are times when the children must act like the adults."

"Thanks, Dr. B. I knew talking to you would make me feel better."

Olivia wasn't certain she was right. She could have M.J.'s parents pegged completely wrong. She hoped not. "Don't thank me. You're the one doing all the hard work."

"That's what you said about my thesis proposal, but I couldn't have done it without you."

"Again, I'm just your cheering section, and maybe your voice of reason."

M.J. finally cracked a smile. "Well, I seem to be in need of both."

Olivia leaned forward. "Can I tell you a secret?"

M.J. nodded.

"You're one of the most together college students I've ever met."

M.J. blushed and looked at her hands. "You're just saying that."

Olivia made a stern face. "I'm not. Your writing is more sophisticated than some of the graduate students I've taught. You're balancing your schoolwork with a job and a girlfriend. And you're the editor of the undergraduate literary magazine. As far as students go, you're a rock star."

"Thanks. It's nice to get a compliment when you feel like your life is a hot mess." M.J.'s grin was shy, but genuine. "How are you doing?"

Olivia smiled. "I'm good, all my classes are great. I bought a house a couple of months ago and it's been quite a project."

"That sounds awesome. Are you doing the work yourself?"

Olivia thought of her escapades in wall paper and carpet removal. "Some of the basic stuff. I hired a pro to do the major work."

"That's so cool. When I'm not working or writing papers, I'm kind of obsessed with *Rehab Addict*, and not just because Nicole is hot."

Olivia chuckled. "You and me both."

"I feel a lot better. Thanks for talking me down."

"Anytime."

M.J. stood. "I'll let you get back to work."

Olivia stood as well. "I'm glad you stopped in. You're welcome anytime. I mean it. I'd like to hear how things turn out."

M.J. opened the door, but hovered, shuffling her feet. "Thanks, Dr. B."

Olivia looked at the young woman who was so different than who she'd been at that age, yet who was so very similar. She turned to leave, but Olivia stopped her. "Hey, M.J."

"Yeah?"

"Everything is going to be okay."

M.J. bolted around the desk to where Olivia stood and threw her arms around her. "You're the best, Dr. B."

Olivia hugged her back, feeling like a cross between a big sister and a cool aunt. "So are you, M.J. Don't let anyone tell you otherwise."

M.J. nodded and left. Olivia smiled after her, feeling confident that things would be okay, at least with time. She glanced up and sighed. It was almost time for the faculty meeting. Olivia shut off her computer and gathered her things. As she pulled her office door closed, she realized Gerald, whose office was across from hers, was hovering.

"Is everything okay?" His voice carried a tone of concern Olivia didn't trust one lick.

"Of course."

"The student you were just with seemed pretty upset. Was her life over because you gave her a bad grade?"

Olivia set her jaw. "Actually, she's one of my best students. She just needed to talk."

Gerald shook his head. "I hate when they do that. That's why there's a counseling center on campus. If I'd wanted to listen to their problems, I'd have become a social worker."

"They're still kids. Sometimes they just need a friendly ear." Olivia pitied any student who sought that out from the likes of him.

"Not in my class. I treat them like adults and expect them to act like adults. If they don't like it, they can drop."

"That doesn't make you a good professor, Gerald. It makes you an ass."

"It's about respect, Dr. Bennett. I command respect in the classroom."

In the conference room, she scanned for an empty seat and an escape route. "That's the tricky thing about respect. Demanding it has little to do with actually getting it. If you'll excuse me, I need to ask Suzanne about something."

She walked away without waiting for a reply.

Chapter Twenty-two

Olivia pulled into the driveway and shut off the engine. She was exhausted. There was something about a department meeting that could suck all the life out of a person. As much as she liked most of her colleagues, they had a way of provoking one another that was reminiscent of a bunch of ten-year-olds. Today's battle had centered around the allocation of teaching assistant hours and who should move into the prime office spot being vacated by a retiring faculty member at the end of the year. In an hour and a half, they'd accomplished, by Olivia's estimation, absolutely nothing of any real consequence.

She picked up her bag, weighed down with the stack of papers she really needed to grade and hand back by the end of the week, and climbed out of the car. Joss's truck was parked in front of her, which made her smile and helped to lighten her mood. As much as she'd had her fill of people for the day, maybe they could go out for a casual dinner. With the kitchen still a mess and the stove—her gorgeous, special-order stove—stuck on backorder, the thought of putting anything together at this point was too daunting.

She opened the side door and was immediately surrounded by the aroma of something warm and savory. She sniffed the air a few times and decided that it was something with sausage and maybe onions. It made her mouth water. Ethel was sound asleep on her bed. Since that meant Joss would likely spend the night, Olivia's mood improved even further. She looked around, but there was no sign of Joss.

"Hello?"

Joss's voice came from upstairs. "I'm in your bedroom. Come on up."

Olivia set down her things and started upstairs. "I don't know what you're cooking, but it smells amazing. I'm suddenly starving." "I took a page out of your book. It's a stew in the crock pot. It should be ready in about half an hour." Joss stepped out of Olivia's room just as she reached the top of the stairs. "But first, I have something to show you." Olivia perked up a little bit more. "Did you get my bed in?" The finish on the floors was supposed to be set. She'd hoped to have Joss help her move in her furniture over the weekend. She'd been sleeping in the office turned bedroom for nearly two months. Although comfortable, it was starting to wear on her psyche. "You could say that." Joss kissed her, then took her hand.

Joss led her into the room and Olivia felt the breath leave her lungs. Not only was her bed in the room, but it was made. The new bed skirt and duvet she'd bought were on it, and her grandmother's quilt was folded over the foot board. Her nightstands sat on each side, complete with lamps. The curtains she'd ordered but had left in the box were hanging from the windows. A braided rug she didn't recognize, but that matched perfectly, pulled everything together.

"I…you…when?"

Joss was grinning. "I asked Ben to swing by after you left this morning. He helped me move the furniture and, because he's better at it, hang the curtain rods. I know it might not be exactly how you want it, but I wanted to surprise you. I figured we could rearrange anything you wanted different this weekend."

"It's perfect. It's utterly and absolutely perfect."

"I know you've been wanting to have this room in particular finished."

"I have. And after the day I've had, coming home to this, you have no idea."

Joss's arms came around her from behind. "I'm glad you like it, that it makes you happy."

Olivia turned so that they were facing each other. She wound her arms around Joss's neck. "I like you. You make me happy."

Joss kissed her again, but more earnestly. "I was hoping you might let me help you christen it later."

She pulled back, locked eyes with Joss. "You said dinner would be a while yet. Does it need any tending?"

"None whatsoever."

"Well, in that case…" Olivia began undoing the buttons of Joss's shirt.

"God, I love the way you think." Joss's hands were in her hair and she pulled Olivia in for another kiss.

Olivia pulled the shirt from the waist of Joss's pants, then ran her hands up Joss's front to her shoulders. She pushed the shirt aside, leaving her in a tight undershirt. She loved the way it showed off the muscles of Joss's shoulders and arms, the way it pulled tight across her small breasts.

She let out a small moan of approval as Joss's mouth went to her neck. She felt the zipper of her dress being pulled down and warm, strong hands on her back. Her moans intensified as Joss slid the material from her shoulders and the dress fell in a pool at her feet.

Joss's arms were back around her, lifting her off the ground. She wrapped her legs around Joss's waist and allowed herself to be carried to the bed. With one hand, Joss yanked back the duvet. Olivia felt the cool, clean sheets on her back and Joss's warm, hard body over her. She couldn't think of a single sensation that had ever been more pleasurable.

She played with the short hairs on the back of Joss's neck while Joss kissed her way down Olivia's torso. Joss stood briefly. Olivia heard the unbuckling of her belt, the rustle of fabric as Joss discarded her pants and underwear. In a flash, Joss was once again hovering over her. Olivia felt her skin flush under Joss's gaze. Unable to contain herself, she began to squirm, desperate for Joss's touch.

Joss pressed her leg between Olivia's thighs. Olivia's hips rose to meet her. Joss began teasing her breasts through the lace of her bra, taking one of her rock-hard nipples between her teeth. She was driving Olivia mad. "Oh, God. Yes, please, yes."

She felt Joss slide down her body, pull off her underwear. The urgency she felt, the need, was overwhelming. When Joss started lightly kissing the insides of her thighs, she thought she might lose it. She was on the verge of begging when Joss's mouth covered her.

Olivia felt her body buck as the heat poured out of her. She grabbed at the sheets, fisting them in her hands and trying desperately not to come. Joss's tongue worked her slowly, with long, firm strokes. The rhythm of it was intoxicating; her hips moved as if under a spell. Despite feeling like she was teetering on the edge of an orgasm, Joss found a way to draw her higher, to continue building the pressure that had taken over her.

Olivia lost all track of time. It was probably only minutes, but it felt like hours. Her body felt like a vessel into which Joss poured a seemingly infinite amount of pleasure. When the orgasm finally swept over her, it felt like her entire being was overflowing; the sensations spilled over all of her edges, leaving her drenched and weak.

"I wanted you here, in this room, like this." Joss was looking at her intently.

"Mmm." It was the only sound she could manage. Real words would need a minute.

"As much as I wanted to surprise you with a finished room, I'd be lying if I said getting you into this bed wasn't my primary motivation."

Olivia summoned the energy to roll over. She traced a finger down Joss's side. "I do hope this isn't how you celebrate every time you finish a project."

There was a devilish gleam in Joss's eye when she responded. "Only the bedrooms."

Olivia rolled the rest of the way until she was on top of Joss, her thighs straddling Joss's hips. "It's not nice to joke about these things."

She thought Joss would laugh, but instead she grabbed Olivia's wrists. "You're right. I shouldn't joke."

"It's okay. I was only teasing you."

Joss swallowed, but didn't ease her grip. "It's you. Only you."

Olivia leaned forward and kissed her. "Yes."

Joss released Olivia's wrists. She hadn't meant to get serious, but something about Olivia's comment overwhelmed her. Olivia cupped Joss's face in her hands, kissed her again. Joss felt a tightness in her chest that hovered on the line between pleasure and pain.

Olivia shifted her hands down, covering Joss's breasts with her palms. The feel of Olivia's skin made Joss's nipples stand erect. Then Olivia started to move, writhing slowly over her. Joss could feel Olivia's wetness, her heat, against her. Joss grabbed her hips, guiding her.

Joss's own hips started to lift, thrusting to meet her. There was something so erotic in the way Olivia looked, the way her red hair tumbled over her shoulders. Her eyes were closed and she'd clearly given herself over to the moment. Her body undulated, putting just the right pressure to make Joss feel like she was really fucking her, filling her completely.

When Joss thought she couldn't take it anymore, Olivia eased back just far enough to slide a hand between them. She pressed her thumb to Joss's throbbing center. Joss came instantly. Her whole body went rigid as the pleasure radiated through her. The speed of it added to the intensity, leaving her weak and panting.

As much as Olivia wanted to stay in bed—for the rest of the night, the rest of the week—she was starving. The aroma of whatever Joss had cooking had made its way upstairs. When her stomach growled for the third time, Joss sat up. "Okay, I think we need to eat now."

Olivia sighed. "Yeah, you're right. It smells amazing."

Joss climbed out of bed and pulled her clothes on. "Your robe is hanging in the closet if you want it."

Olivia walked over and opened the door. As promised, her robe was hanging on a hook on the door. She took a moment to admire the shelves and bars that were just waiting for her clothes and shoes. She'd never had such a nice closet before.

"I didn't dare touch your wardrobe."

Olivia turned to see Joss smiling at her from the doorway. "Oh, I'm going to have fun in here, don't you worry."

Joss chuckled. "I can only imagine."

They sat at the makeshift table, eating Joss's stew of kielbasa and butternut squash and drinking a juicy Shiraz. "I can't thank you enough for putting the room together. It was beyond thoughtful."

Joss cocked a brow. "Even with my ulterior motives?"

Olivia sipped her wine. "Especially with your ulterior motives."

"Well, in that case, let me get rid of these dishes and take you upstairs so we can enjoy it some more."

"I'll put the leftovers in the fridge and take Ethel out. I'll meet you upstairs in a few minutes."

Joss gathered the glasses and bowls. "Deal."

CHAPTER TWENTY-THREE

Olivia was painting the downstairs bathroom when the phone rang. She balanced the roller on the paint tray and wiped her hand on her already splattered T-shirt. She looked at the screen and saw that it was Gina.

"What's up, woman?" She stepped out of the small space to give herself a break from the paint fumes.

It was Kel's voice on the other end. "We're on our way to the hospital."

The meaning of her words registered. "Oh, my God! You're in labor! Are you okay? How far along are you? Is Gina with you?"

"Olivia, breathe. Gina is driving. I've just started having contractions, but since there's a chance they'll have to do a C-section, the doctor wants us there now."

Olivia laughed. Of course Kel would be the one telling her to stay calm. "Clearly you have everything under control. I'm going to wash the paint off me and I'll be right there."

"Take your time. It'll be a while yet." There was a rustling in the background and then she could hear Kel's raised voice. "Gina! Slow the hell down! I'm not going to give birth in the car!"

Olivia couldn't stifle another laugh. "Please be careful—both of you."

"Sorry. We're fine. We'll see you when you get here. Really, no rush."

"Okay." Olivia hung up the phone, then froze for a moment, unsure what to do first. She had to clean up and change and tell Joss and do something with the tray full of paint. She picked up the paint and roller, stepped into the hallway, and ran right into Joss.

Mossy green paint spread across the front of Joss's shirt. It ran over Olivia's hands and up her arms. It pooled on the floor, where Ethel, who'd gotten up to see what the commotion was about, promptly stepped in it. Olivia yelped. Thinking she wanted to play, Ethel danced around, leaving green paw prints everywhere she stepped. Olivia swore. Joss, it appeared, was trying not to laugh.

"And that's why we do floors after we paint."

Olivia, still trying to maintain her easygoing, I don't mind living in a construction zone image, smiled. "Right. You are so very smart about these things."

"I try. Did I hear you say something about labor?"

Olivia walked gingerly to the kitchen with her now-empty paint tray, trying not to drip on the floor any more than she already had. "You did, although it sounds like it's going to be a while yet. I was just going to put the paint away, clean up, and come find you."

Joss raised a brow. "Well, one out of three is a start."

"Jerk." Olivia giggled, taking even the semblance of punch out of the insult.

Despite the additional time it took them to clean up, Olivia and Joss arrived at the hospital less than an hour after Kel's call. After making their way to the maternity ward, they got Kel's room number from the nurse's station and started down the hall. As they approached the room, Olivia detected Gina's voice. She was giving someone orders, loudly.

"You need to be monitoring everything. I want a check-in every half hour. Surely, that's not unreasonable."

She heard murmuring she assumed was agreement, then saw a harried-looking nurse come out of the room. Olivia, knowing exactly how Gina could be when she was worked up about something, caught the nurse's eye and offered a reassuring smile. "She gets like that when she's nervous."

The nurse rolled her eyes but cracked a smile. "She's worse than the husbands!"

She went on her way and Joss grabbed Olivia's hand and headed for the door. Olivia stopped, causing Joss to rock back on her heel.

Joss looked at her. "What? Don't tell me women in labor make you nervous."

She huffed. "Of course not. It just occurred to me that I never asked you if you wanted to come along. This might be the last thing on earth you want to be doing right now."

"Are you nuts? This is great!"

Joss grabbed her hand again and pulled them into the room. Kel was propped up on the bed. Olivia couldn't believe how put together she looked. Gina, on the other hand, was pacing. She'd never seen her mass of curls look so disheveled. Considering she'd seen Gina on the beach and first thing in the morning, it was saying something.

Kel saw them first and raised both hands in the air. "Calm people. Thank heavens."

At Kel's insistence, as well as Joss's, Olivia dragged Gina out of the room for a walk up and down the hall. It was just enough of a distraction to help Gina calm down. When they returned to the room, they walked in on a heated debate.

"I'm just saying," Joss said, "that until the Jets are willing to shake up their offensive line, they aren't going to have a winning season."

"That's such a New England pansy thing to say. You've got a brand-name quarterback and you think the universe owes you a Super Bowl." Kel pounded a fist into the mattress. "It's the arrogance that starts to get old."

"It's not arrogance. The Jets buy a new quarterback every other week, each one worse than the last. Brady is ten times the quarterback of all of them put together." Joss leaned back in the chair she'd taken up near the bed.

Gina shook her head. "I cannot, simply cannot, believe they are arguing about football."

Olivia shrugged. "Whatever does the trick, right?"

"Right." Gina looked over at the two of them, then back at Olivia. "What I really can't believe is how cool and collected she is. I was so sure I was going to be the one over there and she'd be the one fussing and freaking out."

"Are you sad that it isn't you?"

Gina waited a long moment before she answered. "I thought I would be. I was afraid I'd be overwhelmed with longing, and envy. The reality is that this is the best thing that's ever happened to our relationship. It ripped us out of our comfort zones and allowed us to fall in love with parts of each other we didn't even know existed."

"That's really sweet."

"What about you?"

"What about me?"

"Any thoughts or talk of motherhood?"

It was a question she'd asked herself over and over. When she left Atlanta, she grieved for the life and for the family she thought she'd have there. On one hand, not having children with Amanda had made leaving so much less complicated. For that, and for not having to inflict that process on children, she was grateful. On the other hand, she was thirty-two. She had time, but the clock was definitely ticking. Although that fact was often in the back of her mind, she kept it firmly there. It was not a reality she felt ready to accept.

"Yes and no. I'd be lying if I said there wasn't a certain longing. In the moment, though, I'm so glad that I didn't go down that path when I had the chance. I can't imagine being a single mother any more than I can imagine sharing kids with my ex."

Gina tilted her head slightly in the direction of Joss and Kel, who were discussing concussions and what the NFL should or shouldn't be doing to prevent them. "What about Joss?"

Olivia was saved from answering by the entrance of the doctor. She briefly examined Kel, then announced, "I don't think we have much longer to go."

"I think that's our cue to relocate to the waiting room," Olivia said. She gave Gina a hug. "Be calm. She's a champ."

Gina smiled. "Right. Thanks. I love you. Oh, and this conversation is not over."

"Of course."

Olivia walked over to where Joss was helping Kel breathe through a contraction. When it ended, they bumped fists and Joss said, "Like a boss."

Olivia shook her head. Joss had the capacity to perpetually surprise her. She gave Kel a kiss on the cheek and wished her luck. When they were out in the hallway, she said, "Really? A fist bump?"

"What? We're bros."

Joss and Kel had become such fast friends. It still caught her off guard how nice it was to have her girlfriend and her best friends get along so well. She took Joss's face in her hands and planted a firm kiss on her mouth. "You are the best, and I'm pretty sure I'm not the only one who is glad you're here."

"Ditto." Joss grinned. "Now let's go rustle up some junk food to keep us going while we wait."

"You really don't mind hanging around a hospital all night?"

"This is a big deal. Gina is like a sister to you and, even though I give Kel a hard time, I really like them both. Besides, I want to be where you are. Now buy me a candy bar and stop questioning me."

"Yes'm."

They walked arm in arm down the hall. In the waiting area, the vending machine was dark. A piece of paper with the words "Out of Order" in black marker was taped to the glass.

"Foiled! Come on, we've got time to find another." Joss pulled her to the elevator and they went down a floor, where they found two machines well-stocked and in working order. She slid a couple of singles into the machine. "What's your pleasure?"

"Um, Diet Coke and a Twix, please."

"Good choices," she said, nodding. "Is that your usual or just your mood tonight?"

"I suppose that's my usual. There's enough Southern in me that I do love Dr Pepper, but it's rare to find Diet. Sometimes I'll go with peanut butter cups or, ooh, a York."

Joss nodded, as though she were taking in critical information. "Good to know. I'm a Kit Kat woman myself, although I do love a peanut butter cup. And while I don't mind Coca-Cola, I prefer a Pepsi."

Olivia made a face and raised a hand to her chest in horror. "I'm sorry, but I don't know if we can be together." She pulled out her thickest drawl. "I can handle a lot of your Yankee ways, but Pepsi drinkin' may be one step too far."

Joss laughed. She'd come to find many of Olivia's Southern mannerisms charming, but she enjoyed the over-the-top, tongue-in-cheek variation the best. It served as a pleasant reminder that Olivia didn't take herself too seriously.

With hands full of sugar and caffeine, they made their way back to the maternity floor. Once the candy bars were devoured, they sat holding hands in companionable silence. Joss picked up an abandoned newspaper and they got about three-quarters of the way through the crossword before giving up. Olivia rested her head on Joss's shoulder and, despite the sugar intake, started to nod off.

At 2:24 a.m., Gina appeared, looking the perfect combination of elated and exhausted. "They're here. Liam Andrew and Jacob Glenn are here."

The boys weighed a respectable five pounds, four ounces and four pounds, thirteen ounces. They were born six minutes apart and both came out screaming. Gina led them back to the room, where Kel was looking triumphant, but exhausted.

After hugs and congratulations, Gina looked at Olivia and Joss. "Do you want to hold them?"

Joss waited for Olivia to reply, since Gina and Kel were her friends first. Olivia nodded, but seemed a little unsure of herself, and Joss couldn't figure out why. When she saw Liam cradled in Olivia's arms, however, the questions vanished. In their place, a deep and profound longing. For the first time since Cora, Joss could envision being a parent. And she could envision doing it with Olivia.

"Don't you want to?" Olivia's question pulled Joss back to the present moment.

"Of course. Sorry, my mind wandered for a moment."

Gina handed the tiny sleeping bundle to her. Jacob's light brown complexion held a hint of pink and the top of his head was covered in soft black curls. He made faces in his sleep.

"He's beautiful." Joss hoped the emotion in her voice wasn't completely obvious.

Knowing Gina and Kel both needed some rest, Joss and Olivia didn't linger. The roads were empty and the drive was quiet. Joss knew where her mind wandered; she wondered if Olivia's was anywhere in the same vicinity. When they pulled into the driveway, it was nearly four o'clock. Olivia stifled a yawn. "Aren't you glad the babies had the courtesy to arrive at two in the morning on a weeknight?"

Joss shut off the engine and told herself to keep things light. "Lucky for me, my current boss is pretty lenient."

"Lenient, huh? Is that what I am?"

Joss tilted her head. "Flexible, perhaps, is a better word."

Olivia rolled her eyes and climbed out of the car. "I'll take it."

Despite the hour, kisses led to roaming hands. Joss was still surprised by how quickly Olivia stirred up her desire. The need was always there, just under the surface. It was empowering, if a little unnerving.

After they made love, Olivia curled up against Joss's chest in that way she had. It made Joss feel both soft and strong, protected and protective. Given how rocky the start of their relationship had been, it still caught her off guard just how right it felt. But rather than quieting that nagging voice in the back of her head, the feeling only seemed to make it stronger.

Joss still had no idea what Olivia wanted. At first, Joss told herself it was irrelevant, that they wouldn't last long enough to bother having the conversation. With each passing day, however, the connection felt deeper. The possibility of a future no longer seemed absurd. Seeing Gina and Kel tonight with their sons filled Joss with yearning to start a family of her own. She'd known that yearning was there, but Joss had come to realize that Olivia was now—or at least could be—a part of it. Not knowing if Olivia felt the same gnawed at her.

"Olivia?"

Olivia wiggled herself even closer, tightening her grip around Joss's middle. "Mmm. Yes?"

Joss's chest tightened and she realized she was terrified. If Olivia's answer was a flat-out no, what was Joss going to do? As painful as it would be, not wanting children was a deal breaker. "Do you want kids?"

Olivia waited a long moment before responding. It felt, to Joss, like hours. "Yes."

Something in Olivia's tone, something uncertain, made Joss's stomach clench. "You don't sound sure."

Olivia picked up her head and turned, looking Joss in the eye. "I am. I do. It's just that…"

She trailed off. Joss waited for her to continue, but she didn't. "It's just that what?"

Olivia sat up now. She pulled up the sheet to cover herself in a way that seemed strangely out of character. "It's just that I'm not sure if I can do it."

Joss sat up as well. "Carry a child, you mean? Give birth?"

She shook her head. "No. That, ironically, has never frightened me, at least not any more that it should, given what's entailed."

That was a relief. Joss hated to be clichéd, but she'd always assumed—hoped—that her wife would be the one to bear the children. Seeing Kel do it was amazing and had opened her mind to the possibility, but still. "So what do you worry you can't do?"

"Be a parent." Olivia sighed. "Be a good parent."

Joss was surprised. Over the last few months, she'd come to think of Olivia as the type of woman who could do just about anything she put her mind to. On top of that, her energy seemed pretty boundless. "What do you mean?"

Again, Olivia sat for a long minute before answering. "For most of my life, I figured I'd have children one day. As I got older, though, I thought past the want and started to doubt whether I'd be any good at it. The whole unconditional love thing, the energy and devotion that it takes to do it right. I don't think I could be a stay-at-home mom."

Joss thought about her own parents. They'd always both worked. And while the fact that it was a family business probably helped, she'd spent plenty of afternoons occupying herself, or when she was old enough, helping out in the office. She'd never equated love with that kind of constant attention. "I couldn't either. I don't think that means I wouldn't be a good parent."

Olivia didn't seem convinced. "I spent more time with my nanny than I did with both of my parents combined."

"I'm sorry. That must have been really hard."

"It wasn't terrible. Louella was a lovely woman and I adored her. It's just…I think my parents are good people. They provided my sister and me with so many opportunities."

"But?"

"But I think they see their children as an extension of their success. When I decided to push back against their expectations, it created a lot of tension. I love my parents, but there's always something hanging in the air between us. I couldn't stand to recreate that dynamic with my own children."

"So who says you have to?"

Olivia's expression turned sad. "I don't know if I would or I wouldn't. That's what scares me."

"Don't you think that awareness, that desire to be different, counts for something?"

"It would be nice to think so."

"I certainly think so."

Olivia smiled. "Thanks."

"I mean it." Olivia was such a confident woman that seeing her unsure—vulnerable, even—made Joss want to be her champion.

"I can tell. So what about you?"

"Kids, you mean?"

"Yeah."

"I don't feel compelled to carry them, but I definitely want children. Family is the most important thing to me." As nervous as she'd been, it was a huge relief for Joss to say it out loud.

Olivia leaned forward, resting her chin on her hand. "Can I tell you something?"

Joss swallowed. "Of course."

"My ex wanted to get married and start a family. It's one of the main reasons we broke up, in addition to my deciding to move a thousand miles away."

"Oh." Joss felt her heart sink with disappointment. She tried to tell herself it was better to know now than in six months or a year, when she was completely invested in something that wasn't ever going to happen.

"The prospect of doing that with her filled me with an overwhelming sense of dread."

Was this supposed to make Joss feel better? The whole it's not you, it's me routine?

Olivia took a deep breath. "I don't feel that way with you."

Wait. What? "What do you mean?"

"All those doubts I had with her, all the doubts I feel when I think about my own parents. It's different with you. The doubts, they're still there, but they're less somehow."

Joss felt a flutter of hope. "Really?"

"Yeah. I mean, I'd be lying if I said that watching Gina and Kel go through the pregnancy didn't stir up those feelings in me to begin with. But since we've been together, it's felt like less of a vague longing and more like something…concrete."

Joss was pretty sure she understood what Olivia was saying, but she wanted her to keep talking, especially given this turn in the conversation. "Concrete how? Do you mind elaborating?"

"Concrete like I could see it in my mind."

"See what exactly?"

Olivia looked away. She couldn't believe she was having this conversation. It was only a few months ago that Joss couldn't stand her. Winning her over was one thing. Getting involved was another. This, however, this talk about family and future, seemed surreal. For all that Olivia liked to think of herself as fearless, this made her more than a little unsteady.

She forced herself to return Joss's gaze. There was such a sincerity in her face that Olivia found her courage. "I can see what life could be like, what my children—our children—could be like."

Rather than alarmed by her admission, Joss seemed happy, excited even. "Really? What does it look like?"

Olivia wondered if she was blushing. It sure felt like it. "It's not like I fantasize about what our kids look like or anything."

Joss smiled in a way that warmed her from the inside. "It's okay if you did. I want to know."

"It's more like flashes of moments. I see kids running around the yard while I dig in the garden and you build a tree house. Little feet running down the hall and jumping into bed with us. It's silly, really."

"It's not silly at all. It's exactly what I want, what I've always wanted."

"But I'm like the last person on earth you wanted it with." It pained Olivia to say it, but she knew it was true.

"That was only when I first met you." It was Joss's turn to look away. "I was judgmental and a jerk. I'm sorry about that."

As far as Olivia was concerned, it was water under the bridge. It mattered, though, if Joss only thought of their relationship as a diversion. "I'm not looking for an apology. I don't want to make you feel bad, either."

"Okay."

"But since we're having this conversation, I need to know if that still matters."

"What do you mean?"

It felt like their relationship had grown into so much more, but they'd never talked about it. "I mean, am I still someone you'd date, but nothing more?"

Joss leaned forward and kissed her softly. "I wouldn't have asked you if you wanted children if I didn't take you—us—seriously."

Olivia's heart beat uncomfortably in her chest. Her relationship with Joss was shifting before her eyes. Unlike with Amanda, it did not fill her with dread. That was, in itself, a wonder. "I take us seriously, too."

Joss kissed her again. Again, it was soft. Or at least it started out that way. The softness slowly took on an edge. It became more insistent, pleading. Olivia's nervous pulse shifted to desire; it made her feel flushed and out of breath.

Joss shifted to a kneeling position so she could move closer. She cupped the back of Olivia's neck with her hand and held Olivia's gaze. "I want to build a future with you."

It was a somewhat obvious choice of words, but Olivia relished the idea. It wasn't something bought or handed to her. It wasn't packaged up with her parents' seal of approval. It was something they could build, together. "I want that, too."

Joss leaned forward and pulled Olivia into a kiss. Olivia had never experienced something that was at once so tender and yet possessive. It awakened in her a need, a longing, that she hadn't even known was there.

Joss guided her until she was lying on her back. The feel of Joss braced over her, the press of her body, tipped Olivia's scale of feeling back toward desire. As Joss trailed her hand down Olivia's side and along her thigh, Olivia arched, aching to be taken.

"Easy," Joss whispered against her ear. "I'm going to worship you, and it's going to take a while."

Even if Olivia had wanted to protest, she didn't think she could. Joss's declaration turned her into a puddle. She pressed a kiss against Joss's shoulder. "I'm yours."

CHAPTER TWENTY-FOUR

Olivia found herself humming on the way to campus. It had been one hell of a week. The crazy hours and emotional intensity of the twins' birth left her feeling giddy and light. Then there was the subsequent conversation with Joss about their future. For the first time since moving to Ithaca, maybe for the first time ever, Olivia felt like she could have it all. Not only that, she knew what it looked like.

Because she was running a little late, she skipped the usual stop by her office and went straight to her first class. She led a lively discussion on Henry James's *The Turn of the Screw*, inspiring even her most aloof science and economics majors to weigh in on the sexual repression of the story's heroine. The second section went nearly as well, putting her in an excellent mood as she made her way back to her office for office hours.

With no papers recently returned or imminently due, no one was waiting for her. She unlocked the door, thinking she might get a jump start on planning the Eudora Welty unit for her Southern Writers seminar. Not that she needed to do much prep for Eudora.

After flipping on the light and dropping her bag, Olivia noticed a pink message slip sitting on her keyboard. That was odd. It was rare for anyone to call the phone in her office, even rarer for someone to contact the main department line looking for her. Maybe it was some misguided textbook rep looking to hawk the latest anthology. She picked up the paper and recognized Betsy's handwriting.

Tim would like to see you when you get in. (Needs to be today.)

Well, that was really odd. Olivia felt a knot take hold in the pit of her stomach. She hoped it wasn't a student in crisis. Or worse. She scribbled a note that she'd be back in a few minutes and taped it to her door before heading up to the department office. When she walked in, Betsy was nowhere to be seen.

"Hello? Tim?"

"Olivia? Is that you?" The voice came from the Chair's office.

"Hi, Tim. Yes, it's me. Is now a good time?"

As she spoke, he emerged from his office. "It is. Please, come in." She followed him and tried not to flinch as he motioned to the chair across from his desk. With the exception of her interview, every meeting she'd had in this space took place in the sitting area in the corner. Even the second-year review of her tenure portfolio had been in the comfortable wing chairs. She took a seat and tried to read his face for some clue as to what was going on.

"There is no delicate way to put this, so I'm going to come right out and say it. There is an allegation that you engaged in a romantic relationship with one of your students."

Olivia, unable to stop herself, let out a sound that was somewhere between a cough and a laugh. "What?"

He folded his hands on his desk. He wasn't smiling. "There was a report filed through the university's anonymous reporting system that you are romantically involved with one of your students."

The look on Tim's face reflected pure discomfort. He was an unlikely department chair—introverted, nice, and generally loath to deal with conflict in any form. Olivia thought for a moment that she might be part of some sick prank, but Tim would never go along with such a thing. "There must be some misunderstanding."

Tim sighed. "I certainly hope so. Still, the university has a specific policy about investigating all complaints, including reports of harassment and code of conduct violations."

She tried to fight back the wave of nausea that was threatening to envelop her. This was real. She was being investigated. Someone believed she was having an affair with a student. Or she was being sabotaged. The final thought hit her like a truck and made her dizzy. She gripped the arm of the chair. She needed to focus, to cooperate while maintaining an appropriate amount of outrage.

"I'm not involved with a student. I've never been involved with a student. I've never come close. I've never even been attracted to a student, or vice versa, as far as I know."

Tim nodded. Olivia couldn't tell if he believed her or was merely letting her ramble. She racked her brain, trying to remember any student who was inappropriate or needy or anything else that might be misinterpreted. An image of M.J. flashed into her mind. "Who is it?"

"The report was anonymous. I don't know who made it."

Olivia shook her head. "Who am I allegedly having a relationship with?"

Tim opened a folder on his desk. "It doesn't say in the paperwork I've been given. I've been told very little. Everything is being handled by the Director of Employee Relations in the Office of Human Resources, which is probably for the best. I just...I wanted to be the one to tell you."

Olivia got the sense that, in whatever way he could, Tim was looking out for her. That counted for something. Didn't it? "What happens next?"

"This letter explains the process." He handed her a sealed envelope. "It also includes a copy of the complaint. I would imagine the student's name is part of it."

Olivia took the envelope, looked at him. "You don't want to know?"

Tim offered her a sympathetic look. "I'm hoping this is a misunderstanding or a mistake and that it will be resolved quickly. In that spirit, I feel the less I know, the better."

Olivia nodded. Tim had confidence in her. That helped, if only a little. "It is. It will. Thank you."

She went back to her office and closed the door. She read the document Tim gave her three or four times, along with the brief written complaint.

I have seen interactions between Dr. Olivia Bennett of the English Department and Mary Jane Carlton, an undergraduate student, that lead me to believe that there is an intimate relationship between them.

The rest of the details regarding what the person knew, or had seen, were vague. The tone and style of writing, however, made her think it had been written by someone on the faculty. She tried to remember what Tim had said about the procedure, but his words jumbled in her mind.

She turned on her computer and typed "sexual relationship" into the search box on the college homepage. Sure enough, the first result was a link to the policy on sexual harassment, including a prohibition on relationships between faculty and students. The policy page included a link to the procedures for dealing with complaints.

Olivia scanned the page once, then went back to the top and read it again more thoroughly. On one hand, it was disheartening to know there was enough of a need to have a full process in place. On the other, it helped to see it laid out in a straightforward way, including a section on dismissing groundless complaints.

The complaint would be dropped. It had to be. M.J. came to her office hours regularly, but they only talked. She saw her from time to time in town, but they'd never done anything off campus together. Not even coffee, and Olivia had done that with several students during her two years on the faculty. Olivia couldn't think of anything that could be interpreted as romantic, much less sexual.

She wanted to reach out to M.J., to warn her that someone would come asking questions. Given the stress she was under with her parents, the last thing Olivia wanted was to give her something else to worry about. But doing that could be construed as having something to hide, trying to make sure they got their stories straight. She needed to let the process play out. Maybe she could find a way to make it up to M.J. after the fact.

She needed to get through it for there to be an after the fact. She glanced at the clock. It was nearly six. Someone from HR would question her, but that would likely be during regular business hours. She couldn't even call over and try to get it scheduled. At the moment, she was powerless to do anything.

Olivia sighed and looked at the stack of paper on her desk. There was no way she could concentrate enough to get anything done. She left the stack where it was, turned off the light, and left.

❖

Olivia pulled into Joss's driveway and sat in her car for a long moment. As horrible as the conversation with Tim had been, she was dreading having to tell Joss even more. Saying the words out loud would make this whole nightmare more real. And there was the possibility that Joss might doubt her. That was ridiculous. She knew Joss wouldn't believe she'd had an affair with a student. Knowing it didn't seem to help.

She walked up the porch steps and went inside. The house smelled like pizza and she could see Joss standing in the kitchen looking at her phone. God, she didn't want to do this.

Joss caught sight of her and smiled. "I'm so glad you're here. If you'd been a minute later, I think I would have eaten this entire pizza myself."

"Sorry."

Joss's eyes narrowed and she set down her phone. "What's wrong? What happened?"

What should she even say? "I...There's been..."

She must look an absolute fright, given that Joss's worried face had morphed into one that hinted at panic. Joss walked up to her and took her hands. "Come sit down. You're white as a sheet."

Olivia allowed herself to be led to a chair. She couldn't bring herself to meet Joss's eyes. She took a breath and spat out the words. "Someone has accused me of having an inappropriate relationship with a student."

"What?"

"Someone sent an anonymous letter to the Office of Human Resources, raising concerns that I was romantically involved with one of my students." Olivia glanced up and saw Joss's eyes, searching her face for meaning. She couldn't tell if Joss was about to ask her if there was any basis for such a charge. She couldn't bear the thought of it. "It's not true. I haven't—I wouldn't—ever get involved with a student."

Joss scowled. "Of course you haven't. I'm just trying to wrap my head around how someone could say such a thing. Or why?"

"I don't know. It could be someone who saw something innocent and completely misinterpreted it."

"Or?"

Olivia sighed. "Or it could be someone who has a grudge, or wants to see me embarrassed."

"Is that possible? Not that someone would have a grudge against you, but that this could have any weight whatsoever."

"According to my department chair, there will be a confidential investigation. I have no doubt that the official result will be that I'm cleared, but they're going to have to talk to people. And even if they aren't supposed to, those people are going to talk. Professors are worse than little old ladies when it comes to gossip."

Joss squeezed her hands. "Okay, I get that that's a worry, but let's deal with one thing at a time. What happens next? And is there anything you can do to move things along quickly?"

Olivia looked at Joss. She was so calm and had a cool, matter-of-fact way of looking at things. Olivia had expected telling Joss to make her feel even worse. Instead, she felt better. Not only did Joss believe her, she seemed ready and willing to help her through it. She took a deep breath and squared her shoulders. "I'll answer whatever questions they have. I'll give them access to my email, to my office. I think that's all I can do."

"Who's the student?"

Olivia slumped forward. "Her name is M.J. She took American lit with me last semester and is in my Southern writers class now."

"Are you close?"

"She comes to office hours pretty regularly. I helped her start putting together a proposal to do a senior honors thesis."

"That sounds pretty typical."

"It is. She's also gay. She's out at school, but wasn't out at home." Olivia sighed. "Until a couple of weeks ago."

Joss leaned back. "Let me guess. It didn't go well."

"Everything about her screams baby dyke, but her parents were completely shocked."

"Oh, man."

Olivia was recalling the conversation in her office. "Wait."

"What?"

Olivia remembered M.J.'s initial despondence, the hopeful turn as they talked things through. "She came to my office to tell me about it. She was really upset and we talked for quite a while. She hugged me when she left."

Joss folded her arms. "Is hugging a student against the rules?"

Olivia shook her head. "No, but I guess someone could have misinterpreted it. I've been racking my brain for anything that could have looked even the slightest bit inappropriate."

"It seems like a stretch."

"It is, but you never know what people are thinking." Olivia frowned. "Especially if they're looking for trouble."

"I can't believe someone would do that."

Olivia had a flash of Gerald standing right outside her door. "Fucking asshole."

"What? Who?"

"Gerald was there. It was right before a faculty meeting and Gerald was hovering in the hallway."

Joss let out a sound that resembled a low growl. "Would he do that?"

Olivia sighed. "I don't know. Maybe? I wouldn't put it past him."

"Can you press it? File some kind of complaint of your own?"

Even if it was true, she'd probably never be able to prove it. Olivia tried to shove the idea aside and stood up. "I don't know, but I can't think about that right now. I'm going to focus on clearing my name and minimizing the damage."

Joss stood as well. "That sounds like a good plan."

CHAPTER TWENTY-FIVE

For the next several days, Olivia taught her classes, held office hours. She went to a faculty meeting. No one said anything. Of course they wouldn't. It felt as though people were looking at her more, but she might be imagining it. She had no way of knowing who knew, who'd been asked about her.

Her meeting with HR had been oddly anticlimactic. A woman who reminded Olivia of her aunt Phyllis asked her a series of questions. She seemed neither sympathetic nor scandalized. Less than an hour later, she thanked Olivia for her time and assured her a resolution would be forthcoming.

Olivia desperately wanted to tell Gina about the whole thing. Gina would be outraged, but empathetic. She would also have good advice. Gina hadn't endured a scandal, at least not to Olivia's knowledge, but she'd survived the tenure process. In addition to being competent, such a feat required toughness and a certain degree of political savvy. But the last thing she wanted to do was put a damper on the first few weeks she and Kel had at home with the twins. Even as Olivia dreaded that Gina might hear about it from someone other than her, she couldn't bring herself to call her.

After some gentle prodding from Joss, Olivia decided to do it in person. She texted Gina, who sounded thrilled to have a visitor, and headed over after class.

"I'm so glad you're here."

Olivia set down the bags she'd brought and hugged her best friend. "Good. I picked up the things you asked for, but took the liberty of adding a few more." Olivia unloaded grocery items as well as some ready-to-cook and ready-to-eat meals. "If my kitchen was done, I'd have cooked. I've been living on these, though, and they aren't half bad."

"You're an angel."

"I'm no such thing, but I do know my way around Wegmans. How are you?"

"Better than I thought. With Kel home and me teaching my classes online for the month, we've managed to work out a decent system."

"And does decent system mean sleeping for more than two hours at a time?"

Gina grinned. "It does. Kel sleeps from nine to three. I sleep from three to nine. We each try to take a nap during the day, which Kel is doing now. Since we're supplementing with formula, it's working."

Olivia nodded. "I'm impressed."

"Don't get me wrong. Those six-hour shifts can get a little rough, but Kel comes in refreshed and I have the promise of bed to sustain me."

Just being around Gina made her feel better. Olivia chided herself for staying away. "Remind me to get all of my parenting advice from you."

"We certainly don't have it all figured out, but we're a good team. That said, I'm sure the first time one of them runs a fever, I'm going to turn into a crazy person."

Olivia laughed. "That sounds perfectly reasonable."

"What about you, woman? How's school? How's Joss?"

"Joss is amazing. School, not so much."

"Are your students acting like children? Or are our colleagues?"

"At this point, I'd take both of those things, gladly." Olivia launched into an abbreviated version of what had transpired over the last couple of weeks—the conversation with Tim, her meeting with milquetoast HR lady, feeling like she couldn't say two words to M.J. outside of class.

"That is fucking ridiculous." Gina's raised voice made Liam stir. She started bouncing him and pacing, which seemed to soothe him. She lowered her voice. "Completely fucking ridiculous."

"Thanks." Olivia related the one interaction she'd had with M.J. she thought maybe could have been misconstrued.

Gina shook her head. "I don't know. It doesn't sound like a simple misunderstanding to me."

Olivia rocked Jacob, enjoying the faces he made in his sleep. She hadn't planned on saying anything about her suspicions because she knew Gina would flip out. But if Gina already had that thought in her head, she wasn't likely to let it go anytime soon. She cringed a little in anticipation.

"What? Do you smell poop? I just changed them, so it might be gas." Gina lifted Liam and smelled his rear end.

"No. Gerald."

"What about Gerald?" Gina stopped pacing and looked at her.

"When M.J. came to my office to talk about her parents, Gerald was there."

"Like in your office?"

Olivia could see his face, the disdain for students he considered needy. She remembered her irritation, getting in a dig. Could that have been enough to set him off? "No, when M.J. left, he was hovering outside my office. I don't know if he saw something or if he decided he wanted to see something. And I don't know if it was him. He's the only one I can think of."

"Fucking son of a bitch." Gina resumed her pacing. "Well, I'd put nothing past him. Especially if it stood to benefit him in some way."

Olivia's mind turned it over for the billionth time. Did Gerald dislike her that much? Did he have something to gain? "I don't see what it could be, other than making my life difficult. We had a little tiff, but I don't think I antagonized him to the point of needing revenge."

She could tell that Gina was mulling over the different angles. "You know what? Philip is on the same tenure cycle as you."

Olivia couldn't see what Gerald's little acolyte had to do with things. "So?"

"So making you look bad could make Philip look good."

The tenure process could feel like a popularity contest, but Olivia was loath to think it might be as fickle as that. "Could that possibly make a difference?"

"Probably not at the departmental level, but sometimes the university-wide committee will do a compare and contrast if there are two people up from the same department."

It seemed insidious, even for Gerald. Not to mention a long shot. "I don't know."

"I'm not saying he did, or that if he did that was his motive. I'm saying you should watch your back."

"Yeah." Olivia hated it, but Gina was right. "Thank you so much for listening."

Gina set Liam in a bassinet that had been placed in the corner. "I wish you'd told me sooner. I mean, I get it, but I wish you'd told me sooner."

"You've had your hands full." Olivia handed Jacob to Gina, who set him down next to his brother. "Hopefully, it will be over sooner rather than later, but I didn't want to chance you hearing about it from someone else."

"If anyone dares whisper anything to me, they'll have a black eye to show for it."

Gina was kidding, but it was nice to hear. "You're the best."

"I know. I'm also dying to hear about Joss. You guys seemed awfully cozy when you visited at the hospital."

"Yeah." Olivia flashed to the conversation she and Joss had after the hospital. "We're good."

"Are you in love?"

Olivia sighed. "Yeah."

"But?"

"I'm not sure she's in the same place. I think she might be getting there, but I'm not sure."

"I'd say anyone who spends half the night keeping you company in the maternity ward waiting room is pretty far gone."

Olivia smiled at the memory and their debate over junk food. "I hope you're right."

"I usually am. I'm also starting to get stir-crazy. We agreed to start venturing out once the boys hit four weeks. Maybe our first outing can be to your house."

"It really is in the home stretch. The upstairs was finished right before the boys were born. Most of the furniture is in, floors done, walls painted. I'm just waiting on the stove."

"Still on backorder?"

Olivia sighed. "Still on backorder."

"And no other stove will do?"

"You know me. Once I have my heart set on something…"

"Wait, are we talking about the stove, or about Joss?" Gina always knew exactly what to say.

"I'm going to go with both."

Olivia peered in on the boys before leaving. She seemed to be getting her heart set on a lot of things these days.

By the time Olivia got home, it was after seven. She was so glad that she'd told Gina everything, not to mention spending some time with the babies. She was drained, though, and tempted to crawl directly into bed. Joss's truck was still in the driveway, which surprised her.

Joss greeted her at the door with a kiss. "How was your day?"

"Exhausting. How about you?"

"It was pretty good. I have something that I think might make you happy."

"Whatever it is, I'll take it."

Joss rubbed her hands together. "Close your eyes."

"What? Why?"

Joss rolled her eyes. "I have a surprise for you. Don't you trust me?"

Olivia lifted her hands defensively, but laughed. "Okay, okay. Sorry."

She closed her eyes. Joss took both of her hands and slowly guided her into the house. Olivia had lived there long enough to know they were heading down the hall and toward the kitchen. Joss led her to what felt like the middle of the room, then turned her toward the island.

"Open."

Olivia did as she was told and found herself looking at a stove. No, not a stove. The stove. The stove she'd set her heart on that turned out to be on backorder. The stove that had held up completion of the kitchen for nearly a month. It was top of the line and completely modern, but designed to look like an antique, complete with white enamel finish and side-hinged oven door. It was beautiful. "Joss."

"I know. I was skeptical at first, but it really is cool, and perfect for this room."

"It is perfect. I love it."

"It literally came in this afternoon. I called in a couple of favors to get it brought straight here. I haven't had a chance to hook it up yet, but I knew you'd be excited to see it."

"I am. Thank you."

"I'll connect the gas lines and do all the safety checks in the morning if that's okay with you."

"Of course."

"I didn't want to invite myself to stay, but I picked up some steaks to grill for dinner, along with stuff for salad. With everything going on, I wanted you to be able to have a relaxing evening."

Olivia looked at Joss and her chest grew tight. Joss seemed to know exactly what she needed, even when she didn't always know herself. It was the first time in her life she'd been with someone like that and it still caught her off guard. Combined with the emotional roller coaster that had been the last few weeks, Olivia felt herself tumble over the edge. Before she could stop herself, the tears started. "That sounds great."

When Olivia began to cry, Joss panicked. She crossed the room and wrapped her arms around Olivia. The gesture seemed to make things worse; Olivia's whole body shook with sobs. "I'm so sorry. I thought the stove would cheer you up."

"It did cheer me up." Olivia choked out the words one at a time as she continued to cry. Joss could barely understand her.

"Okay. What is it then? Did something bad happen?" Joss hadn't pressed Olivia to talk about things at work. She was confident everything would work itself out. The possibility that wasn't the case made her stomach turn uncomfortably.

Olivia sniffed, took a couple of choppy breaths, and pulled away. "No, nothing happened. I'm just on edge. And you're being so sweet to me."

Joss studied her. Even with splotchy cheeks and smeared mascara, Joss thought she was the most beautiful creature she'd ever seen. "Hey, I didn't do anything special. I love you."

It was only after seeing the look on Olivia's face that Joss registered what she'd said. Olivia blinked a few times, but didn't say anything. Joss couldn't decide if it was better to backpedal or plow forward. "I'm sorry. I didn't mean to say that."

Olivia tipped her head to one side. "Didn't mean to say it or didn't mean it?"

Could her timing be any shittier? Joss knew she was in love with Olivia from the moment they talked about building a family. The night had already been so intense, she hadn't wanted to add another layer to it. Then the investigation started and everything seemed up in the air. She was planning to wait until the dust settled, then plan something romantic. With that plan now squarely out the window, Joss knew she couldn't withhold her feelings. Nor was she going to lie about them. "I didn't mean to say it, not like this."

It was still impossible to read Olivia, to know what she was thinking. "Not like how?"

"Not casually, not while everything is still going on at work." She touched a hand to Olivia's cheek. "Not when you're teary-eyed."

Olivia let out a small chuckle and smiled. "Well, that's where you're wrong. It is absolutely the most perfect time to say it."

Olivia threw her arms around Joss and squeezed. Joss felt a wave of relief wash over her. Or at least as much relief as she could feel without having Olivia say it back. "I'm glad."

Olivia leaned back and sniffed. "I'm sorry. I'm such a dolt."

"You're not. It's okay to feel overwhelmed. You have to let it out."

She shook her head. "No, I mean I'm a dolt for not saying it back. I love you, too. I've loved you for quite a while, actually, but I was afraid of sending you running for the hills."

Relief turned into elation. Joss experienced a swelling in her chest that she hadn't felt in such a long time. "I love you, Olivia. I'm in love with you and I want to be right here, with you, until the cows come home."

Olivia smiled again, although it was more of a grin this time, accompanied by a playful gleam in her eye. "We can get cows?"

Joss couldn't help but laugh. "One thing at a time, babe. One thing at a time."

CHAPTER TWENTY-SIX

The kitchen—and with it, the house—was officially finished. The stove, which had stubbornly remained on backorder even three weeks longer than originally promised, had finally arrived. Joss installed it, connected the gas line, and earned a one-woman round of applause when she tested the burner and got fire on her first try. As frustrating as it had been, it seemed fitting that the final touch was, perhaps, the single most important element of the entire renovation.

Between that and Joss telling Olivia she loved her, it was almost enough to make Olivia forget everything that was going on at work. She decided she was going to set aside the weekend and refuse to worry at all. After giving Joss a drawn-out kiss, Olivia shooed her from the house. "I know you have other projects. Go work and come back at 6:30. I'm making dinner."

She drove to town despite generally refusing to set foot in the grocery store on Saturdays. She bought a latte from the café and wandered leisurely, enjoying rather than being vexed by the jumble of carts and kids and moms and senior citizens in motorized scooters. She paid for her purchases and loaded them in her trunk. She made a stop at the wine store and arrived home in a ridiculously good mood. Mind over matter. That was her mantra for the day.

Back in the kitchen, she put on her favorite black and white hostess apron and started prepping. When everything was in place, she went about setting the table. She was just lighting candles when she heard Joss's truck in the driveway. When she walked in, Olivia was pouring wine.

"Hello, darling."

Joss looked her up and down and up again. She swallowed hard and then smiled. "Hello."

Olivia sashayed over and handed Joss a glass. She gave her a long and teasing kiss before asking, "How was your day?"

"Um, drastically improved in the last two minutes. Otherwise, not bad. You?"

"It was lovely. I shopped like I had a kitchen to cook in, I took a long bath, and I've been puttering around my absolutely perfect, perfectly finished house."

Joss sipped her wine. "If I'd known this was how you were going to react to having your stove delivered, I would have driven to the factory and built it myself."

Olivia laughed. "Are you saying I've gotten carried away?"

"Maybe, but you should feel free to get carried away anytime the mood strikes you."

Olivia returned to the stove and added vegetables to a hot skillet. "I can't tell you how happy that sizzle makes me. Is that silly?"

"Not at all. I'm sorry it took so long to get to you."

Olivia waved a wooden spoon at her. "Don't apologize. I'm the one who picked out the stove. I know the perils of special order."

They ate chicken Marsala with roasted potatoes and green beans at the dining room table. There were real plates and real wineglasses. It felt both ordinary and elevated at the same time. Joss talked about her next big project, an addition on a Cape Cod in Dryden. Olivia told Joss about the little boy who'd run headlong into her at the grocery store, clutching a box of Cheerios like it was the Holy Grail.

"I made dessert, too," Olivia said as she cleared the table.

"Did you now?"

"Chocolate molten cakes."

"Oh, please tell me there's ice cream."

Olivia smiled. "Vanilla and coffee, because I didn't know which you'd prefer."

"You're a goddess. Either, both, surprise me."

"Okay. They'll only need fifteen minutes or so in the oven."

"Just enough time for me to make a fire."

"Oh, yes please."

Olivia went to the kitchen to bake her cakes. When they were just shy of being set, she pulled them from the oven. She put both of the miniature cakes into a large soup bowl with two scoops of ice cream. She grabbed two spoons and returned to the living room. Joss had not only built a fire, but she had spread a blanket on the floor next to it. She took the bowl from Olivia, set it on the coffee table, then tugged at the bow of her apron.

"As much as I'd like to see you in nothing but this, I've got other things in mind."

Joss removed the apron and pulled Olivia close. Olivia took in her scent and the way Joss's body molded against hers. It felt so familiar, so natural, it was hard to imagine that she'd only known Joss for a few months. When Joss's fingers slipped under her shirt and traced over the skin of her lower back, all the tension of the last week melted away.

Joss unbuttoned Olivia's blouse, slid down her skirt. Joss then took off her bra and panties. "Lie down."

Olivia looked at her curiously, but did as she requested, watching Joss remove her own clothes.

"Now close your eyes."

Again, she obeyed. The next thing Olivia knew, there was something ice cold on her breast. She gasped. It was quickly followed by the warmth of Joss's mouth. She gasped again. On her other breast, Joss spread something hot. The sensation was followed again by Joss's mouth, this time cool from the ice cream she'd just eaten. Joss did this a couple more times—on Olivia's belly, her thighs. Olivia squirmed, both from the sensations as well as from the anticipation of what she would do next.

When Joss slipped inside her, Olivia sighed. The pleasure was intense, but without the edge it usually held. Joss's fingers were slower, more gentle, as well. Instead of aching for more, each thrust made Olivia feel complete, whole. When she came, it was a wave of warmth that enveloped her. Olivia let it take her. As she floated weightlessly through it, she whispered Joss's name.

When she opened her eyes, Joss was watching her. "I love you so much."

"I love you, too."

Joss's leg was draped over her and Olivia could feel her wetness. She shifted, pressing her thigh into Joss. Joss moaned, moving against her. Olivia lifted her hips so that she could slide her skin up and down Joss's slippery and swollen lips.

"Oh, God." Joss rolled onto Olivia, bracing herself on her elbows and straddling Olivia's thigh.

Olivia continued to arch into her, trying to provide just the right amount of pressure and friction. Joss thrust against Olivia with increasing speed. Olivia watched her, loving the look of fierce concentration on Joss's face and the way her breathing grew more and more ragged. When Joss came, the heat poured out of her. Olivia wrapped her arms around Joss and pulled her close. She fell asleep with tangled limbs and the warmth of the fire on her skin.

CHAPTER TWENTY-SEVEN

As usual, students lingered after class. There were a few questions about the upcoming paper, an apology for coming in late. Two students had wanted to talk more about one of the day's short stories. She encouraged them to make appointments so they'd be able to have more thorough conversations. Dorothy Allison's work often struck a raw nerve and Olivia had learned the hard way that, whether good or bad, reactions to her could be emotionally intense.

She gathered her things and nudged the stragglers along to make way for the next class using the room. She realized that Tim was waiting for her in the hallway. Olivia felt her stomach turn over and she was pretty sure she flinched.

"Do you have some time to talk?" His voice sounded encouraging, but Olivia couldn't tell if he had good news or was trying to seem upbeat.

"Of course."

She'd been lucky to have all of her classes that semester scheduled in the building, so they made the short walk down the hall and up to the department office. Tim gestured to the chairs in the sitting area and Olivia tried not to read too much into the gesture. They sat down and he handed her an envelope. Olivia took it and looked at him. Tim nodded.

Olivia broke the seal and pulled out the letter. She skimmed the contents, catching phrases like "no evidence of wrongdoing" and "allegations determined to be without merit." She let out a breath and realized that she was trembling. She took a moment to read the letter a second time before looking back to Tim.

"It's over," he said. "You've been cleared, completely."

Olivia nodded. "Yes. Thank you."

"There's no need to thank me. I'm sorry you had to go through it in the first place. I hope you understand that the investigation was protocol. It was required by university policy."

Olivia sat opposite Tim, wondering why she didn't feel more relieved. "I do understand. I'm grateful you pushed to move things more quickly."

"There won't be any record of the allegation, neither in your department file nor with Human Resources. It will be like it never happened."

She wanted to believe him. More than anything, she wanted to believe that she would leave his office and it would be as though the last three weeks had never happened. Even if it was true in the official sense, she knew better than to think that people's minds would be wiped clean as easily as the relevant documents would be shredded. The truth was that for some people on campus, especially those she didn't know well, her name would be associated with something unseemly if not illegal. And when it came to things like tenure, even a flawless publication record couldn't undo the effects of rumors.

"I appreciate your saying that," she said, trying make her voice sounds sincere.

"What is it? What's wrong?"

"It's just that I'm sure part of the investigation was talking to people. Clearly those people said the right things, but I can't help worry that the questions themselves planted some seed of doubt or, at the very least, wondering."

"Those conversations were confidential, and everyone involved was explicitly informed of that."

She nodded, not at all convinced.

"Olivia, you're a respected member of this department. Even as junior faculty, your research is solid. Your teaching evaluations are consistently high and you're serving on a couple of key committees."

"I know." She also knew how much faculty loved to gossip. Even when the intent wasn't malicious, juicy stories seemed to make the rounds.

"This will blow over as quickly as it blew in. I'm sure no one will even remember it by the end of the semester."

"You're right." Even if she didn't believe him, the last thing Olivia wanted to do was process her feelings with the man who'd be writing her annual review letter.

"Try to put this out of your mind. You have plenty else to focus on that is a better use of your time and energy."

Olivia smiled, not so much because of what Tim said, but because he sounded like her father. "Yes, absolutely."

"If there is anything you need, you know where to find me."

Olivia stood, squared her shoulders. This was not the time to seem weak. "Thank you. I'm fine, really. I'm ready to move on and focus on what's important."

Tim seemed relieved to hear the shift in her tone. "That's the spirit."

❖

Olivia drove home, still feeling unsettled. Seeing Joss's car in the driveway should have lightened her mood, but she found herself not wanting to talk, even to share the good news. She sat for a long moment, trying to muster the mental energy to go inside.

Joss must have been watching, because eventually the front door opened. Joss stepped out onto the porch. With the porch sconces now working, Olivia could see the concerned expression on her face.

"It's fine," she said out loud to herself. "The worst is over."

Olivia climbed out of the car and forced a smile onto her face. She walked to where Joss was standing and handed her the letter. She watched as Joss's eyes moved back and forth, then looked up to her. "It's over?"

Olivia nodded. "It's over."

"Thank God." Joss wrapped her arms around Olivia and squeezed, lifting her off the ground for a brief moment. "Baby, I'm so glad. I mean, I knew this would be the outcome, but it's good to see it on paper."

Joss's enthusiasm helped to lift Olivia's mood. She'd been so supportive, so willing to listen as Olivia strategized her meeting with HR and vented about it after. Olivia wasn't sure she would have managed it without her. "It is. And as far as these things go, I think it moved through the process pretty quickly. I think my department chair helped on that front."

"Well, I'm glad. He should be looking out for you. You're one of his rising stars."

Olivia had to chuckle at the choice of words. In the few months they'd been together, Joss had gone from disliking her, at least in part, because she was an academic to deciding she was one of the best. It was sweet and kind of adorable.

Olivia made dinner while Joss touched up some trim work in the living room. She poured wine and piled pasta onto plates, pulled out napkins and utensils so they could eat right in the kitchen. As they ate, Olivia found her mind wandering back to the conversation she had with Tim. Although the outcome was exactly what she'd hoped for, she couldn't shake the nagging feeling of being on edge.

"You still seem stressed."

Apparently, the feeling was clear on her face as well. "I am, but I'm not sure why. I thought I'd feel more relieved."

"You're not?"

"I am relieved. It's just…"

"Do you feel jaded about the whole thing?"

Olivia considered. "Maybe that's part of it. I can't help but worry that, even though it's over, the ripples of it aren't."

"What do you mean?"

"I worry that just enough people know about it, there will be talk. It'll be quiet for sure, but salacious accusations have more sticking power than anticlimactic exonerations."

"Maybe you should file a complaint of your own."

"The university was following protocol. I can't fault anyone for that."

Joss shook her head. "It just seems wrong."

"I know. I'm going to try to set it aside, though. Obsessing about it isn't going to get me anywhere and, as my chair said, it's just a distraction from what I really need to be doing."

Joss looked confused. "Really need to be doing?"

"Teaching, research, service—all the stuff I need to do to get tenure."

"Right."

"So I'm going to shake it off and put my head down and do my work."

Joss nodded. "That sounds like a good plan."

"But not tonight."

"No?"

"No. Tonight I'm going to drag you to bed and have my way with you."

"Hmm. That might be a problem."

"Problem? How so?" Olivia desperately wanted to make love to Joss, to give herself over to the physical and the way being with Joss made thought or worry impossible.

Joss raised a brow. "Because I already had plans to have my way with you."

Olivia reveled in the way Joss's eyes sparkled when she spoke. "I see. Well, perhaps we'll have to negotiate some sort of a compromise."

"I'm quite fond of compromise, actually. It's required in my line of work."

Olivia thought of her initial negotiations with Joss, the ideas she'd had as the work progressed, the goat pen. Despite their rocky start, they'd managed to sort everything out—on so many levels. Tonight, Olivia realized that the thing she wanted most was to cede control entirely, to follow wherever Joss wanted to lead. "You know what? I've changed my mind."

Joss took a deep breath. "It's okay. I'm sure you're exhausted after everything."

Olivia set their plates in the sink. "No, that's not what I meant."

Joss looked at her expectantly.

Olivia walked over to her, took Joss's hand and placed it around her waist. "I meant that I don't want to compromise. I want you to have your way with me. Tell me what to do. Take what you want."

Joss swallowed hard, but she didn't speak.

"You can be rough or gentle, fast or slow. It doesn't matter. All that matters is that you do exactly what you want, tell me what you want me to do. I want you to call all the shots."

Joss searched Olivia's face, trying to understand what she needed. What she saw was pleading. Joss realized that what Olivia wanted was a break from having to think, having to make decisions. For a woman so very much in control of her life, it couldn't be something she asked for lightly.

Joss tightened her grip around Olivia's waist, placed her other hand on Olivia's hip. "Kiss me."

Olivia smiled and leaned forward. She took Joss's lips, pulling the bottom one into her mouth and sucking gently. It was easy to get lost in Olivia's kisses, but Joss pulled her attention back to the moment and to Olivia's request. "Lead me to your bedroom."

Olivia took one of Joss's hands and pulled gently until Joss stood. She walked them both down the hall and up the stairs. Once they were there, Joss kissed Olivia again. Without a word, she reached around and slid down the zipper of Olivia's dress. She tugged at the sleeves until Olivia's arms were free, letting the dress fall to the floor. "Step out of your shoes."

Olivia obeyed.

"Lift your arms."

Olivia did as she was instructed and Joss lifted the satin slip over her head. Joss then removed her bra, slid black tights and lace panties down her legs. Joss started to unbutton her own shirt, but then dropped her hands. "Undress me."

Olivia went to work on Joss's shirt, undershirt, and jeans. It was unnerving for Olivia to be so quiet, so compliant. She'd never thought much about power play, but something about Olivia's request gave her courage. Now that she was in it, Joss realized how sexy it could be.

With both of them naked, Joss's instinct was to please Olivia. She took Olivia's breasts in her hands, rubbed her thumbs over each nipple. She leaned forward and took one of them into her mouth, loving the way it became puckered and hard. Joss glanced up at Olivia. Her eyes were closed, but her face was otherwise blank. Joss realized that, while Olivia's body was in the moment, her mind remained elsewhere. She was going to have to change tactics.

Joss stood and pulled her hands away. That caused Olivia's eyes to flutter open. Joss could see worry in them, mixed with a hint of alarm. Rather than pointing that out, Joss took Olivia's hands and placed them on her breasts. "Touch me. Make me want you."

Olivia nodded and began to massage Joss's breasts. She pinched Joss's nipples gently, then rolled them between her index finger and thumb. Joss groaned, struggling to keep her mind focused. She slowly walked backward toward the bed. "Don't let go."

Olivia kept her hands on Joss, continued pinching and tugging in a way that sent a throbbing ache straight to Joss's clit. Joss eased herself onto the bed, pulling Olivia with her. She lay flat on her back and said to Olivia, "I want you to straddle me."

Olivia released Joss's nipples and complied, placing a knee on either side of Joss's torso. Joss put her hands onto Olivia's hips and guided her down. When she felt Olivia's wetness against her, she groaned again. It seemed as though her plan was working. Now if only she could remain coherent long enough to see it through. "Do you like that? Does it feel good?"

"Yes." Olivia's voice was barely above a whisper.

"Good. I want you to move against me, but I don't want you to come. Do you understand?"

Olivia locked eyes with her. "Yes."

Olivia began to move, slowly at first. The thrust of her hips against Joss's pelvis made Joss ache to be inside her, to fill her and feel her come. When she thought she couldn't stand it anymore, Joss grasped Olivia's thighs. "I need you to stop now."

"But." The word came out and then Olivia seemed to remember herself, the role she'd created. She didn't say anything else.

"I want you to please me," Joss said. "You can use your fingers, but not your mouth."

If Olivia was bothered by the instructions, she didn't show it. Joss didn't say it was because if Olivia put her mouth on her, she'd be done. Olivia moved to a kneeling position next to Joss. She ran her hand over Joss's abdomen, down her thigh. Joss shifted to give her access and Olivia wasted no time sliding her fingers to where Joss needed her most. Joss watched Olivia, the focus and determination evident on her face. It was clear that everything else that had happened that day was forgotten, at least for the moment.

As Olivia stroked, Joss gave herself over to it. She was even more turned on than she'd realized and the orgasm hit her, hard and fast. Joss worked to regain her breath, aware that Olivia was still kneeling beside her. "Lie down," she said, trying to keep her tone gentle, but firm.

Joss rolled onto her side, propping herself up so she could look into Olivia's eyes. "That was amazing. You are amazing."

Olivia offered a small smile. "Thank you."

"Did you like being told what to do?"

"Yes." Olivia blushed when she said it, turning Joss on all over again.

"Do you want me to please you now?"

A barely perceptible nod. "Yes."

Joss made a trail of kisses from Olivia's collarbone to her navel. Olivia writhed beneath her. "Okay. But not yet."

Olivia's eyes, which she had closed, opened, revealing a combination of longing and apprehension. Joss moved back up her body and lay next to her. "Like I told you before, I don't want you to come. Do you understand?"

Another nod.

Joss trailed her hand down Olivia's body and between her legs. Without even touching her, Joss could tell how wet she was. After only a grazing caress, she moved her hand away. She traced Olivia's ribs, the soft skin on the underside of her breasts. She moved so that she was braced over her, enjoying the position of dominance.

Olivia moaned and moved against her, burying her hands in Joss's hair. Joss continued her assault, reveling in Olivia's incoherent mumbling. She moved over her, letting her sweat-soaked skin glide over Olivia's body. After a while, words ceased and Olivia's breath grew short and fast. Joss slid into her, felt her clamp down. Even more than her own orgasm, this was what she wanted. The melding of their bodies made Joss feel powerful, like anything was possible.

She pushed into her again and again. Olivia's body bucked and writhed. It was a good thing Joss had come or the sheer force of Olivia's need might have pushed her over the edge.

"Now. Olivia, come for me now."

Within seconds, she felt Olivia stiffen, heard her scream.

When Olivia went lax, Joss shifted and took her into her arms. Olivia trembled for a long while, to the point Joss worried that something was wrong. She kissed the top of Olivia's head, stroked her back. "You okay?"

Joss felt Olivia nod against her. "Can we stay just like this?"

"Of course." Joss reached over and turned off the light. It didn't take long for Olivia's breathing to even out. Relieved that she was asleep, Joss kissed her again and allowed herself to drift off.

CHAPTER TWENTY-EIGHT

The magic of the worry-free weekend gave way to Monday and all its typical concerns. Olivia taught her two American lit sections, held office hours. With the second paper due at the end of the week, the line outside her door was long. There were quick questions about formatting and panicked students who'd yet to decide what they were writing about. By the time the last one left, she had a pounding headache and was almost late for the faculty meeting.

Olivia walked into the conference room, scanning for Gina. She didn't notice Gerald slide up next to her.

"I know we're not supposed to talk about it, but I wanted to tell you how glad I am that this whole unsavory mess is behind you." His smile was an unsettling mix of condescension and smarm.

"Excuse me?" Olivia had heard just fine, but the comment had caught her off guard and she needed a moment to get her wits about her.

Gerald leaned in conspiratorially, as though they were the oldest and dearest of friends. "I never believed a word of it. Maybe a few people did, but no one of real consequence. Do you have any idea who started the rumors in the first place?"

Olivia had no way of knowing whether he'd heard about the allegations through the grapevine or knew because he'd instigated them in the first place. She set her jaw. "I really don't. If you'll excuse me, I need to talk with Gina before the meeting starts."

Olivia had expected the meeting to be awkward. Mostly, she expected people to avoid her, offer uncomfortable but reassuring smiles. Leave it to Gerald to go for the jugular not thirty seconds after she walked into the room. Apparently, she should have taken Gina up on her offer to walk in together and remain engrossed in conversation until the meeting was under way. At least Gina was there. She didn't have to come in for the meeting, but she did. She said it had nothing to do with offering moral support, but Olivia knew better. Gina wasn't that invested in committee elections.

Olivia made her way over to where Gina had secured a pair of seats and flopped down next to her. "I'm officially a punch line."

"You are not."

"Gerald couldn't wait to assure me he never doubted my innocence."

"Gerald is an ass and a half."

"Still."

"Still nothing."

Tim called the meeting to order. After approving the minutes of the prior meeting and congratulating Gina on the recent birth, he launched into the agenda. Two members of the department were scheduled to be on sabbatical in the spring and one had taken an emergency medical leave to have a hernia operation. That left holes on one departmental and two college-wide committees. Olivia had planned to volunteer for the departmental curriculum committee. Since there were no major curricular changes on the horizon, it would boost her service record without demanding an inordinate amount of time. Gerald chaired that committee, though, and Olivia could no longer bear the idea of spending any more time with him than was absolutely necessary.

Tim read the description of the Academic Coordinating Committee. It met two Fridays a month starting at three p.m. and was responsible for university-wide curricular and academic policy decisions. Of all the committees on campus, it had the reputation of being one of the most arduous, so much so that junior faculty were often advised to steer clear of it because it could suck so much time away from research. When he asked for volunteers, no hands went up. Olivia decided it was just the sort of commitment that could help her regain her footing. She raised her hand.

"I'll do it."

Tim looked at her like she'd grown a second head. Gina kicked her under the table.

"That's a very generous offer, Olivia," Tim said.

"I second the nomination." Olivia glanced over and realized it was Gerald who'd spoken.

"Are there any other nominations?" Tim look physically pained.

"I nominate Professor Stevens." Gina's voice dripped disdain.

Gerald chimed in. "While I appreciate Professor Morello's vote of confidence, I'm not eligible to serve based on my position as chair of the Curriculum Committee."

Tim nodded. "This is true. Are there any other nominations?"

Silence.

"All those in favor of Olivia's appointment say 'aye.'"

There was a chorus of "ayes."

"All opposed?"

Silence.

"Olivia Bennett is hereby the English Department representative to ACC."

The meeting dragged on for another half hour. Olivia half listened to the other committee appointments, discussion of a cleaning schedule for the departmental refrigerator, and the upcoming retirement reception for Leonard Barken. The larger part of her mind was consumed with the formulation of her new plan.

She'd serve on ACC. She'd be the most thorough, collegial member in the history of the committee. She'd also revamp the annual Freshman Essay Prize that she'd been tasked with overseeing the year before. She'd market it, promote it, and make sure her name was attached. She'd do that and kick her research into high gear. If she could get a new draft ready to send out and a couple of conference papers, her portfolio would go from solid to noteworthy. Even if there was gossip, it would drown in the sea of her accomplishments and she'd be granted tenure. At the end of the day, that's what mattered.

After the meeting, Gina headed home to the boys and Olivia went back to her office. She put on some music and told herself she couldn't leave until she'd graded ten of the nineteen papers stacked on her desk. An hour later, she'd only managed to plow through four of them. Realizing she'd been hunched over her desk, she leaned back and tried to stretch out the kink that had developed in her neck and shoulder blades. If she could just get to the halfway point tonight, she could finish tomorrow and hand papers back on Thursday. She cracked her knuckles and got back to work.

The next time Olivia looked up, the sky outside her window had gone dark. She glanced at the clock just as her phone pinged. The clock said it was 7:15 and the text message was from Joss. Shit.

Dinner is almost ready. Will I see you soon?

Between Joss having to help Ben with a project and Olivia having a lot of student meetings, they hadn't seen each other for a couple of days. Since they'd been spending so much time at Olivia's, Joss had offered to make dinner at her place. Olivia quickly typed a reply and gathered her things.

I'm on my way!

Olivia caught herself speeding on the way and forced herself to slow down. When she pulled into the driveway, the lights were burning and the whole house seemed to emit a welcoming glow. She grabbed her bag and hustled up the porch steps. Just as she reached for the knob, Joss opened the door.

"I'm so sorry I'm late."

Joss kissed her firmly on the mouth. "It's all good. I'm glad you're here. Is everything okay?"

"Yes, yes. I was grading after the faculty meeting and completely lost track of time."

Joss shook her head and smiled. "That is such a teacher thing to say."

Not only was dinner made, but the table was set and a fire crackled in the fireplace. Ethel was curled up on her bed, snoring away. "A girl could get used to this."

Joss served two plates of lasagna. "I know the last couple of weeks have been rough. I wanted you to have one less thing to worry about."

"That means a lot to me." Olivia took a bite. "Wow, this is good."

"Thanks. I've got your back. Remember that."

"I will."

"How was the faculty meeting?"

"Gerald got a dig in, but it's fine. Gina came in to offer moral support, which was great. I also had an epiphany."

"An epiphany?"

"Yes, and now I have a plan."

Joss had no idea what she was talking about, but was happy that Olivia felt back in control of her life at school. "All right. What's the plan?"

"I don't know how many people know about the investigation, nor do I have any way of finding out."

"Right."

"So what I need is some good PR. Having something good will balance out the negative if there is any. If not, it will only make people think more highly of me."

Joss understood the logic. She wasn't sure about the agenda, or the need, but it wasn't her call to make. "What's going to be your good PR?"

Olivia smiled, clearly proud of herself. "I volunteered for the crappiest committee on campus."

"Okay." Joss wondered if she was missing something or if that was the entirety of Olivia's plan. Even now, she did not get academia.

"Someone in the department had to do it, so I raised my hand. It will look good on my C.V. and it will give me more name recognition across campus."

"So why is it the crappiest committee, then?"

"It's time consuming and the meetings are notorious for running long." Olivia glanced away briefly. "And they're on Friday afternoons."

"That doesn't seem terrible."

Olivia perked up. "It really isn't. I figure if I do that, ramp up my research a bit, and kill it in the classroom, I'll be back on track."

Joss frowned. Something in Olivia's tone worried her. She sounded almost manic. "Babe, I'm all for doing a great job, but, well, were you ever really off track?"

Olivia considered for a moment. "No. I'd say I hit a bump, slowed down a little. I just need to pick up steam again."

Joss still had an uneasy feeling about the whole thing, but she wanted to be supportive. She lifted her glass. "Here's to picking up steam, then."

Olivia clinked Joss's raised glass. "I'll drink to that."

CHAPTER TWENTY-NINE

Over the next week, Olivia worked late more nights than not. Joss worked plenty of late nights herself, but she tried to be considerate if someone was waiting—or cooking—for her. And as much as Joss loved to cook, she was getting a little tired of making things she could keep warm until Olivia showed up. But Olivia always seemed to have one more meeting, one more paper to grade, one more email to send. Olivia seemed to be loving it, though, and her week off for Thanksgiving would be here soon enough. So Joss tried to stay positive, offering words of encouragement and back rubs, listening to stories about people who, had she worked with them, would have driven her nuts.

The first Friday Olivia had an ACC meeting, Joss suggested dinner out. She decided it would be a way of celebrating Olivia's new committee appointment. Even if it made her uneasy, Joss wanted to support Olivia's take-charge approach to her career. Besides, they hardly ever went out on dates. While that fact had never bothered her, at this point she thought they could stand to shake things up a bit.

Joss suggested they meet at Maxie's at 7:30, figuring Olivia would have more than enough time to finish her meeting and wrap up whatever else she needed to do before the weekend. She hoped the happy-hour vibe would help to set the tone for a work-free, stress-free couple of days. That would be good for both of them.

Feeling upbeat, she invited Ben to join her for a beer at the Westy at 6:00. Since they were working on different projects again, Joss hadn't seen him all week. The weather was promising winter more than lingering fall, so they bypassed the patio and headed inside. Joss ordered a couple of pints and then joined him at one of the hi-top tables in the corner.

"To Friday night." Ben lifted his glass.

"I'll drink to that." Joss tapped her glass against his. "How the hell are you?"

"Can't complain. I have a fourth date tonight, so that's something."

Joss raised a brow. "That is something. You think it might be serious?"

Ben shrugged. "You know, I'm kind of hoping it is. Becca is great and I'm feeling a little tired of the dating scene."

"Wow, that's even more serious than I thought."

"I'm not shopping for rings or anything, but I feel like there's potential. And the potential feels good."

Her little brother was growing up. It made Joss proud, if a little wistful. "That's great, Ben. I hope it only gets better."

"Thanks. I think she might be a keeper."

"I look forward to meeting her."

"All in good time. Perhaps a nice Sunday dinner like you did with Olivia. That seemed to go over well."

Joss nodded. "I was nervous, but it was great. I didn't do it with the idea of taking us to the next level, but it definitely helped things along."

"Speaking of, how are you?"

Joss smiled. "I'm good."

"That didn't sound all that convincing. What's up? I thought things were settling back down."

Ben knew about the turmoil at Olivia's job, as well as the ostensible resolution. "That's just it. Olivia was completely cleared, but she's acting like she has something to prove."

Ben cocked his head to one side. "What would she have to prove?"

"I think she's convinced there are lingering rumors about her. She's decided that the best way to deal with that is to go into some kind of professional overdrive."

Ben nodded. "Like overcompensation."

Ben was more perceptive than Joss gave him credit for. She regretted not confiding in him sooner. "Yes, exactly. She's working on two articles and has joined this insanely demanding committee. She's actually at a meeting right now."

Ben made a face. "On a Friday night?"

"Afternoon, technically, but they're known to run long."

"So work is sucking up all her time."

Joss shook her head. "That's part of it. I'm not unreasonable, though. I know there are times when work is demanding, when a deadline is looming and a project has to get done. I don't begrudge her that or expect her to be available whenever I am."

"But?"

She sighed. "But it feels like a bigger shift than that. What seemed like a good balance is all out of whack."

"All work and no play…"

"I'd finally started to believe we were on the same page and now I'm not at all sure."

Ben gave her a sympathetic look. Perhaps he was remembering the last time Joss fell for someone whose priorities were different from hers. "You don't think it's just the aftermath?"

"I'm hoping that's what it is. I know the whole incident really shook her. And in her work, being in the right isn't always enough. This whole tenure thing is nuts."

"So I've heard. So what are you going to do about it?"

Joss didn't know. She'd been asking herself that for the last couple of weeks and had yet to come up with an answer. "Be patient, I guess, at least for a while. Now that her house is done and I'm working on other projects, we'd be recalibrating anyway. I want to give her time, be supportive."

"Because there's potential?"

Joss had to chuckle at his choice of words. When she'd been hesitant to date Olivia in the first place, he'd harped on the idea of not worrying too much about whether Olivia had potential to be The One. Letting go of the expectations had opened the door and Joss had come around to seeing just how much potential was there. Somewhere along the way, between talking about kids and building goat pens, she'd started planning their lives together. Just how much Joss had done that, how much she'd invested in it, hit her like a punch to the gut. She looked at Ben. "I think I've got myself way beyond potential."

"Well, then I'm sure you'll find a way to work it out. Olivia is special, what you have is special. You'd have to be blind not to see that."

"Thanks, man. I appreciate that."

"I just calls them as I sees them."

After finishing their beers, Ben left to meet Becca and Joss started the walk over to Maxie's. Their conversation—and the feelings it stirred up—played over and over in her mind. She wanted to be with Olivia. She wanted to build a life and a family and a home. Well, they'd already built a home. Only, it was just Olivia's home.

Joss realized how easy it would be to think of the house on Davis Road as theirs. For one thing, it was a great house, exactly the kind of thing she'd choose. For another, she and Olivia had done so much of the work together. Between the carpet and wallpaper, the painting and the decorating, Olivia had been around. Unlike clients who made decisions from a distance and stayed away until there was a finished product, Olivia had her hand in things every step of the way.

And then they'd spent so much time together not working. Other than a casual lunch here and there, she wasn't in the habit of having meals in a home she worked on. She sure as hell didn't do sleepovers. Or bring Ethel along. Or get chummy with goats.

Having never dated a client, she wasn't sure if all this was a normal reaction to mixing work with pleasure or if it was something unique to Olivia. It had to be Olivia. Not only could Joss see herself living in the house, she saw her future with Olivia. Olivia's visions of tree houses and little feet had become her own, along with big family barbecues and morning after morning of waking up with the woman she loved.

Joss had already started thinking about moving in with Olivia. She'd thought about proposing, too. The last couple of weeks had put a bit of a damper on that, but the thoughts were still there. She needed a sign, something that told her Olivia was all in. Joss didn't know what that would be, but she hoped she'd know it when she saw it.

Maxie's was hopping. People waited outside for tables and crowded the bar, sipping drinks and sampling raw oysters. She didn't see Olivia anywhere, so she put her name in with the hostess and stepped back outside. The evening air was cold and snow was in the forecast, but it hadn't started yet. People came and went, but still no sign of Olivia. Joss pulled out her phone to check the time and realized she'd missed a text from her.

Fell into a conversation with chair of ACC, who's also on Tenure & Promotion! Amazing luck, but just finishing now. Sorry. Dinner still?

The text had come in just a few minutes before. Joss was working on a reply when the hostess came out to say their table was ready. Knowing it would take Olivia at least twenty minutes to get to the restaurant from campus, she apologized to the woman and told her to give the table to the next people in line. She'd suddenly lost her appetite.

Restaurant packed. I'll meet you back at your house.

She'd typed "at home" and then corrected herself. This sure as hell wasn't the sign she was hoping for.

❖

Olivia read the text from Joss and frowned. She couldn't tell for sure, but it seemed like Joss was irritated. She hoped not.

The ACC meeting had, as predicted, run long. Afterward, Arun Dutta, who was from the Physics Department and chaired ACC, had come up to her. He was welcoming and friendly, asking about her background and how long she'd been at the university. It was only after talking for a while that she learned he was also on the Tenure and Promotion Committee. It wasn't like she would—or even could—campaign for herself, but knowing members of the committee couldn't hurt. They'd chatted for nearly an hour and Olivia completely lost track of time.

She walked to her car trying to think of how she could make it up to Joss. A good starting point was probably dinner. She called an order in to the Chinese place in Collegetown, knowing the food would be ready by the time she got there to pick it up.

Olivia pulled into the driveway, relieved to see Joss's truck there. She grabbed the bag of food and made her way inside. When she walked in the front door, Joss switched off the television and stood.

"I feel so bad about our dinner plans. I thought I'd bring a peace offering of General Tso's and dumplings."

Joss sighed, but she did crack a smile. "If there's shrimp lo mein in there, too, I suppose we could work it out."

Olivia grinned. "But of course."

She walked to the kitchen and set down the bag, got out plates. When Joss came in behind her, she turned her attention and wrapped her arms around Joss's neck. "Forgive me?"

"I wasn't mad in the first place."

"Oh, admit it. You were annoyed. It's okay to say so."

Joss sighed again. She was sighing a lot lately. "I'm really not. I'm…I guess if anything, I'm worried."

Olivia stepped back and gave her a puzzled look. "Worried? Why would you be worried? I was just on campus."

"Not worried about your safety. I know campus is safe."

"Worried about what, then?" Getting Joss to open up was like pulling teeth. Why was she being so vague?

"You've been spending so much time at work. I thought that after you were cleared, things would settle down. Instead, work seems to be getting even more of your attention."

Olivia put her fists on her hips. "Honey, I told you about my plan. You knew I was signing up for this."

"I know. I guess I underestimated just how consuming it would be."

In the whole time they'd been together, Joss had never been clingy. Olivia found it odd that she'd start now. She couldn't decide if it was cute or irksome. She settled on the former, closing the distance between them and putting her arms around Joss's waist. "Aw, you miss me."

Olivia thought that would earn her a smile but it didn't. Instead, Joss frowned. "It's not like that."

Olivia fought to keep her patience. "Well, what is it, then? I am a woman of many talents, but reading minds isn't one of them."

Joss weighed her options. Telling Olivia how she felt might clear the air. It might also start a colossal fight. Did she want to risk it? "I guess I miss you some."

Olivia kissed her. "That's very sweet."

"With the house done, both of us are having our attention pulled in other directions." Joss didn't add the fact that this terrified her.

"I know what you mean. I'm so glad the house is done, but I miss working on it together. It was fun, but it was also what brought us together."

Joss cringed inwardly. Great, now Olivia thought she missed working on the house together. She did miss working side by side on projects, but that wasn't the point. Joss felt like the moment for baring her soul had passed. "It's all good. Let's eat before things get cold."

"Yes. I'm starving."

Olivia went about filling their plates from the takeout containers. Joss poured wine, not having the heart to say she wasn't the least bit hungry.

"Was that a football game you had on when I got home?"

"Yeah. Nothing exciting. LA Tech at Rice."

"That's okay. I'm not picky. Shall we put it back on?"

Joss decided the game would be preferable to talking, even if it was a snoozer. "Sure."

By the time they crawled into bed, Olivia was lamenting how exhausted she was. Rather than bothered, Joss was relieved that Olivia wasn't feeling amorous. She took some ibuprofen for the headache that had been simmering at the base of her neck and joined her. When Joss finally fell asleep, it was after midnight and the questions were still swirling around her mind.

Chapter Thirty

The next morning, Joss woke with the same headache she'd had the night before. She took two more ibuprofen and downed a cup of coffee in addition to filling her travel mug. She kissed Olivia and headed out to the Patel house, dreading having to deal with the consultation and walk through with such pounding in her head.

She wasn't sure if it was the coffee or the pills, but by the time she arrived at the site, she felt better. Mr. and Mrs. Patel were very friendly. And with their three kids approaching their teens, they were desperate for a space for the kids to hang out with their friends. Basement remodels weren't Joss's favorite, but the Patels were going all out. In addition to finishing the space, they were putting in a bedroom, a bathroom, an efficiency kitchen, and a media room.

After talking with them, Joss realized they were essentially looking for an in-law apartment. They wanted a space for the kids, but they also needed a place for their parents to stay when they visited from India. Since those visits lasted a month or more, having more than a guest room was important.

They had ideas, but were content to let Joss make a lot of the decisions. And while they didn't give Joss a blank check, doing the job well and quickly were clearly their top priorities. By the time she left, Joss had a vision for the project and a two-week window when the family would be traveling to the West Coast to get started on the work.

When she was done with the consultation, Joss drove back to the shop to work up a more precise rendering of her plan and start making a supply list. Although the task could have waited until Monday, she liked getting things on paper while they were still fresh in her mind. The office was quiet and she worked quickly. Within a couple of hours, she had everything sorted out, including a bright and functional laundry room where the washer and dryer currently sat. It would only add a small percentage to the overall budget, and she thought the Patels would go for it.

Feeling pleased, she drove back to Olivia's in a good mood. Maybe she'd overreacted the night before. Olivia was doing her best, just as Joss was doing hers. It was hard to fault Olivia for not giving family priority when there was no family yet that needed tending. She'd give it time and see how things went, at least for the next few weeks. She'd be plenty busy anyway.

She walked in the house to find Olivia standing in the kitchen, staring into space. She was wearing leggings and an oversize sweater; her hair was pulled into a clip that exposed her neck. The stir of arousal was both exciting and reassuring.

"Hello, gorgeous."

Olivia turned and blinked at her a few times. Clearly her mind had been elsewhere. "Hi."

Olivia smiled, but Joss thought she could see a shadow of worry behind it. "Everything okay?"

"It is. I love you, you know."

Joss smiled, more concerned rather than less. "I love you, too."

"I'm sorry the last few weeks have been so hectic. I know I've been putting more energy into work than into us."

Joss relaxed a little. "It's okay. I don't need all your attention all the time."

"Yeah, but I've hardly been giving you any."

"I do love your attention, but I hope you know it's not about that."

Olivia raised a brow. "What do you mean?"

"I'm a big believer in balance—work, life, family. It's felt a little lately like all your focus is on work. I worry about you burning out, you know?"

"That's sweet. You're sweet."

"I mean, if you felt compelled to lavish me with attention, I wouldn't say no."

"Ah."

"For your well-being, of course."

"Of course." Olivia closed the distance between them. She'd just started undoing the buttons of Joss's shirt when her phone rang. "Shit."

"What?"

Olivia took a step back and sighed. "That's my mother."

Joss had to laugh. "Answer it so you won't have to call her back later. I'm not going anywhere."

Olivia gave her a quick kiss. "You're the best."

Olivia snagged her phone and answered it. Joss headed to the living room so it wouldn't seem like she was eavesdropping. She wandered over to the mantle she'd crafted from a reclaimed beam. Olivia might love the kitchen, but the living room was Joss's favorite.

About fifteen minutes later, Olivia appeared. She looked shell-shocked. Joss's first thought was that someone had died. "What's wrong?"

"My parents are coming for a visit."

Joss smiled, relieved. "That's great. I've been hoping to have the chance to meet them. And they'll get to see the house and all of your hard work."

Olivia nodded, as though she was trying to convince herself that was true. "Yes, they will."

"Are you not looking forward to it?" Joss got that she was unusually close to her parents because they worked together, but Olivia seemed to be on the complete opposite extreme. She knew Olivia and her parents weren't close, but maybe it was worse than that.

"I am. Of course I am. They haven't visited since I moved north, so it's a bit of a surprise. That's all."

"They haven't visited at all?"

"Well, it's only been a couple of years. I went down for my youngest nephew's christening. And I was in an apartment for a while, so I would have had to put them in a hotel. It just didn't work out."

Joss smiled again. "I think it's great that they're coming. When?"

"Thanksgiving."

"Thanksgiving? That's really soon." It was in a week and a half, to be exact. Joss did her best to hide her surprise.

Olivia took a deep breath. "I know. They'll fly in on Tuesday, then drive to New York City on Friday to take in a couple of shows. I think my mom might be more excited about doing her Christmas shopping in the city than anything else."

Joss willed herself to stay positive. The more she learned about Olivia's parents, the less she liked them. But still. They were Olivia's parents. Meeting them was important. And seeing how Olivia was with them might answer some of the questions that had been nagging at her. All in all, it would be a good thing. It had to be. "The city does have a certain thrill. But they'll be here for the holiday. That's so nice. I'm sure my mom would be happy to have them if you all wanted to come over for dinner."

A look of alarm passed over Olivia's face.

"Or not."

Olivia must have realized she'd made a face. She quickly backpedaled. "It's such a sweet offer. And as much as I'd love to spend Thanksgiving with your family, I'm not sure it would be ideal."

"Okay." Joss was trying to make sense of the hesitation and the real meaning behind it.

"They can be kind of high maintenance. I love them, but I'm not sure inflicting them on your family at a big holiday dinner is the way to go."

Joss nodded. "I understand."

"Maybe we could do something casual on Wednesday night. Here, even. Drinks and hors d'oeuvres."

Joss loved finger food and cocktails as much as the next person, but it was the last thing she thought of when she thought of family. Maybe Olivia was right and colliding the worlds wasn't such a good idea. "Sure. You can decide whether you want to invite my parents, too, or have it just be the four of us. Introduce them in small doses."

Olivia chuckled. "That's the phrase I usually use to talk about myself spending time with them. But yes, I think you're right. Small doses."

Olivia seemed genuinely happy with her new plan and Joss was relieved, mostly. "You just let me know what I can do to help you get ready."

Olivia smiled for real. "Thanks. I know I've said so already, but you really are the best. I'm going to go make some lists. That always helps."

Joss nodded. "How about I go out and take care of the goats. I haven't seen them in a couple of days, and since we're supposed to get some snow tonight, we want to make sure they've got enough bedding to stay warm and cozy."

"They'll be thrilled to see you." Olivia walked over and kissed her. "I'll be in my lovely office that is no longer a makeshift bedroom."

Joss wanted the whole thing to feel homey—Olivia preparing for guests while she tended things around the house. Something was off, though. As much as she wanted them to feel like a team, it seemed like Olivia was just happy to have another pair of hands. Maybe she was overreacting. Joss put her coat on and headed out to the barn.

Olivia walked down the hall and into her office. While her computer booted, she grabbed a notepad and started jotting things down. She made one list for groceries, another for the liquor store. She'd stop by the mall to pick up some new towels. Were the guest sheets nice enough? Thinking about linens made Olivia's mind jump to the furniture in the guest room. It was pretty tired. She hopped online and started looking for stores that could do immediate delivery. After finding a store that delivered locally and had photos of their full inventory, she chose a set that she liked. She picked up the phone, chatted with a very nice sales guy and, within fifteen minutes, had it ordered and delivery scheduled.

Olivia walked into the kitchen feeling satisfied with everything she'd accomplished. She looked at Joss, who had just come in and was taking off her boots. "I ordered new furniture for the guest room."

Joss raised a brow, unsure how making lists had turned into buying furniture. "You did? Is there something wrong with the furniture that's in there now?"

Olivia made a face. "No, it's just old. It was the furniture I had in my apartment when I was in grad school."

To Joss, that was exactly the kind of furniture you'd put in the guest room. "Oh."

"I convinced my parents to stay with me instead of in a hotel. I want it to be nice for them."

Olivia was making less sense rather than more. It wasn't the first time in the last couple of weeks, so Joss decided to let it go. She also shoved aside the weird feeling she got at the realization that Olivia had and would spend money on new furniture at the drop of a hat. "I'm sure it will be really nice."

"I think so. Unfortunately, the only day they can deliver it is next Monday, but I have my last class before break and a meeting. And my parents will be here the next day. Any chance I could sweet talk you into being here for the delivery guys?"

Joss hated to give up a whole day of work, but the Patels were out of town, so there was no reason she couldn't go over later in the day or over the weekend to make up the time. "Sure."

"Thank you, thank you, thank you. I'll leave instructions on where I want everything and money to tip them."

Olivia was probably trying to be thoughtful, but Joss cringed. It felt like a clear statement about who was in charge. Olivia saw it as a favor and not as something Joss would do because they were in it together. "What about the furniture that's in there now?"

"Crap. I knew I was forgetting something."

Joss shook her head. She'd tried not to notice how flighty Olivia had been in the last couple of weeks. At least, flighty about everything that wasn't school. "Even if you're tired of it, it's a nice set. I can take it to the secondhand store in town for you if you want to put it on consignment."

"That would be great. When it sells, I'll take us out for a nice dinner."

"You don't have to do that. I offered to help."

Olivia kissed her. "Think of it as a token of appreciation."

Olivia went back to making her lists and Joss stood in the kitchen. Again, she didn't think Olivia meant it in a bad way, but the choice of words made Joss feel more like a hired hand than Olivia's partner. Joss had a flashback to the party with the people from Olivia's department—the awkwardness and the insinuation, the queasy feeling it gave her. Then there was the way Olivia reacted to it. After the fight that ensued, Olivia had convinced her it was an anomaly, that some of the people she worked with brought out the worst in her. Could the same be true of her parents?

Joss shook her head. She hoped not. For one thing, it could make the next couple of weeks close to unbearable. For another, it would say things about Olivia that Joss wasn't sure she could accept.

CHAPTER THIRTY-ONE

Since she'd promised to wait for the furniture delivery, Joss stayed in bed and watched as Olivia flitted around getting ready for work. Since she was always heading off to work herself, she'd never taken the time to study Olivia's routine. It was fun to watch her pick out clothes, put on makeup in just a bra and panties.

"I have to run. I'm meeting with a student before class. See you tonight? I'll make dinner."

Joss smiled. See? That was better. "Sounds great."

"I'll pick up wine, too, and we can enjoy a relaxing evening before my parents descend."

"And by relaxing, I hope you mean sexy."

"You know it." Olivia kissed her long and slow. "I'll see you later."

When she heard the back door close, Joss climbed out of bed and pulled on yesterday's clothes. Since she was stuck at Olivia's until the furniture guys arrived, Joss decided to head out to the barn. Pierre and Bill were happy to see her, which made her smile. She freshened their water and hay, gave them a brush and some attention. When they bleated, she talked back, enjoying the nonsensical banter. She'd never have bought—or adopted—goats herself, but she was starting to understand their appeal.

After, she took a snow shovel to the driveway. Although Olivia hired a service, they couldn't help but leave a mess at the garage door. She cleaned up the edges, then shoveled the sidewalk. Even though there wasn't much, keeping it clear would prevent ice buildup as winter trudged along. She didn't know if Olivia didn't understand that or if she'd let it slide in her perpetual state of hurrying to campus.

Feeling like things were in order, Joss headed back into the house. She took a shower and dressed, then powered up her laptop. She pulled up the plans for the Patel project. She was still struggling to come up with a floor option. Because the space was small, she wanted to do a single material throughout, including the kitchen area and bathroom. The Patels weren't crazy about tile, but Joss always hesitated to put hardwood in a basement. A single sewer backup or water heater blowout could mean having to rip everything out.

Joss suddenly remembered something she'd seen at her last home show. She went online and did a search. Although she had yet to use it in a project, it looked like wood grain tile was becoming quite popular. She browsed the options, pleased that some of them looked more natural than laminate. And with the radiant heat in the floor, it wouldn't even have the cold feel of tile underfoot.

Pleased with herself, she jotted down a couple of brands and styles to check out. She was plugging away on an email to the Patels outlining her thoughts when the doorbell rang. She opened the door and found two lanky guys standing on the porch. They didn't look much like delivery guys to her, but she resisted making judgment.

"Hi. Uh, we've got some furniture for you."

Joss smiled at them, trying to be nice. "Yep. We've been expecting you."

"Great. So, like, where...where do you want us to put it?"

Joss led them upstairs to the room she'd emptied the day before. She pointed out where things generally needed to go, then stepped back to let them work.

Twenty minutes later, she wished she'd never have agreed to be the one to deal with them. Joss gritted her teeth and willed herself not to yell at the delivery men who acted like they'd never moved a piece of furniture before. In truth, the two guys—boys, really—didn't look much over sixteen. And while they were nice enough, they clearly had no idea what they were doing. She couldn't imagine what company would hire them to maneuver heavy and expensive merchandise into small spaces. Joss didn't know where Olivia ordered from, but she was certain it wasn't one of the handful of local companies she knew and trusted.

By the time they left, there were marks on three walls, a gouge in another, and a huge scratch across the guest room floor. Apparently it hadn't occurred to them to check the feet of the dresser for staples before sliding it across the room. They apologized, but it was clear they had no interest or investment in making it right.

She gave them half the tip money Olivia had left. As irritated as she was, she blamed the company more than the kids. In addition to poor training, she guessed they weren't paid very well either.

Joss cleaned up the snow they'd tracked into the house and up the stairs. She peeked in the room, hoping it was maybe not as bad as she thought. No, it wasn't as bad. It was worse.

She stood for a moment and rubbed her temples. It wasn't anything she couldn't fix, but it still drove her nuts. She decided to head over to the Patel house and bang out some of her annoyance. Joss jotted a quick note for Olivia and left.

❖

Olivia pulled into the driveway. It was empty; there was no sign of Joss's truck. Her first thought was one of worry. She hoped nothing had happened. When she got inside, Olivia found Ethel dozing and a note on the island.

Delivery boys a mess. Furniture looks great. Floor less so. I'll be back in a couple of hours.

Olivia had no idea when Joss wrote the note, so she had no idea when to expect her. She set down her things and went upstairs. She saw the marks on the walls, the dent at the top of the stairs. When she walked into the guest room, she didn't even notice the furniture. A huge scratch—probably three feet long—arced right across the middle of the floor. Fuck.

Olivia traced her fingers over the line. It wasn't wide, but it went all the way down to bare wood. She took a deep breath. It would be okay. Joss would know how to fix it. She stood up and took in the furniture. At least it looked good. The detail on the white headboard matched the trim on the dresser. The handles of the dresser drawers matched those on the nightstands. Perhaps it was a little Pottery Barn for her tastes, but it looked clean and fresh. And her parents would like it.

She headed downstairs, trying not to be annoyed that Joss had taken off. Maybe she was getting whatever she needed to fix the scratch.

Olivia hoped it didn't require sanding the whole floor. She went to the kitchen to start dinner. Once Joss got home, they could make a game plan.

Olivia stood at the kitchen island chopping vegetables for a riff on ratatouille. Each time her mother's face invaded her thoughts, complete with raised brow of judgment, Olivia willed it away. By the time she was sautéing garlic and onions, she felt a little bit calmer.

She hated being so on edge. The last month had felt like an endless tightrope walk. Her body and mind seemed stuck in overdrive and she had to keep reminding herself that the worst was over. She was in control and wasn't going to get shoved out of the driver's seat again. Everything was going to be fine.

Joss walked in an hour later, just as Olivia was pulling her casserole from the oven. Apparently, Joss had gone to work on another project as a distraction. Olivia swallowed her annoyance that she didn't have any floor-fixing supplies in hand. They went upstairs and stood in the doorway, surveying the damage.

"Can't you just put the rug over it until after they leave?"

Before coming back, Joss had gone to her house and picked up one of the rugs from her bedroom. It was a thoughtful gesture, but still. Olivia could just see her mother flipping it back, then lamenting how hard it was to find good help these days. She cringed at the thought, considering her girlfriend and the help were one in the same. "I don't understand why you can't just fix it."

"I can, but I kind of have my hands full at the moment with a project that's on a tight deadline."

Olivia fisted her hands on her hips. "Will it even take you that long?"

Joss huffed. "It will to do it right. What's the big deal? I thought you didn't care what your parents thought."

"I don't."

Joss merely raised a brow.

"I need them to understand that I made a good decision. I don't do things their way, but I still do them well."

"Are you talking about the house? Or me?"

Olivia rolled her eyes. Why was Joss being so unreasonable? "Of course I'm talking about the house. What a ridiculous thing to say."

Joss shook her head. Given how things had been between them for the last few weeks, it didn't feel ridiculous at all. It felt perfectly, painfully in line with how Olivia had been treating her. The hallway, the guest room, began to feel claustrophobic. Joss turned away and walked downstairs, taking deep breaths and trying to calm the anger that seemed in danger of consuming her.

Olivia followed her into the kitchen. "I can't believe you're picking a fight right now."

"I'm not picking a fight and I'm sorry if my timing isn't convenient for you. Clearly your convenience is the utmost priority."

"I thought you said my job was the utmost priority."

"Actually, you said as much last week when you were apologizing for putting all your energy into your job."

"And now you're turning it around on me just because you're annoyed."

"I'm not annoyed."

"Then what are you?"

What was she? Joss wasn't sure she could—or wanted to—put it into words. "Olivia, you've stood me up two nights in the last week. On top of that, you've just assumed I would be around and wouldn't mind taking care of the furniture delivery, the damage from said delivery. Not to mention shoveling snow, feeding the goats, and whatever projects are still laying around."

"I thought you liked the goats."

"I do like the goats. That's not the point."

Olivia's hands went to her hips. "Then what is the point?"

"I'm not your hired hand." Just saying the words made Joss's stomach turn over.

"Oh, I'm sorry. Is the problem that I'm not paying you?"

Something in Olivia's eyes sent a chill through her. It wasn't anger so much as condescension. "That's not what I said, or what I meant."

"Because if being here—being with me—is just an extension of the job, you should say so."

"That is completely out of line. You're the one who expects that I, or someone, will be around to take care of everything. I have a job and responsibilities beyond your house. And my work is just as important as yours."

"Don't you get it? Everything relies on me getting tenure. If I don't get it, all of this," Olivia spread her hands to either side, "goes away."

"You've got a serious case of tunnel vision."

"What is that supposed to mean?"

"It means that if your job is the only thing you're worried about, all of this," Joss moved her hands up down to indicate herself, "goes away."

"Is that a threat? Or an ultimatum?"

"It's me being honest with you. I understand that your career is important. It's one of the things I love about you. But if it's the most important thing, then we are not going to work out."

"You're telling me that your work is not your highest priority? That's bullshit."

"No, it's not. Family comes first, always."

"The family you work with every day."

"Family no matter what. There is no project or contract that would trump family, especially the family I build with my wife. I can't be with a woman who doesn't feel the same." When it came down to it, it was as simple as that. And if Olivia felt differently, no amount of talking or negotiation could resolve it.

"You're making it sound black and white. It's more complicated than that." Olivia's anger took on a shade of fear. She tried to pull the edge out of her voice. "Isn't family what started this whole fight? Me freaking out about my family?"

"We aren't fighting about your family and you know it. And if your version of worrying about your family is trying to make your house seem like a high-end bed and breakfast to impress them, we don't even have the same definition of family."

The criticism nudged Olivia back toward being angry. "That's unfair. Just because I don't have the same perfect relationship with my family that you do, you don't have to be so judgmental of mine."

Joss pressed a thumb to her temple. "I'm not being judgmental."

Olivia's indignation grew. "Really? Because it sounds like you have a problem with my family and my job and pretty much everything else about me right now."

"Look, we're not getting anywhere. I don't want to do this with you."

"What does that mean?"

"It means I don't see any resolution to this right now and I need to walk away before I say something I really regret."

Olivia swallowed. "Are you saying we're breaking up?"

"I'm saying if this is who you are, who you want to be, we can't be together."

"You know who I am."

Joss's face softened, the anger giving way to something that looked more like sadness. "I thought I did. Now I'm not so sure. I don't know if you are, either. And until you have that sorted out, there isn't much I can do."

"I don't know what you want from me."

Joss nodded slowly. "Yes, you do. What you have to figure out is whether you want the same thing. When you do, you know where to find me."

Joss put on her coat and boots, picked up her keys. She hooked a leash up to Ethel, who must have heard their raised voices and had come lumbering into the kitchen. When the dog hesitated to step out into the blowing snow, Joss scooped her up. She didn't slam the door, but she didn't look back either.

CHAPTER THIRTY-TWO

Olivia was left standing in the kitchen. Hurt and anger vied for dominance. She couldn't believe Joss had walked out on her. Even worse, Joss was leaving her in a lurch to deal with everything and didn't seem to care. And even though she said she did, Joss clearly didn't understand why Olivia needed things to be just so for her parents' visit. Just like she didn't get why work needed to be a priority right now.

It was like Joss wanted her to be everything to everybody at once. Olivia was a lot of things, but she wasn't Wonder Woman. Of course, that wasn't what Joss wanted, either. She wanted Olivia to focus all of her energy on their relationship, and that simply wasn't possible. She wasn't going to be some doe-eyed wife who sat around all day, tending the house and waiting for the bread winner to come home. She'd seen enough of that in the girls she grew up with. And she refused to be handled, either. Her ex had tried to handle her, gently coaxing her towards the friends and activities and job that she decided were suitable. She'd fought tooth and nail to be her own woman, and she sure as hell wasn't going to change that now.

Olivia worked herself into quite a state, pacing around and having to resist the urge to throw something. Indignation made her feel strong, told her she was right. Those were the feelings she held on to. She couldn't allow her mind to focus on the alternative—that Joss was right and Olivia was pushing her away and ruining their chance of being together. If she thought about that, she might fall apart completely. And with her parents coming and the semester nearly over, falling apart wasn't an option.

Olivia squared her shoulders. She had just under twenty-four hours until her parents arrived and plenty to do. She'd start upstairs and work her way down.

She began in the bathroom, scrubbing every surface, every nook and cranny. In the guest room, she made the bed with the new sheets she'd run through the wash a couple of times and the duvet she'd bought to go with the new furniture. Because she didn't have anything else, she placed the rug Joss had brought over next to the bed. It pulled the room together and completely covered the scratch in the floor. Olivia swallowed the lump in her throat and moved on, tidying her closet and cleaning her room so she could show them off to her parents as well.

Downstairs, she dusted and vacuumed, scrubbed and polished. On one hand, the work distracted her from the constriction in her chest and the dull ache behind her eyes. On the other, everything she touched reminded her of Joss. The perfect lines of the trim, the colors on the walls. Joss's work was everywhere. There probably wasn't a thing in the house she hadn't touched during the three months they'd worked on the renovations.

By sheer force of will, Olivia kept it together. Until she got to the kitchen. She looked at the stove and her mind raced through their initial conversations about Olivia wanting it, the frustration of waiting, the favors Joss called in to get it delivered when she knew Olivia needed something to celebrate. She thought about the first meal she cooked on it, the night that followed. Unable to hold on to her composure any longer, Olivia sat on the floor and cried. Anger took a backseat to hurt, leaving space in the front for fear to settle in.

By the time she cried herself out, it was nearly two in the morning. She was still sitting on the kitchen floor, a fact that added a layer of pathetic to the hollowness inside her. She replayed the fight with Joss in her mind, trying to pinpoint the moment the conversation derailed. Joss had been so unreasonable. Olivia wished she'd handled things better, but clearly Joss was hankering for a fight.

She pulled herself off the floor. She felt weak and achy. Even if she didn't sleep, going to bed was probably a good idea. She took a shower that was a few degrees too hot and a couple of aspirin. She resisted the urge to pull on one of Joss's T-shirts, settling for a tank top and pair of flannel pants.

After crawling into bed, Olivia realized she'd hardly spent a night alone in her new bedroom. As much as she'd designed the space to feel like a sanctuary, it suddenly felt cold and sterile. It struck her just how much Joss had become a part of the house. It wasn't only the work she'd done. It was as though she'd seeped into the very essence of it. The idea riled her. She'd bought the house to make it hers. And now Joss was everywhere. Given that everything with Joss was a giant question mark, it made the house feel unsettled, like an unknown. She couldn't stop her mind from jumping to a whole string of what-ifs. If she and Joss broke up, Olivia wasn't at all sure she could stay in the house. As much as she loved it, the house had become completely entwined with Joss and their relationship. It was a feeling she was sure she wouldn't be able to shake, and one she didn't think she could bear.

Olivia realized she was being dramatic. She and Joss had a fight. Fights didn't mean relationships ended. If anything, fighting meant the relationship mattered. And having Joss so engrained in the house made it feel more like theirs. That was what she wanted, wasn't it? Yes, without a doubt. They'd find a way to work it out, even if Olivia wasn't sure how.

She tossed and turned for several hours before giving up on sleep. She finished cleaning the kitchen, showered, and tried to get herself ready for the arrival of her parents. She'd focus on that, try to make things as pleasant as possible. Once they were gone, she'd figure out the rest.

Joss slept fitfully and was up before five. Part of her wanted to call Olivia, to show up on her doorstep, so they could hash things out. The other part screamed at her to steer clear, at least until Olivia's parents had come and gone. She'd been half dreading meeting them anyway. Now the thought of spending time with the Bennett attorneys filled her with foreboding.

She'd let the dust settle. Olivia was so amped up anyway, trying to have a meaningful conversation would be pointless. It might even make things worse. They'd talk after the holiday and figure things out.

Joss wasn't entirely sure what there was to figure out. Based on how they'd left things, compromise felt unlikely. And if either of them tried to be something they weren't for the sake of the relationship, it would be a recipe for disaster. It was a hard lesson she'd learned once in her life and one she didn't feel the need to repeat. Joss reminded herself that her relationship with Olivia was different. Just the fact that Olivia had bought a house meant she was more settled, more committed to staying in one place, than Cora had been. And they'd talked about starting a family. Even without a wedding ring and a game plan, that meant something.

She showered and dressed, then headed over to the Patel house. She was grateful to be able to work alone and in an empty house. After arriving and making a mental to-do list for the day, she put in her ear buds and cranked the music.

Mid-afternoon, Ben showed up bearing sandwiches. Even though she hadn't said anything to him, he seemed to know something was up. And although she had no desire to eat, putting something in her stomach would probably make her less edgy and ease the painful gnawing that had been there all morning.

As they sat on the floor, eating turkey subs and drinking Pepsi, she weighed whether or not to confide in him. He understood her, maybe better than anyone else. He was her best bet for getting some perspective. She gave him an abbreviated version of the last few weeks, as well as the culminating fight.

"So was it a 'we are breaking up' kind of fight or an 'I need some space and we'll work this out later' kind of fight?"

Joss shrugged. "That's just it. I don't know."

"What do you want it to be?"

She sighed. "The second."

"You're in love with her?"

"Oh, yeah."

"The 'marry me and have my children' kind of love?"

Joss scrubbed her hands over her face. "Yes."

"What are you going to do?"

"For the next two days, nothing. Her parents are in town. It was their impending arrival—and how worked up about it Olivia was—that tipped us to the breaking point. I can't imagine being able to talk things through with her still in that state."

Ben nodded. "It sounds like they do a real number on her."

"Yeah. She talks about how much she isn't like them, but then she works herself into a frenzy trying to impress them. I don't get it."

Ben crossed his arms. "Kind of reminds me of a difficult client."

"What do you mean?"

"Think about it. Super demanding, high expectations clients. You don't really like them, you don't agree with what they want or like necessarily, but you still want to wow the pants off them. Maybe even more so because they make it clear they're hard to impress."

Joss frowned. "I don't think it's really the same thing."

"No, it's even worse, because in Olivia's case, she's related to them. The relationship is permanent and I'm sure, at least on some level, she loves them. That's a hard line to walk."

Joss hadn't thought about it that way. It made it a little easier to understand. "Maybe. But that doesn't say anything about how obsessed she's been with work. Not only has she had no time for us, she's expected me to take care of things at her house, like her work is more important than mine. Or like..." God, she hated to say it. "Like I'm still working for her."

Ben offered a sympathetic look. "I hear you. That part really sucks. I'm not saying you should let her off the hook."

Joss raised a brow. "What are you saying?"

He shrugged. "Maybe she's way more stressed out than she's letting on. And maybe trying to control everything is what she's doing instead of falling apart."

Joss thought about the last few months. Olivia was definitely a woman who prized being independent and in control. On one hand, it was a trait Joss admired. On the other, it made her feel like they weren't a team. If they were going to make things work, they had to be a team, complete with give and take. "Maybe you're right. Of course, I might prefer her falling apart, at least a little, over trying to control everything."

"Have you told her that?"

Since when was Ben the relationship guru? It was weird. He was right, but it was still weird. "Not in so many words."

"Well, when you do talk to her, it might be a good place to start."

"Thanks, oh wise one. How about you channel all that wisdom into helping me frame some walls?"

Ben stood, patted her on the shoulder. "At your disposal, grasshopper."

CHAPTER THIRTY-THREE

Her parents would have been content, if not happier, to go to a restaurant. Olivia was adamant about cooking, though, and content to do it on her own. After setting out the breakfast they ate every morning—grapefruit juice, boiled egg, yogurt—she got to work. The smallest turkey she'd been able to find was fourteen pounds. There would be a ton left over, but she didn't mind. Olivia could eat a turkey sandwich every day of her life and never grow tired of them. She'd put it in a honey brine the night before, so all she needed to do was drain the liquid, dry the skin, and rub a little butter on it. After sliding it into the oven, she got to work on sides.

While sausage browned in a skillet, she chopped onions, celery, and garlic. Olivia added them to the pot, enjoying the way everything sizzled and steamed. Despite promising herself she wouldn't, Olivia found herself thinking of Joss. She wondered if Joss was already at her parents' house, helping her mom in the kitchen or watching the Macy's parade with her nieces. Olivia was content to be in her house, in her kitchen, preparing the meal. At least, that's what she firmly told herself as she dumped the contents of her skillet into the bowl of crumbled cornbread that was going to become dressing.

Olivia's mom came in while she was prepping the Brussels sprouts. She topped off her cup of coffee and took a seat on one of the stools at the island.

"I still can't believe you enjoy all this fuss." She waved her hand to indicate the tools and ingredients piled around.

"I guess it must have skipped a generation." Olivia made sure to keep her voice light.

Sharon smiled. "You're right. Your Nana was the queen of the kitchen. And between the cooking, the baking, and all her craft projects, your sister could practically be Martha Stewart."

Olivia gritted her teeth. While she had no desire to be compared to Martha Stewart, it irritated her that her sister would, of course, win the nonexistent contest.

"Speaking of your sister, did she tell you she and Beau are trying to get pregnant again?"

Olivia sighed. She hadn't heard, probably because they were still in the trying phase. Tara tended only to tell Olivia things once they were settled. Like sibling rivalry in the extreme, Tara seemed intent on collecting all gold stars on the chart of life accomplishments. "I hadn't heard."

"Well, even though she was pretty set on stopping at three, she really wants a girl."

Olivia raised a brow. "And what if she ends up with a fourth boy?"

Sharon laughed. "Beau says he can fit five in his fishing boat, so they'll be fine."

Olivia shook her head. On one hand it was sweet. But it felt so utterly foreign to her that it was hard to relate. "Hopefully, she'll have a girl."

Sharon nodded. "Hopefully so. I'm simply dying to buy all those frilly dresses and hair bows. Baby girl things are so much more fun."

Olivia was actually partial to the stuff for boys—shirts with dinosaurs and tiny sweater vests. Again, thoughts of Joss flooded her brain. Images of Joss picking out baby clothes and putting together a crib combined with the memory of her holding one of Gina and Kel's sons at the hospital. The flashes, and the feelings they churned up, were so strong Olivia didn't realize her mother was talking again. "I'm sorry. What did you say?"

"I asked if you had anyone on the horizon."

Olivia hadn't told her parents much about Joss. At first, it had been because she knew they'd not approve of her being with someone who was a contractor. Then, she hadn't wanted to jinx things. It was too late for that now. "No, no one worth mentioning."

"Well, I hate to be doom and gloom, but you're not getting any younger."

Olivia cringed. "Thanks, Mama. That's exactly what I wanted to hear."

"Oh, sweetie. I'm not trying to make you feel badly. It's just, well, if you want babies of your own, you're going to have to get to it in the next couple of years."

Olivia couldn't decide if she wanted to scream or cry.

"I thought Ithaca was known for lesbians. There have to be plenty of nice professors at school. Someone in engineering, maybe, or business."

"It's a little more complicated than that."

"Weren't you dating someone? She had something to do with you buying the house or the remodeling you had done?"

Even without saying her name, the mention of Joss sent a pang through Olivia's chest. "Joss. Her family's company did the renovations. Joss did a lot of the work."

"Joss. What an interesting name. So you were dating, but you aren't anymore?"

Were they officially broken up? Olivia didn't know. It was hard to imagine being with her after their last argument. It was even harder to imagine not being with her at all. Olivia longed to share the confusion and hurt with her mother, to confide in her and get in return some empathy or maybe even advice. She knew better than to try. "Things are a bit up in the air. We both have a lot on our plates right now, different priorities."

Sharon shook her head. "That's why it's a terrible idea to get involved with the help. Other than whatever project you hire them for, you've got nothing in common."

Olivia's hurt transformed into anger. The switch was instant and the indignation she felt toward her mother overshadowed whatever frustration she had for Joss. They had plenty in common. Joss got her, at least until recently. Olivia set down her knife.

The truth of the situation hit her like a sucker punch. Joss hadn't changed in the last couple of weeks. She had. Olivia had an overwhelming urge to run from the house and drive straight to Joss's.

She resisted it because doing so would be impulsive and crazy. It was Thanksgiving morning. Joss might even be at her parents' house already. She might have no desire to see Olivia. Or to talk.

Olivia realized her mother was still sitting there, waiting for a response. She knew better than to start an argument. Her mother would dismiss whatever she said as sass and Olivia would only end up angrier. "I have a hell of a lot more in common with Joss than I ever did with Amanda."

"You're so quick to say that, but I could never figure out why. She's from an excellent family, she's professionally ambitious, and she was crazy about you."

Olivia huffed. "She was crazy about the idea of us being together. She thought I'd be a suitable second half of her power couple."

"You say that like it's the most horrible thing in the world."

"Is that what you and Daddy are?"

"What do you mean?"

"Are you two suitable halves of a power couple?"

Sharon considered for a moment. "I suppose you could say that. We complement each other, personally and professionally."

To Olivia, it sounded pragmatic and completely devoid of passion. "Are you happy, Mama?"

Sharon set down her coffee. "Of course I'm happy, darling. Why would you ask that?"

"Does your heart beat a little faster when you think about Daddy? Did it used to, at least?"

"You're asking if I have passion for your father?"

Olivia shrugged. "Maybe."

"Probably not in the way you're thinking. I grew up with the expectation that I would get married and have children. I only went to college because my parents figured it would be the best way for me to secure a husband with a solid future. When I met your father, he opened my eyes to something different. He wanted a wife who would be his partner, in every sense of the word. He respected me, and that was a lot more important than someone who made my insides fluttery."

Olivia realized she'd never heard that story before. It didn't resonate, necessarily, but she understood it. "And you want the same thing for me."

"Being madly in love is overrated, darling. You need someone you can count on, someone with the same priorities as you."

Olivia thought about her fight with Joss. It had been all about priorities. Joss had become convinced that Olivia's priorities were completely different from her own. They had, Olivia realized with dread, morphed into exactly what she'd spent her whole life trying to avoid—ambition and status over everything else. With Joss, she could have the balance of life and work. She could be successful, but still manage to have fun. And, perhaps most importantly, she could have all that and passion. The idea of waiting until after the holiday to sort things out no longer felt acceptable. Olivia needed to do it now.

"I have to go."

"What?"

"I need to go find Joss. I have to talk to her."

"Olivia, it's Thanksgiving morning. You're in the middle of making dinner."

"I don't think this can wait."

"You're being impulsive. There isn't anything that couldn't possibly wait until tomorrow."

"I love you, Mama, but you couldn't possibly be more wrong. I'm going to get dressed."

Olivia ran up the stairs two at a time. She took a two-minute shower and got dressed, not bothering to dry her hair or put on makeup. When she reentered the kitchen, both of her parents were standing there.

"Darling, if you're going to go chasing after Joss, shouldn't you put yourself together a little more? At least try to look nice?"

Olivia was already picking up her purse. "I'm fine, Mama. The turkey needs at least two more hours. The alarm is set on the digital thermometer. If it goes off while I'm gone, just pull it out and cover it loosely with foil. I'll take care of the rest when I get back."

"Good luck, sweetheart," Olivia's father called when she was halfway out the door.

"Thanks, Daddy."

Olivia called, but Joss didn't answer her phone. Olivia had no way of knowing whether it was because she was occupied or avoiding her. She drove to Joss's house and found an empty driveway. Instead of being disappointed, Olivia was relieved. If Joss was already at her parents', it was more likely that she wasn't intentionally ignoring her.

When Olivia arrived at Sandy and Frank's house, Joss's truck, along with Ben's and a car she assumed was Daphne's, filled the driveway. She parked on the street and took a deep breath. She had no idea what she was going to say. Or if Joss would even speak to her. This was not the time to chicken out. She took a deep breath and climbed out of the car. She knocked on the door with no idea what would happen next.

Ben answered. After the briefest flash of surprise, he smiled at her as though she was both welcome and expected. "Olivia. Happy Thanksgiving."

"Hi, Ben."

"Come in." He stepped aside so she could enter. "I didn't realize you were coming. I thought your folks were in town."

"I wasn't. They are. I mean…" Great. She was blubbering and she wasn't even talking to Joss yet. "I just needed to talk to Joss."

If Ben was curious, he didn't show it. "She's in the kitchen. Follow me."

Joss was standing at the stove with her back to the doorway. Before Olivia could say anything, Ben got her attention. "Joss, someone wants to talk to you."

"Well, tell them they'll have to come in here. I'm busy." Joss turned and Olivia froze. Maybe this was a terrible idea. Not only did she have no clue what to say, she was interrupting a family holiday to do it.

Joss figured it was one of her nieces, or maybe her dad. When she realized Olivia was standing there, looking nervous and uncertain, Joss's throat went dry. "Olivia."

"I'm sorry to barge in, but I really needed to talk to you."

"Okay." She turned to her sister. "Daphne, can you take over here?"

"Of course." Daphne took the spoon and stepped in front of the stove.

"Let's go down the hall." There weren't many places in her parents' house for privacy. She led the way to the bedroom she'd shared with Daphne for fifteen years. Not the ideal place to hash things out, but it was quiet. She closed the door and turned to Olivia. "What are you doing here?"

"Apologizing." Olivia offered her a pained smile. "Groveling, maybe."

Joss took a deep breath. "Let's start with the first. I'm not really interested in the second."

"Joss, I'm sorry."

As much as she wanted to hear those words, they weren't enough. "What exactly are you sorry for?"

"For having my priorities all wrong, for making you feel like you aren't the most important person in my life, like our relationship isn't the most important thing."

Now they were getting somewhere. "Sorry that I got that impression or sorry that's how you actually feel?"

"I'm sorry that my behavior made it seem like that's how I feel."

"So how do you really feel?"

Olivia seemed to choose her words carefully. "I feel like you're the best thing that's ever happened to me."

Joss softened. She felt the same way, or at least she had until recently. But it still didn't mean they wanted the same things.

Olivia took a deep breath and continued. "It's been over two years since I've spent more than twenty-four hours with my parents. You were right. As much as I told myself I was nothing like them, I was. I got so caught up in what people thought of me, of what my parents would think of me, I started acting like a crazy person. And I took you for granted. I acted like you didn't understand my job, but really, I was the one who didn't understand."

The pocket of hope Joss had for them grew. "I know that your work is important to you. And I know that getting tenure is a big deal and not a given."

"I know. I lashed out at you because I could. I've been feeling so out of control. I think a part of me knew that I was being unreasonable and I was looking to you for validation. The fact that you called me out sent me over the edge."

Olivia was taking more responsibility than Joss expected. And her words echoed the conversation she'd had with Ben the day before. The fact that Olivia seemed to understand, and not merely apologize, meant a lot. "It felt like you were saying I couldn't possibly wrap my head around something so far removed from my little world."

"Oh, Joss. I'm so sorry. You have to know that was never my intention."

Joss sighed. "I know. I can admit that I'm overly sensitive to that kind of thing. I probably gave you a harder time than was necessary."

At that, Olivia cracked a smile. "So we're okay?"

Joss allowed herself to feel relief. "I think we are."

"Thank God."

"I'm not going to lie, I kind of love that you drove over here on Thanksgiving morning to make up."

Olivia smiled for real now and made Joss's heart do a flip in her chest. "Well, then don't forget to add the fact that I ran out of my house, abandoning my parents and a half-cooked meal, to do it."

Joss chuckled. "I love you, Olivia. So very much."

"I love you, too, Joss. More than anything."

Joss liked to think of herself as a woman who preferred actions to words, but hearing Olivia say "I love you" made her feel almost giddy. She stepped forward, took Olivia's face in her hands, and kissed her. She meant it to be tender, affirming. It didn't take long, however, for the heat to take over. The worry of the last few days gave way to longing laced with urgency.

Remembering where they were, Joss broke the kiss reluctantly. She enjoyed the way Olivia's eyes fluttered open, as though she was coming out of a pleasant dream. "You know, I'm sure the invitation still stands if you want to bring your parents here. The more people she has to feed, the happier my mom is."

Olivia laughed. "I'm having a really good day here, let's not push it."

"Fair enough. Does that mean you need to leave now?"

"It does. They leave in the morning. Can I see you then?"

"I think that could be arranged. What do you say we go pick out Christmas trees together?"

Olivia's eyes lit up. "It's a date."

"Okay. I shouldn't keep you now, then." Joss opened the door and caught a flash of Ben and Daphne scurrying down the hall. "I see you," she called. God, it was like being a teenager again.

Joss walked Olivia out. They stood in the driveway with snow swirling around them and Joss kissed her again. "Drive carefully and have a good day with your parents."

"You, too. Feel free to tell everyone I'd rather be here."

Olivia climbed into her car and drove away. Even though she was standing in the cold without a coat, Joss waited until Olivia's car was out of sight before going back inside. When she did, she found seven pairs of eyes looking at her expectantly. "Everything's good. Nothing to see here."

Immediately, everyone turned their attention to something else. Joss knew she'd have to give more details later, but for the moment, it sufficed. She returned to the kitchen and resumed her place at the stove with a smile on her face.

CHAPTER THIRTY-FOUR

Joss pulled into the driveway at ten the next morning. Olivia had seen her parents off less than an hour before, happy to see them go. Thankfully, the snow had stopped and the roads were clear. Since neither of them had experience driving in winter conditions, bad weather would have likely prolonged their stay.

Olivia stepped onto the porch, anxious to see Joss. She felt good about their conversation the day before, but it didn't completely ease the worry, the disquiet that came from realizing how close she'd come to losing Joss. When she climbed into the passenger seat, Joss's smile was warm, as was her kiss hello. Olivia felt some of the tension leave her body.

"Your parents get off okay?"

"They did. I guess a couple of their friends from the country club are also in the city for the weekend, so they're going to go to the Four Seasons and *Phantom of the Opera*." Joss nodded, but didn't say anything. Olivia had to laugh. "I promise that if we ever go to New York City, those will be the absolute last two things I want to do."

Joss shrugged. "I'm not opposed to theater or anything."

"Of course not. But I like to think we'd be at least a little more original."

It was Joss's turn to laugh. "Did they have a nice time here?"

Olivia weighed the question before answering. It hadn't gone exactly as she'd hoped, but it wasn't a disaster either. "I think that they enjoyed themselves. We had some nice conversations, dinner turned out well despite my abandoning it halfway through."

Joss smiled. "I'm glad."

"And even though I realized it doesn't matter, they were very impressed with the house."

Joss didn't want it to matter, either—to Olivia or to her—but it did. "Good."

"Don't get me wrong. They still think I'm nuts, for buying it and living out in the country in the first place, but they said the house was beautiful and the work impeccable."

Joss reached over and squeezed her hand. They rode for a while in contented silence. Olivia looked over at Joss. She refused to let herself dwell on how closely she'd come to letting Joss walk away. She'd made a huge mistake, but had found a way to fix it. She didn't plan to take that chance again.

Joss glanced over at her, raised a brow. "You look pensive. What are you thinking about?"

Olivia smiled and rubbed her gloved hands together. "Do you know I've never had a real Christmas tree?"

Joss turned her truck onto yet another road Olivia had never been on, taking them farther out of town. She appeared to be scandalized by the statement. "You mean never ever?"

"Never. Isn't that terrible? My mother put up six Christmas trees every year—every one of them fake and every one with a different, very specific theme." The idea came from an issue of *Southern Living* and Olivia had always hated it.

Joss scowled. "Like side by side?"

"No, no." Olivia laughed. "They were all in different rooms. The one in the dining room was done up with blue and silver to match the wallpaper and her china. The one in the formal living room was all gold and pink. She had a small one for the kitchen that she covered with food-themed ornaments."

"That's intense."

Olivia had the feeling Joss was thinking of a different word entirely. "It fed her deep need to decorate. She could redo the rooms of our house only so often, I think, without driving my father crazy."

"That's so strange to me. My family and I are in the business of remodeling, but I can only remember one major overhaul to our kitchen. And we repainted the living room when we got a new sofa, but that only happened two or three times in my memory."

"It's probably different when you do the work yourself. For Mama, I think it was mostly a status thing, and maybe her creative outlet."

Joss turned the truck into a gravel parking lot with a small trailer at one end. "Well, my lady, those days are over. Let's find us a couple of real, live, amazing-smelling pine trees."

Olivia took a deep breath. This was her opening. She had to grab it. "Joss?"

Joss looked over at her. "Yeah?"

"What if we only got one tree?"

Joss chuckled. "Are you having second thoughts?"

"No, I mean, what if we picked out a tree together for my house?"

She raised a brow. "Are you implying I won't be spending much time at my place? I like the sound of that."

"What if we picked out a tree together for our house?"

Joss looked at her searchingly, but didn't say anything.

"I mean, I love your house. If you feel really strongly about it, I'm open to that, but well, we put so much work into mine, it sort of feels like ours already."

Joss swallowed the lump in her throat and tried to keep her voice even. "Are you asking me to move in with you?"

Olivia looked down and seemed to be shy all of a sudden. Joss couldn't decide if she was nervous or wishing she hadn't opened her mouth in the first place. When she looked up again, her eyes were wet. "I've been wanting to ask you for a while and then, well, chaos happened and I was afraid we might break up. I was planning to do it over a romantic dinner, or maybe in bed, but, well, I don't want to get two trees."

A tear spilled over and fell down Olivia's cheek. Joss's heart was beating so hard, it made it difficult to breathe. "Olivia."

"I'm so sorry for everything. You are what I want. A life and a family with you."

It was exactly what Joss wanted. It was what she'd been planning for when things got so out of control. "It's what I want, too. It's what I've wanted all along."

Olivia sniffed and laughed. "Except when you were adamant you didn't want it with me."

Joss smiled. "A momentary lapse in judgment."

"So is that a yes?"

"It is."

Olivia leaned towards her and Joss took her face in her hands. "I love you, Olivia."

"I love you, too." The tears were flowing in earnest now, but Joss got the feeling they were the overwhelmed, but also relieved, but also happy sort. She knew the feeling.

"Let's go pick out a tree."

They got out of the truck and Olivia looked around. Next to the trailer were a few dozen cut trees leaning against makeshift sawhorses. There were tall ones and short ones and plump ones and gangly ones. Beyond them were rows and rows of trees, interspersed with a few stumps. As they got closer, the door of the trailer opened and a woman stepped out. She offered them a wave and said, "Good afternoon! Welcome to Pulaski's! I take it you're in the market for a tree."

"We are. If you could point us in the direction of the Frasier firs, we'd be thrilled."

The woman nodded. "The cut ones closest to me are all Frasiers, and then the first four rows here. They go back quite a ways. Pre-cut are forty dollars, cut-your-own are thirty."

Olivia was unable to contain her excitement. "We can cut our own?"

"It's the only way to go," Joss said.

The tree woman nodded in agreement and gestured toward a dozen or so saws hanging from hooks on the side of the trailer. "Help yourself to a saw and just knock on my door when you're all set."

Joss picked one up and they started making their way down the rows of trees. "The thing to remember is that they always look smaller out here than they will in your living room."

"You mean our living room."

Joss grinned at her. "Our living room. My reach is a little over seven feet, so you can pick one that's a foot or so taller than that, but no more."

Olivia nodded. "That sounds good. I imagine it would be very easy to get carried away."

They wandered for fifteen minutes or so. The snow from the day before gave the whole scene a Currier and Ives feel. And there were so many trees to choose from, Olivia had a hard time deciding. Each time she found what she thought was the one, another one in the distance would catch her eye. She darted from one tree to the next, extolling its virtues. "I want one that's nice and full, but also has character. I don't want it to look like it came out of a box."

Joss followed her around good naturedly, raising her arm on demand so Olivia could assess proportions. Olivia was pretty sure Joss was indulging her at this point. "Take your time. It's supposed to be an adventure."

When they were about three-quarters of the way down the row, Olivia spotted a tree that was quite wide for its height. Its top, instead of tapering to a perfect point, spread out slightly, sort of like a pineapple top. Without any hesitation, she declared, "This is it. This is the one."

Joss came over to assess her find. She gave it the once-over. "This is it? You're sure?"

Olivia shrugged and shuffled her feet. "I mean, only if you like it."

"I think it's perfect. I'm happy to cut it down myself, but if you want to help, I can get down and get it started for you. Using a saw while lying on your side can be tricky."

Olivia beamed. "I would love to help and I would love it even more if you got it started."

Joss got on the ground and scooted under the lower branches. Olivia heard the sound of wood being cut and the whole tree began to vibrate slightly. After a couple of minutes Joss emerged, pine needles stuck to her coat and gloves. They were also in her hair and stuck to her forehead. "Are you sure you want to go in there?"

For all of Olivia's newfound handiness, she had never actually used a saw. She wasn't about to let that stop her. "Gimme," she said, holding out her hand for the saw.

Wiggling under the tree was easy, as was getting the saw blade into the nice groove Joss created for her. Placing both hands firmly on the handle, she began working the blade back and forth. Flecks of sawdust went flying and the scent of pine filled her nostrils. It was exhilarating. It was exhausting. Her neck cramped and her biceps began to burn. She continued at it until she gauged she was more than halfway through the trunk.

"Is it okay if I stop now?"

"Of course." Joss chuckled. "Excellent effort. Also, your ass looks amazing when you do that."

Olivia wiggled out from under the tree, adding an extra shimmy or two for Joss's benefit. She handed back the saw and Joss made quick work of finishing the job. Olivia stuck her hand into the tree, holding it steady so it didn't fall on Joss's head. When Joss told her to let go and push it away from her, the tree landed in the snow with a satisfying thwack.

"Timber!" She said it about ten seconds too late, but with great enthusiasm.

They each took an end and carried the tree back to the parking lot. They hoisted it into the back of Joss's truck and Olivia tapped on the door of the trailer. She handed the woman three twenties and picked up a pair of rustic evergreen wreaths for the front and back doors. She laid them in the back with the tree and climbed into the truck to join Joss.

"I always want to do this with you."

Joss smiled. "I want to do this with you always, too."

After getting the tree in the house, in the stand, and watered, they stopped for leftover turkey sandwiches. Olivia pulled out her bins of Christmas decorations. Joss shuffled around the tree behind her, holding the lights while Olivia tucked them between the branches. Olivia refused to put on any ornaments until Joss could bring hers over and they could all be put on together.

The snow started up again and it got dark outside early, even for November. Olivia poured wine and they sat on the sofa with only the light from the tree and the fire illuminating the room. Ethel snored on her bed. On one level, Olivia couldn't imagine being more content. On another, she worried about how quickly Joss agreed to move in with her. Given everything that had happened, the last thing she wanted was for Joss to feel like she was trying to control everything, or have things her way.

Olivia took a deep breath, let it out. "Are you sure you're okay letting go of your place? It's such a great house."

Joss kissed the top of her head. "I'm sure. It was a great project and a good investment, but it's small and doesn't have much land. I never intended it to be the home I raise a family in."

It made sense. And she desperately wanted to believe it. Olivia leaned back and looked at her. "And this place?"

Joss smiled. "This place is absolutely perfect. And we made it that way, together."

"We did." Olivia thought back to the first time she'd seen the house. Even in a state of disrepair, it stirred something in her. It was as though her soul knew something the rest of her still had to figure out. It was the same with Joss, really. Despite getting off on the wrong foot, Olivia persisted. What she thought was a physical attraction was the spark that started a much bigger fire.

Joss leaned back and looked into Olivia's eyes. "Things mean so much more when you work for them. Don't you agree?"

Olivia smiled. "Are you referring to the house? Or us?"

Joss offered a playful shrug. "Both."

Olivia thought about the last few months. There'd been plenty of sweat, some tears. She'd even shed a little blood in her battle with the carpet staples. She'd never poured more of herself into a project, or a relationship. She'd never felt such a deep connection, either. "In that case, I couldn't agree more."

About the Author

Aurora Rey grew up in a small town in south Louisiana, daydreaming about New England. She keeps a special place in her heart for the South, especially the food and the ways women are raised to be strong, even if they're taught not to show it. After a brief dalliance with biochemistry, she completed both a B.A. and an M.A. in English.

When she's not writing or at her day job in higher education, she loves to cook and putter around the house. She's slightly addicted to Pinterest, has big plans for the garden, and would love to get some goats. She lives in Ithaca, New York, with her partner and two dogs.

Books Available From Bold Strokes Books

A Reunion to Remember by TJ Thomas. Reunited after a decade, Jo Adams and Rhonda Black must navigate a significant age difference, family dynamics, and their own desires and fears to explore an opportunity for love. (978-1-62639-534-3)

Built to Last by Aurora Rey. When Professor Olivia Bennett hires contractor Joss Bauer to restore her dilapidated farmhouse, she learns her heart, as much as her house, is in need of a renovation. (978-1-62639-552-7)

Capsized by Julie Cannon. What happens when a woman turns your life completely upside down? (978-1-62639-479-7)

Girls With Guns by Ali Vali, Carsen Taite, and Michelle Grubb. Three stories by three talented crime writers—Carsen Taite, Ali Vali, and Michelle Grubb—each packing her own special brand of heat. (978-1-62639-585-5)

Heartscapes by MJ Williamz. Will Odette ever recover her memory, or is Jesse condemned to remember their love alone? (978-1-62639-532-9)

Murder on the Rocks by Clara Nipper. Detective Jill Rogers lives with two things on her mind: sex and murder. While an ice storm cripples Tulsa, two things stand in Jill's way: her lover and the DA. (978-1-62639-600-5)

Necromantia by Sheri Lewis Wohl. When seeing dead people is more than a movie tagline. (978-1-62639-611-1)

Salvation by I. Beacham. Claire's long-term partner now hates her, for all the wrong reasons, and she sees no future until she meets Regan, who challenges her to face the truth and find love. (978-1-62639-548-0)

Trigger by Jessica Webb. Dr. Kate Morrison races to discover how to defuse human bombs while learning to trust her increasingly strong feelings for the lead investigator, Sergeant Andy Wyles. (978-1-62639-669-2)

24/7 by Yolanda Wallace. When the trip of a lifetime becomes a pitched battle between life and death, will anyone survive? (978-1-62639-619-7)

A Return to Arms by Sheree Greer. When a police shooting makes national headlines, activists Folami and Toya struggle to balance their relationship and political allegiances, a struggle intensified after a fiery young artist enters their lives. (978-1-62639-681-4)

After the Fire by Emily Smith. Paramedic Connor Haus is convinced her time for love has come and gone, but when firefighter Logan Curtis comes into town, she learns it may not be too late after all. (978-1-62639-652-4)

Fortunate Sum by M. Ullrich. Financial advisor Catherine Carter lives a calculated life, but after a collision with spunky Imogene Harris (her latest client) and unsolicited predictions, Catherine finds herself facing an unexpected variable: Love. (978-1-62639-530-5)

Dian's Ghost by Justine Saracen. The road to genocide is paved with good intentions. (978-1-62639-594-7)

Soul to Keep by Rebekah Weatherspoon. What won't a vampire do for love... (978-1-62639-616-6)

When I Knew You by KE Payne. Eight letters, three friends, two lovers, one secret. Can the past ever be forgiven? (978-1-62639-562-6)

Wild Shores by Radclyffe. Can two women on opposite sides of an oil spill find a way to save both a wildlife sanctuary and their hearts? (978-1-62639-645-6)

Love on Tap by Karis Walsh. Beer and romance are brewing for Tace Lomond when archaeologist Berit Katsaros comes into her life. (978-1-62639-564-0)

Whirlwind Romance by Kris Bryant. Will chasing the girl break Tristan's heart or give her something she's never had before? (978-1-62639-581-7)

Love on the Red Rocks by Lisa Moreau. An unexpected romance at a lesbian resort forces Malley to face her greatest fears when she must choose between playing it safe or taking a chance at true happiness. (978-1-62639-660-9)

Tracker and the Spy by D. Jackson Leigh. There are lessons for all when Captain Tanisha is assigned untried pyro Kyle and a lovesick dragon horse for a mission to track the leader of a dangerous cult. (978-1-62639-448-3)

Whiskey Sunrise by Missouri Vaun. Culture and religion collide when Lovey Porter, daughter of a local Baptist minister, falls for the handsome thrill-seeking moonshine runner, Royal Duval. (978-1-62639-519-0)

Dyre: By Moon's Light by Rachel E. Bailey. A young werewolf, Des, guards the aging leader of all the Packs: the Dyre. Stable employment—nice work, if you can get it…at least until silver bullets start to fly. (978-1-62639-662-3)

Fragile Wings by Rebecca S. Buck. In Roaring Twenties London, can Evelyn Hopkins find love with Jos Singleton or will the scars of the Great War crush her dreams? (978-1-62639-546-6)

Live and Love Again by Jan Gayle. Jessica Whitney could be Sarah Jarret's second chance at love, but their differences and Sarah's grief continue to come between their budding relationship. (978-1-62639-517-6)

Starstruck by Lesley Davis. Actress Cassidy Hayes and writer Aiden Darrow find out the hard way not all life-threatening drama is confined to the TV screen or the pages of a manuscript. (978-1-62639-523-7)

Stealing Sunshine by Tina Michele. Under the Central Florida sun, two women struggle between fear and love as a dangerous plot of deception and revenge threatens to steal priceless art and lives. (978-1-62639-445-2)

The Fifth Gospel by Michelle Grubb. Hiding a Vatican secret is dangerous—sharing the secret suicidal—can Felicity survive a perilous book tour, and will her PR specialist, Anna, be there when it's all over? (978-1-62639-447-6)